Anchoring Annaveta
By Lorna Faith

To my Dad and Mom

For your faith and bravery.

Chapter One

Russia, August 1, 1914

Someone watched Annaveta. She felt it.

The back of her neck tingled, her skin prickled in rhythm with the rumble of the train. Alex continued to breathe deeply, sound asleep on the seat beside her. With deliberate slowness, she turned her head for a clearer view of the passengers around her. Loud snores came from the gray-haired couple in the seat in front of her, and a young mother tried to calm her two young children who fought over a toy in the seats across the aisle. She turned her head to see who sat behind her. Three young men wearing Navy uniforms talked in low tones. A man wearing wire glasses read a newspaper in the seat behind them. She started to turn back around to face the front when she saw the cuff of the man's sleeve roll up. A tattoo of a skull and crossbones was imprinted on his arm.

Her whole body shivered, trembled, quaked. She couldn't stop thinking about her family burning to death in their izba, about the written notes sentencing her to death. And she couldn't stop thinking she would swear—she would swear—Misha and the Black Hand sat there with her on the train.

She swallowed the scream that wanted to erupt.

Annaveta turned her head around, grabbed Alex's hand, and squeezed.

"What is it?" Alex pried her fingers loose from his and rubbed her shaking arm.

"That man behind us has the same tattoo as Misha and other Black Hand members." Annaveta's whispered words were strained. A familiar lump of panic rolled up her throat. She turned to look into Alex's steady blue eyes, and it took the edge off the fear. She trusted Alex. He had been the one to save her from Misha's jealous rage. When Misha stalked them and shot at them both in the forest between Pleve colony and Annaveta's old Russian village, he had protected her. Later, when Misha had locked her in Baron Yakov's cold, dark basement and Alex had been taken from her at gunpoint, an angel had opened the door for her after three days in that dungeon-like prison. When Annaveta found Alex lying in the shed, bruised and beaten, they had escaped from that place of horror as fast as they could. The horrible memories of that time flashed through her mind as she thought of the tattoo of the dark haired man behind her.

The squeal of the breaks from the iron-wheeled locomotive filled Annaveta with relief.

"Shh. I know you're scared. I'm right here with you. Stay close by my side. I'll protect you." Alex whispered to her and moved her in front of him as they walked down the aisle off the train. As they stepped onto the platform of the Odessa train station, she turned to look behind her to see if she could spot the thin man's black fedora hat among the crowd. She couldn't see him, but that didn't ease her worry. Not knowing where he was seemed worse somehow.

Annaveta turned forward and kept her focus on Alex's tall, broad-shouldered form in front of her. She hurried to catch up.

"You don't frighten easily. I'm glad." Annaveta hooked her arm through Alex's. He felt so good. Warm. Soft. And not threatening.

"I don't see him anywhere, but we should keep moving all the same." She felt the heat of his whispered words against her hair. It soothed her harried nerves, and his tender smile and soft blue eyes calmed the threat of danger.

"We just need to get to Aunt Esther and Uncle Roman's place." Annaveta quickened her pace, hurried as fast as her long skirt allowed. Amid the chatter of the crowd, dogs barked and impatient horses whinnied. Smells of horse flesh mingled with the sweet aroma of tobacco drew her gaze to an old man leaning against a well-used buckboard puffing on his pipe. The smoke curled into the air toward them, like an invitation to join him. A well-dressed man approached him, and the old farmer pointed to the back of his wagon.

Annaveta was intrigued.

"Come, Alex." She pulled on his hand and walked toward the wooden cart that seemed to attract so many. "This man seems to know a lot of people. He might know where my aunt and uncle live."

The gray-haired farmer bent his already crooked body to push the last of the crates filled with bottles of wine and milk along the splintered wood. He pressed some hay around them and walked to the front of his wagon, checked his horses' halters, then climbed onto the bench seat as if ready to leave.

"Wait, sir." Alex spoke loudly in his stilted Russian, which got the old man's attention. He waited until they reached him. "We've just arrived on the train. We were wondering if you knew where we could find the home of Roman and Esther Levinson?"

The man sat there, brooding. He puffed more smoke from his pipe. "How do you know the Levinsons?" He tipped up his straw hat, a skeptical look on his face. His keen gray eyes searched each of theirs.

"Esther Levinson is my mama's sister." Annaveta silently beseeched Heaven to make this man help them. "We've just arrived from St. Petersburg and are very tired. Please, if you know where they live, would you point the way?"

The old man leaned over, his weathered face nearly touching her own. His gaze lingered on her features until at last a toothless smile appeared. "You do have the look of Roman's wife, Esther. It's in the eyes." The man patted his hat firmly on his sweat-moistened forehead and nodded. "Now that I've gotten a good look at you, I can see you must be family." He waved his hand for them to come join him on the wagon seat. "How about I give you a ride to their home?"

"Oh, thank you, sir. That would be very agreeable." Annaveta sighed in relief and gratitude as she reached up to get on the wagon. Alex sat down on her other side. "First, let us pay you for your help."

The old farmer shook his head. "Wouldn't be right. I'm helping a neighbour. One look at the happiness on Esther's face when she sees you will be all the thanks I need." With that, he flicked the reins and clucked to the two dappled mares. The smart-looking horses' ears perked, and they started up the twisted streets of Odessa toward the Levinson's estate.

The man beside them talked about the many different folk who lived and worked in Odessa. Alex's smile grew wider as this old man, whose name they found out was Boris Rusnak, explained about the crops they could see on both sides of the narrow road. Alex talked at length to the seasoned farmer about the Volga German method of farming and the new way of heating their homes with manure mixed with mud instead of wood. The Volga German farmer who had discovered it had been honoured by the Russian Government. Alex looked pleased when Boris Rusnak seemed suitably impressed with his colony's inventiveness.

Soon the wagon reached the top of a wide hill that overlooked the port city of Odessa. Annaveta sucked in her breath to see the reflection of the morning sun on the water, shimmering like little diamonds on the rooftops. Moisture on waiting merchant ships added to the sparkle of this city. The sky's subtle change from an airy blue to gray, accompanied by the rumble of a storm headed in their direction, sent a foreboding wave of fear that settled like chains in her stomach. Annaveta was awe-struck and disquieted all at the same time. She felt the tickle of sweat on her neckline—her body's response to what seemed both threatening and beautiful.

Boris led the horses up a well kept tree-lined lane toward a large estate. Annaveta could hardly believe her eyes when the wizened old farmer stopped the wagon in front of an enormous three-story brick mansion with two turrets on either end, complete with a sprawling balcony and large pillars. The entire property suggested comfort and elegance.

Memories flooded Annaveta as she stared at the large stately home. She remembered when she first arrived at Count and Countess Tashkova's estate as Nanny. This vast home looked every bit as intimidating as that. She rubbed her clammy hands on her nubby skirts.

Alex got out of the wagon and held his hand out to help her down. They followed behind the old farmer. She smoothed her hair with shaky hands, nervous to see her aunt and uncle for the first time in many years. It was Boris Rusnak who knocked on the door and stepped back when a maid in black uniform opened the large door.

"Yes?" Her crisp voice matched the starched look of her uniform.

"Hello, Maria. I've brought family to see Mrs. Levinson." Boris Rusnak stood there, looking out of place. His threadbare trousers, worn suspenders, and wrinkled off-color farmer's shirt a stark contrast to the maid's pressed uniform and the pristine décor of the foyer behind her.

"Hmm. I'll see if Mrs. Levinson is receiving callers. Wait here, if you please." She spun on her heels, closing the door firmly behind her.

Annaveta paced the driveway. The maid's clipped greeting made her tense. Doubt ambushed her, and she wondered if Aunt Esther would remember her. More fears coursed through her. Would they be turned away at the door?

"Don't worry too much about Maria."

Annaveta jumped at the sound of Farmer Rusnak's throaty voice behind them.

"She's always in a gripe. Has been all the years I've known her. She doesn't mean anything by it." His toothless half-grin had her smiling back.

Without warning, the door opened and a slender, middle-aged woman stood in the large door opening. She stood for several minutes just staring at Annaveta, not saying a word.

Annaveta held her breath and waited.

Aunt Esther's eyes misted. Her silky blonde hair, now highlighted with gray streaks, was gathered in a loose bun. Her neck-high white lace blouse gathered close at her slim waist, and the navy blue skirt hung in smooth lines to her kid leather shoes.

This was the same picture of elegance Annaveta remembered from when she was young and saw her Aunt Esther for the first time at Bubbeh and Zaydeh's home on the outskirts of Odessa. As she gazed at Aunt Esther's face, she found bright blue eyes—so similar to Mama's—smiling into her own.

"So it's true. My dear sister's only daughter is here at last." Aunt Esther hurried toward her, and she wrapped her arms around Annaveta in a tight hug. "I'm so glad you're here. Uncle Roman will be so pleased you decided to visit. We'll see him later on. Sorry our son Jude isn't here. He's been working on one of the Imperial Navy ships, so most of the time he's out at sea."

"I'm happy to see you again, Aunt Esther. I'm sorry we just showed up here without any word of warning."

"Nonsense, child. You're family. Our door is always open to you." Aunt Esther kept her arm around Annaveta's shoulders as she turned to look at the men who waited. "Who is this young man you have with you?"

"This is my good friend, Alex Wagner. He has saved my life at least two times in the past year, and he brought me here so I would be safe." Annaveta watched as her graceful aunt walked over to Alex.

"If you have been such a good friend to our niece, then you are very welcome here." Aunt Esther took his hand between both of hers. His cheeks reddened when her tone changed over the words "good friend." Annaveta grinned, and her aunt's silvery laugh floated upward, breaking the hush of the morning air.

"And Boris Rusnak, I have you to thank for bringing these two in from the train." Annaveta watched the old farmer pull off his dusty straw hat, pulling it against his chest and bowing his head in response. "Well, why don't you come inside? Boris you go ahead into the kitchen. From the smell of the air, Edda has just baked a batch of that bread you love so much." Aunt Esther put her hand on the old farmer's arm and waved them all inside. "Dmitry, you'll see to their bags, won't you? Annaveta will stay in the green room in the East Wing, and we'll put Alex in the West Wing's Fireside room." She nodded to a young twelve-year-old boy who quickly did as she asked.

Her aunt took the old farmer to the kitchen to enjoy Cook's bread while two of the maids led them to their rooms. Alex followed Maria to the West Wing and a younger maid led Annaveta down a long hallway in the opposite direction.

"Mrs. Levinson asked me to tell you a warm bath is on its way for you, as well as a breakfast tray." The maid busied herself hanging up the few clothes in her small travel bag while

Annaveta waited, unsure of what to do next. "I'll come back to show you to the bathing room when your bath is ready, miss." The maid curtseyed and left the room with a light click of the door handle.

Annaveta fell back onto the bed with a sigh. A smile hovered on her lips as she thought of Aunt Esther's warm welcome. It didn't take long until the maid was back, and then she enjoyed a long bath, almost falling asleep in the steamy water. Afterward, she relaxed on the bed and promptly fell asleep.

A knock at the door startled her awake.

"Mrs. Levinson said I was to come help you get dressed. She wants you to join her and Mr. Wagner for luncheon." The maid brought her only other clean clothes out and helped her put them on, quickly brushing out her hair and putting it up in a loose bun. "You look very pretty, miss."

"Thank you for your help. What's your name?" Annaveta asked as she followed the maid down the hallway toward the eating room.

"I am Tatyana, miss."

"Well, thanks for all your help, Tatyana."

The maid gave her a quick nod and a small curtsey as they reached the luncheon room.

"Ah, good. You look well rested." Aunt Esther looked her over as the butler pulled out a chair for Annaveta to sit at her aunt's right hand side. Alex sat to her aunt's left.

"Let us give thanks." Aunt Esther bowed her head. "Blessed are You, HaShem, our God, King of the Universe, by Whose

Word everything comes to be."

Listening to the Jewish blessing brought Annaveta back in time. She remembered sitting on her Bubbeh's lap as he read her stories from the Torah while her mama and Zaydeh sat nearby stitching the delicate laces they sold.

Annaveta's aunt reminded her of her mama, and her heart felt a familiar longing to know more of Mama's family.

"So, you lived in St. Petersburg. What made you decide to live there away from your Mama?" Annaveta's heart lurched inside her chest as she realized that her aunt still didn't know about the death of her only sister. Heat rose from her neck up to her cheeks as she scrambled to find the right words. She swallowed and looked at Alex, whose tender expression was nearly her undoing.

"Aunt Esther, there's something I need to tell you."

Her aunt put her spoon on her plate and sat there looking at her, a grave expression on her face.

Annaveta cleared her throat. "A little over a year ago, both my parents and my two younger brothers died in a fire that destroyed our izba. Your sister, my mama, is no longer alive."

Aunt Esther gaped and covered her mouth.

"Since that dreadful day, I lived in a Volga German colony with Alex's family until it was time to leave. I met Alex and his sister Clara before our house burned to the ground, and it's where I needed to go to be safe. Then I left there to live in St. Petersburg because an evil man from my village who wanted to marry me found me in Pleve colony, and it was too much trouble for the Wagner family for me to stay. In St.

Petersburg, I was able to secure a position as a nanny for a wealthy family. However, because I was chased by men who have hurt me again and again, Alex thought it best if we left the city secretly to come and stay with you for awhile. I hope that's okay?"

"Of course you should come here, you needn't ask. Oh, you poor dear. How awful for you to go through all of that." Aunt Esther put her hand on Annaveta's, and she didn't speak for the longest time. Tears trickled down her cheeks unchecked. A maid brought her a hand cloth, and she dabbed at her eyes. "You came to the right place, my dear. From now on you will be treated like our own daughter. My sister would have wanted that. And Alex, there's always room at our table for you because you've kept our dear girl safe."

By Alex's sober expression, she could tell he was moved by her aunt's words. Annaveta was too overcome with emotions to speak. She squeezed her aunt's hand, swallowed, and tried again.

"You're every bit as nice as Mama said." Annaveta gave Aunt Esther a shaky smile and wiped away a stray tear.

"We'll have a lot of news to tell your uncle when he gets home for supper." Aunt Esther looked at them, then she pushed back her chair, stood up, and threw her napkin on the table. "Let's not wait. Your uncle is at the port this afternoon, checking the cargo to be exported on the ships. Let's surprise him."

Annaveta's aunt's enthusiasm was easily caught. They left the table and followed her down the hallway to the front entrance. Aunt Esther pointed to a dark green waist-length shawl, and the butler pulled it along with a black shawl from the corner closet. He helped put the green shawl on her shoulders and brushed off the lint. It seemed so strange to have help with the smallest of tasks.

"It's cooler by the beach area." Annaveta watched as Larson, the butler, helped her aunt with her shawl, repeating the motions he had made on her own shoulders. She noticed that Aunt Esther was also wearing a dark blue skirt and blouse and realized she was dressing in dark clothes out of respect for mama's passing. She admired the depth of her aunt's feelings for her departed family.

"Larson, would you ask Cook to have supper ready a little earlier tonight? I think six o'clock would be best. Thank you."

He nodded. "Will that be all ma'am?"

"Yes, thank you, Larson." Her aunt nodded to the butler, and then Alex and Annaveta followed her out the door. The slightly windy but warm Odessa weather greeted them.

"I hope you two have good walking shoes on. I know of a short cut to the port." A smile brightened Aunt Esther's face.

They followed her down a well-used trail. Annaveta walked fast to keep up with her aunt. Finally coming through the maze of trees, Annaveta drank in the vivid picture before her—the blue-gray horizon, the golden rays streaming through the clouds, the deep shimmer of the ocean. No artist could paint a picture so bold and so breathtaking.

"It's beautiful, isn't it? I never get enough of being near the ocean." Aunt Esther looped her arm through Annaveta's, and they walked to the bottom of the hill onto the sandy beach.

Annaveta breathed in the warm salty air. The sound of waves lapping against the shoreline breathed new life into her.

They were close to the port when she heard a man yell. He ran down the long Odessa staircase, waving a newspaper in his hands, and he stopped when he got to where most of the men worked.

"I wonder what he's saying?" Aunt Esther motioned for them to move closer to the peer where men started to gather. "Ah, there's your uncle. He'll sort it out."

Annaveta looked where her aunt pointed and saw the man with the newspaper talking to a tall, distinguished man with gray-streaked dark hair. She had forgotten what a handsome man Uncle Roman was.

"Let's get closer so we can hear what he's saying," Alex said. Apparently he wanted to hear the news, too.

They walked closer until they stood at the edge of the crowd of men. The guy with the newspaper shuffled his feet until Uncle Roman held up his hand to quiet everyone. The grave expression on his face gave her a sense of foreboding.

"I just received some sobering news from St. Petersburg this morning. Today, Germany has declared war on Russia. Men, we are at war!"

August 1, 1914. The day life changed forever. For a few moments, the silence was deafening. After that, it seemed everyone talked at the same time.

She looked at Alex, saw his face turn an ashen color. The gray mask – that many other men in the crowd wore – was the color of fear.

The gravity of this moment struck her speechless.

What will happen to us now that we are at war?

Chapter Two

Roman Levinson finished his meal and leaned back on his chair. "So, tell us, Alex, how did you meet our niece?"

Alex saw the frown that creased the otherwise smooth features on Annaveta's uncle's forehead. Mr. Levinson stared into Alex's own eyes employing the skilled tactics of a drill sergeant.

He carefully considered his next words.

"Annaveta and I met on a day I was helping my sister hunt for herbs. We saw her a few more times before the tragic fire. It wasn't long after that Annaveta came to live with my family at Pleve colony." Alex shifted his gaze between Mr. and Mrs. Levinson. Annaveta's aunt nodded at Alex. He took it as a sign to continue, until he looked over at Mr. Levinson.

Tension crawled up Alex's spine at Mr. Levinson's glacial stare. He took a sip of tea to calm his nerves, still Annaveta's uncle didn't move. Mr. Levinson didn't drink the tea in front of him. He didn't squirm in his chair. He didn't avoid eye contact.

"She lived in your family's home?"

"Ja, only until the she was sent threatening notes from the man she refused to marry back in her village. So Annaveta escaped to St. Petersburg." Alex glanced over at the subject of their conversation to see her wiping her fingers across damp cheeks. He found his own tea cup to be of sudden interest, and he swallowed the anger that flared whenever he talked about this. "Your niece worked as a nanny and then as a nurse in the city, and that's where I found her. When the Black Hand locked her in that dungeon in St. Petersburg—and we finally got free—we escaped and came here to you, Annaveta's only living relatives."

"That's an amazing story. So how do you know this man didn't follow you to Odessa?" Mrs. Levinson asked her niece.

"When we left the city, he had been put in jail. So he couldn't have followed us. I hope we aren't causing you trouble by coming here." Annaveta lips quivered as she continued the story.

Alex hurt for Annaveta and her discomfort. He wished they would both stop all the questions so she could relax again.

"I'm sure you will be safe here, and we are so glad you came, aren't we Roman?" Mrs. Levinson looked at her husband, who had uncrossed his arms and sat up.

"I was unsure about your accent, but now I understand you have a German background." Roman made the word "German" sound so dirty. Like it was something to be ashamed of. Alex didn't know if he read it right—it sounded so subtle—but he was sure there was an undercurrent of disapproval in his tone.

"Our son Jude began his tour of duty already last year. Just last month he was promoted to Lieutenant in the Imperial Navy. We're proud of him." Mr. Levinson leaned toward Alex, his forehead a torture of grooves above that hook of a nose. "And what about you, Alex? Now that the war has begun, when are you planning to sign-up to fight?"

Alex's mind raced with a thousand excuses for why he couldn't fight in the war. In fact, it was all he had thought about since they heard the news. He knew he would likely be conscripted when he turned twenty, which was only three months away, but right now he knew deep inside himself that he couldn't deal with the aftermath that choosing to fight would cause. He was terrified of getting killed or maimed, that was true. But there were more reasons. He knew it was his responsibility to fight for his country, but if he left, how would Annaveta be safe? He decided to tell Annaveta's uncle a version of the truth that hopefully wouldn't make things worse for him or for Annaveta.

"It's all I've thought about today. We're really at war with Germany, it's just so hard to believe." Alex looked around the table and was encouraged by an understanding smile from Annaveta. "Right now, I'm not quite twenty, the age of conscription, so I guess that gives me time to think. The thought of fighting against other Germans, some of whom are my relatives, seems like an impossible situation to me. How could I do that? And yet, I was born and raised in Russia. This is my country, and my loyalty is here. I know those in my family back home feel the same way, because we've had conversations about what would happen if there was war. But I still feel this inner conflict about killing my relatives. There's also Annaveta to consider. I have a responsibility to keep her safe. How can I do that when I would be far away?"

"None of those is reason enough to not do your duty. And as for keeping Annaveta safe, she will be safe enough with us."

Mr. Levinson's disapproval sent waves of guilt and confusion through him. He could tell Annaveta's uncle didn't care how difficult the decision was—duty came above all.

"Roman, our guests haven't been with us very long. I think a little more generosity might be in order?" Mrs. Levinson's tone along with her words landed like a fist on the table between them.

Mr. Levinson stared at his wife overlong, before a slight nod revealed his surrender.

Alex felt the strain of heightened expectations.

"Now let's stop talking about war, shall we?" Annaveta's aunt said. "It would be much more exciting to talk about the dinner party we'll have in Annaveta's honour. We should plan for Friday night, two weeks from now. What do you think?" Her eyes were bright as she talked of gown fittings for Annaveta and hiring extra workers to help with food preparation and decorating their great room for the big day.

Annaveta's face flushed and her smile glowed. He was glad her aunt and uncle wanted to make a big deal of their only niece's arrival. Sort of like the prodigal child coming home. He only hoped he wouldn't be tossed aside like day-old bread as Annaveta's uncle and aunt killed the fatted calf.

Alex longed for sleep. He longed for the unconscious state of lying still for hours, for one day—and night—free from worry or fear. His deepest thoughts had been exposed, and he had been found wanting. His thoughts twisted and turned in rhythm with his restless movements tonight.

He sat up in bed. He needed to get out of this room to think.

Two days ago, Mrs. Levinson had asked if he wanted to move out of the West Wing and into the guest house. It was nearer the stables and his woodworking shop, so he agreed.

However, it wasn't only the new sleeping arrangements that made him unsettled. Since the dinner yesterday evening, Alex realized that somehow he wasn't measuring up to Mr. Levinson's high standards. It had almost seemed like he couldn't wait for Alex to go to war, so he wouldn't be around Annaveta anymore.

He paced, frustrated and restless from his own insecurities. The dim light spiraled its long fingers through the window of his small room in the guest house, beckoning him to come outside. He sat on the edge of the bed and rubbed his eyes. Without too much fuss, he finished dressing and walked out the door, not wanting to miss the beauty of the sunrise. His rapid steps followed a path that led to the small hill on the estate that overlooked the city and the ocean.

Alex reached the summit and saw long auburn hair flowing in the gentle breeze. His heart raced faster, like it always did when he saw Annaveta. He just stood there for moment, drinking in the sight of her. The sun glinting on her hair turned the long strands into a golden-orange hue matching that of the sunrise. She turned her head as his foot kicked a rock.

"You're awake." She smiled up at him. A rare peace shimmered in her sea green eyes that he hadn't seen for a very long time.

"Ja, I couldn't sleep any longer." Alex sat next to her, stretching his long legs beside her much shorter ones. He looked at her again, amazed that she loved him. He knew that, but even now he couldn't help the insecurities that plagued him. They were now living with very different people from what he was used to. Last night, hearing Annaveta's aunt talk of shopping for and planning this big event, made him realize he had walked into a different mindset and culture. Reality of this new moneyed world took him out of his usual place of comfort.

"Are you glad we came to stay here with your relatives?" Alex looked at her, curious as to how this first day had been for her.

"Oh, Alex. I'm so happy." Annaveta's face beamed with pleasure. "I can't believe how nice and welcoming Aunt Esther and Uncle Roman have been. They have fed us, and now they are going to invite their friends to a party in my honour. I don't think I have ever had any sort of celebration that was just for me, Alex. All my childhood years, Mama had to give me something in secret, usually a handkerchief she had stitched or clothes that had been remade. I was grateful to her for doing even that, because Papa drank away any extra money we ever had. So you can understand that I'm so surprised and really looking forward to spending time with my aunt and uncle." A stray tear made its way down her cheek. She wiped it away and smiled at him. "Something in me just wants to have a chance at a deeper relationship with my uncle that I never had with my papa, and just to get to know the aunt that Mama talked about with such fondness." She looked up at him and laughed a little. "You must think me silly."

"No. I think that's really great. And it's probably something that's long overdue." Alex put his arm around her, pulling her close to his side. He kissed the top of her head, letting her lavender scent fill his senses. He put his cheek against her head and breathed in his fill of this amazing and sensitive woman. He was happy that she was getting closer to her aunt and uncle, but his heart held a sense of fear. What if this couple, the very people that Annaveta loved, took her away from him? What if they decided they really didn't like him at all and did all they could to separate Annaveta from him? Who would Annaveta choose?

"I'm so happy to be surrounded by people I love and who love me back." Annaveta let out a long sigh of contentment.

Alex hoped it would always be so for her. However, insecurities about Annaveta's love and whether her aunt and uncle thought he was good enough for their niece created knots of endless worry inside of him. He hoped that somehow he could show them he was someone who would be good for their only niece.

As Alex walked toward the main house, he could hardly believe two weeks had already gone by since they had arrived in Odessa.

That night, Annaveta's aunt and uncle would host a dinner party and a ball to introduce Annaveta to their friends. Mrs. Levinson had somehow managed to find the right size trousers for him with a new fitted jacket. He had found them on his bed late this afternoon with a note asking if he would please wear them to tonight's dinner. So there he was, all dressed up like a peacock.

In the past week, Alex felt like an unwelcome guest. He didn't know really what it was he had done to upset Mr. Levinson. Well, that wasn't completely true. Annaveta's uncle shunned the things that Alex found important—his relationship with Annaveta, his identity as a Volga German, and his loyalty to his family.

Once Annaveta had told her aunt that Alex was very good at making furniture, he'd been given the opportunity to use the old carriage house to work. He designed and crafted new chairs for their dining room. There, amid the tools and the sawdust, his troubled mind soothed.

It felt good to let the scent of the oak fill his senses, to run his hands down the unfinished surface of the wood. Touching it and forming it into something reminded him of home. He loved creating with his hands. However, he wished he could have a little more time with the woman he loved. Instead, these past two weeks it seemed like he didn't really get to see Annaveta most of the time, except for meals and that one morning they'd shared alone on the ridge of the mountain. He had the feeling her uncle and aunt were trying to keep him as busy as possible so he wouldn't have so much time with Annaveta. He missed her. He would change that, starting tonight.

Alex entered the Levinsons' manor just as a carriage drove up to the stately front entrance. He walked through the door and Larson whispered to him that Annaveta was in the drawing room. He walked to the large room that was just off to the side of the grand Ball Room.

Looking around, he saw Mrs. Levinson talking with a well dressed, middle-aged couple. Beside them was a dark-haired man who looked to be around his own age and a much shorter blonde girl whose face would have been pretty if she didn't wear so much makeup.

Annaveta stood next to her aunt, looking more beautiful than he ever remembered seeing her before. She wore a long flowing gown of dark purple, and with her auburn hair up and a simple string of pearls around her neck, she looked like a natural socialite.

Born to privilege.

For a second, it felt like someone had punched him in the gut. He liked the Annaveta who had lived those months with his family, and he hoped living with her aunt and uncle wouldn't change her too much. To him, this world of the rich seemed too strange, and he knew he didn't fit in. If he was honest with himself, deep inside he hoped Annaveta wouldn't get more attached to her aunt and uncle than she was to him. But he knew that was probably a selfish thought.

Alex saw another man, along with a young lady, walk over to Mrs. Levinson and Annaveta. The dark haired man looked vaguely familiar in an unsettling sort of way. Alex was about to walk over there when the two of them moved away and began talking with others. He decided he would ask Annaveta later if she knew the man.

He walked over to the punch bowl, and one of the maids poured him a drink. He looked up so Annaveta could see him from where she was standing, and when she noticed him, he nodded at her. She turned back to talk to a young man who her uncle brought over.

Alex tensed when he noticed three other young men waiting to meet her. So this was really what the ball was about. It wasn't really about introducing Annaveta to their friends. It had more to do with Annaveta meeting the right kind of man, someone who her aunt and uncle thought was worthy of her hand in marriage.

Alex stood there drinking his punch, watching and inwardly hating it as those men fawned over the woman he loved. What could he do? Annaveta was desperate to please her aunt and uncle. Yet he also had a need to please Annaveta—to do what he could to make her happy.

The music started, and Annaveta danced the first dance with her uncle. Alex watched the way her eyes mirrored the smile on her face as she looked up at her uncle. He was happy she had found a father-figure at last who treated her well and loved her in return. As they twirled around, Mr. Levinson looked at him and frowned.

Alex stiffened at his tough features and the look of pure dislike. The soaring strains of Tchaikovsky's "Violin Concerto" began. Then Annaveta's uncle, a big smile lighting his face, gave her hand to a tall, dark-haired, well-built man. Alex studied his face and recognized him from a dinner party Mr. and Mrs. Levinson had hosted the week before. Alex right away noticed two traits that stood out about the families the Levinsons were friends with—they were wealthy and they had eligible sons for marrying Annaveta.

Alex studied Annaveta's dance partner and remembered his name. Sacha Yudin. He seemed over-confident and tried in subtle ways to make people around him—people he thought were beneath him—look and feel small.

It took all of Alex's discipline not to walk up to him and pull him away from her. It seemed to take forever for their dance to finish. Alex walked up to take his turn with Annaveta just as the sound of the last violin rang through the air. He held out his hand for her. She curtsied first to Sacha, who bowed and kissed her hand.

"You don't need to hold her hand longer than necessary, Sacha." Alex lifted one eyebrow and glared at Sacha, who released her hand with a lingering "come-hither" smile.

"Your problem is you're not cultured enough to know how to treat a lady." Sacha smirked at him. "It's time you realized you need to go back to the fields—taking care of cows and mucking out stalls, where you belong."

Alex glared at him. When the music started again, Alex took Annaveta's hand. Sacha stood and stared at him for a long time before he swaggered away, heading toward his friends at the side of the room.

Alex looked down at Annaveta, glad to finally have her in his arms. She was frowning at him.

"What?" Alex wasn't sure why she would be mad at him.

"I don't like to see you like this. Angry and impatient." Her eyes searched his own. "Why are you being like this?"

"Sorry. I just don't like how your aunt and uncle seem to be throwing all these single men in your direction ever since we got here." He closed his eyes to calm his frustration, thankful it was a slow dance. He looked into her shiny sea green eyes and spoke his heart. "Doesn't your uncle realize we are more than just friends? That I love you?"

Annaveta looked at his shoulders and around the room instead of into his eyes.

"No, Uncle Roman doesn't know that, and neither does my aunt. Alex, can you be patient, please? I'm doing all I can to be a good niece and not cause trouble. I'll talk to them when the time seems right, okay?"

Someone tapped on his shoulder. The music had stopped, and he didn't even realize it.

"Okay." He kissed her hand and walked away, more frustrated than when he started. It felt like he was losing her, and he didn't know what to do about it. All he could do at the moment was wait.

He seemed to be thwarted every time he tried to get closer to Annaveta. And that thought made him irritated.

Chapter Three

Annaveta covered her mouth to smother a laugh when she saw her wealthy aunt kneeling in the garden and digging in the dirt with her hands. She loved that her aunt was a mixture of culture and practicality, besides being unexpected. She walked closer, knelt down, and started to help pull the weeds.

"I used to help Mama in the garden at home." Tears formed in her eyes, and she looked over at her aunt. "We didn't have beautiful flowers like this, but I remember planting potatoes, carrots, and onions, and even though we didn't have much, it was good to be together."

"Ah, child. How I wish she was still on this earth." Aunt Esther hugged her close to her heart. "I'm so happy you are here with us. She's most likely looking down from Heaven with a smile right now."

Annaveta looked up at the clouds and imagined her mama's smile. She closed her eyes for a second to soak it all in. "I love that thought. Especially being here with you and Uncle Roman. It feels like coming home."

Warmth tingled up the length of Annaveta's arms as she thought of her mama. Her soft hugs, her loyalty, and most of all, her love. This reminded her of the many conversations she had as she helped Mama in their small garden. Even through all the really hard times with Papa's drunkenness and their poverty, she would talk of her loyalty to her flesh and blood and to her Jewish roots.

When Annaveta was still little, Mama had a special box where she hid things that she treasured. Once she reached into it, retrieved a metal Star of David, and showed it to her daughter. That was the first time Annaveta heard her explain that the double triangle in the star was a symbol of the connection they have to Yahweh. And that it represented all she held dear in her Jewish identity.

She could still hear Mama's voice echoing in her ear to this day. "The Star of David is a picture of who you are. Its roots go deep into your soul. It will give you your strength to be the woman you were always meant to be. It's the only thing in the world that amounts to anything, for 'tis the only thing in this world that lasts. And don't you forget it. It's the only thing worth working for, worth fighting for—worth dying for."

It was something Mama had learned not to talk about in front of her husband. Papa got very angry whenever Mama mentioned anything about her Jewish heritage. So she talked to her children about those things she held closest to her heart. She was glad Mama had talked to her about her Jewish background, but she didn't feel as passionate about it as her mama did back then.

Since Mama's death, she longed to find out more about her background and to really know where she came from. Her identity. Somewhere along the way, through all the trauma, she had lost who she was. She had to hide herself so many times from people who rejected her, called her names, and considered her worthless, that she had begun to believe them. She was lost in her longing to understand herself. Her voice and the essence of who she was and what she had to offer to the world had been snuffed out like a candle in a hurricane of blustery wind.

She hoped while she lived with her aunt and uncle she would find out more about the heritage her Mama loved so dearly. She wanted to know why her mama loved her Jewish roots so much, and why it should matter to her. She meant what she said to Aunt Esther, that being there felt like coming home.

"I'm so happy to hear you say that, my dear." Aunt Esther finished weeding the last few flowers and stood. "Many of my friends at the ball last night thought you looked enough like me to be my own daughter. I know Uncle Roman and I both think of you as our own."

"Thank you, Aunt." Annaveta stood and helped carry the bucket and tools to the large garden shed close to the old carriage house.

"Ah, good," Aunt Esther said. "Alex is working on the dining table. It will be nice to have the old one replaced."

She heard the sounds of scraping wood as they walked toward the shed. She thought of their dance last night. She didn't understand why Alex was putting all this pressure on her to tell her aunt and uncle of their relationship. His anger last night was a sign of his jealousy.

He had done this before at the Oktoberfest they had in Pleve colony when she lived with his family. But that time he'd been drunk and punched another man who had shown an interest in her. And then she had stormed out of the

29

building. But this time she had just stood there, not really knowing what to say. She knew he was afraid of losing her, and that had prompted his anger. But she hated how he reacted. She loved him, and believed that nothing would change her feelings for Alex. If only she knew how to make that obvious to him. One way would probably be to tell her aunt and uncle about their relationship.

She thought about why she hadn't told them. Although she hated to admit it, she realized she worried once she told them about Alex and their promise to each other, that it would change her relationship with her aunt and uncle.

The way her uncle had demanded answers from Alex when they first arrived, she could tell he disapproved of Alex's German background, as well as the fact that he hadn't signed up for the war yet. Secretly, Annaveta was happy about that. She didn't want him getting hurt. But she didn't like that Uncle Roman continued to pressure him about it. Right now, she wanted to grow her relationship with her uncle and aunt, and she didn't want to do anything that would make them disappointed in her or to disapprove of her. She longed for a man in her life that was like a father, that she respected and loved and would love her back. She thought of her own father and the abuse she and the rest of her family went through for years, and she was glad he was dead. She felt guilty for even thinking it, but it was true. That was why she craved her uncle's acceptance and love.

"So, what did you enjoy most about last night's ball?" Her aunt closed the doors to the shed and looked at her, a smile lighting her eyes.

"I liked dressing up and being treated like a princess. Thank you for inviting all those people. It was good to meet so many new friends. My feet are still sore from all that dancing." Annaveta giggled as she thought of the many men she had danced with.

"I saw you were almost danced off your feet." Aunt Esther winked. "Well, I'm happy you enjoyed yourself. Don't be surprised if sometime soon, some of those young men come to the house asking to court you."

Annaveta's eyes grew large. She didn't want that. "Why would they do that?" She blurted out the first thought that came into her head. "I was just having fun meeting new friends last night. Do you think they thought it was something more?"

"I'm sure most of them are hoping for just that." Aunt Esther's musical laugh seemed to float over their heads. "Well, we'll just see what happens."

As they entered the house, the maid came to let them know that luncheon would be served in a few minutes.

"Well, we should change into something more suitable and get the dirt off our hands, I suppose." Aunt Esther rang the bell that was nestled on the table near the hallway. Soon a young maid came.

"Yes, Ma'am?" She curtsied and gave them both a small smile.

"Would you assist Annaveta into one of those day dresses that came yesterday? Oh, and we'll be going out for the afternoon."

"Right away, Ma'am."

"See you soon." Aunt Esther and Annaveta each walked to

their separate rooms. Annaveta's maid had three beautiful dresses for her to chose from by the time she got there—a light cream, a light blue, and a dark green. Since her Aunt had yet to tell her where they were going, she chose the dark green, as it was more practical than the other two.

It didn't take long for Annaveta to wash up and for her maid to fix her hair. She looked in the mirror as Tatyana buttoned her dress in the back. She could hardly recognize herself. With the form-fitting dress, her hair in a loose bun, and a few loose tendrils framing her face, she looked like a lady. But she didn't feel like what the mirror suggested. Instead, she felt quite the opposite. More like a fraud dressed as a princess, one who wouldn't fit in no matter how hard she tried.

She determined to do all she could so her aunt and uncle wouldn't have reason to be ashamed of her. At a few luncheons with Aunt Esther and her high society friends and again at last night's ball, it was all she could do to smile and try to act and say the right thing. When she was unsure what to say, usually she said nothing at all. Learning the social graces expected of her was a balancing act. Skill for which she had no talent.

Annaveta walked down the hall toward the luncheon room, wondering what her aunt had planned for the afternoon. She sat in her usual place, across from Aunt Esther.

"Looks like it's just us two for lunch today. Your uncle has a business meeting, and Alex said he was in the middle of something, so he was going to eat a little later." The maids put sandwiches on the table and ladled soup into their bowls. Hot tea soon appeared in front of them, as well.

She wondered at Alex's absence. She knew he was upset with

her last night, so maybe he was avoiding her. She would need to find him later and talk to him.

"So, today I thought we'd go someplace you haven't been before." A stoic look crossed her Aunt's face. "But I believe you can handle it. Today we'll be going to the hospital to do what we can for the wounded soldiers who are there."

"Helping in a hospital is something I've done before." Mixed emotions flooded Annaveta's senses as she thought of babies born, as well as those suffering from disease whom she had done all she could to help. In some ways she felt like she failed when those who were sick died. Fear gripped her at the thought of people dying under her care again. But it was her duty to her country and to her aunt and uncle. With shaky breath she added, "I will help however I can."

"I know you will, my dear. It won't be pleasant, but it's our duty to help those who are sick and less fortunate. However, some of my friends and the young ladies you met last week at our luncheon will be there, too. We are part of the Russian Red Cross Society. We do what we can to help our soldiers in the war."

"Well, I'm glad I can help in some way too, Aunt."

They finished their tea and got up, ready to go.

"Larson, see to it that the carriage is brought around, please."

Outside, a beautiful black carriage waited for them, with two beautifully matched black Frisian horses. Annaveta admired the proud lift to their heads and shiny coats. She recognized this type of horse because Count and Countess Tashkova had a similar pair who seemed to dance when they walked.

A short ride, and the carriage came to a halt. The door opened to a large building, long and three floors high. Annaveta stepped out aided by Alfred, her aunt's groom and driver.

She matched her aunt's brisk pace as they climbed the stairs to the old building. The red cross symbol was placed in the middle of both doors, bringing back memories of her time at the St. Petersburg hospital.

A nurse recognized her aunt. She gave them each an apron to wear, then she took them to where the wounded soldiers were. At first Annaveta followed Aunt Esther around and listened as she talked to each soldier. Then she left her aunt and went to the far end of the room where the men who had the worst injuries were.

Annaveta choose to do what she could for these dying men, in spite of the knot that formed in her stomach from being back in a hospital. She gave them water to drink, read their letters from home, and wrote letters to their girlfriends, wives, and parents. As she talked with them, she asked them what they needed help with, and she wrote down all the things the men named. Socks, handkerchiefs, and warm clothes. A few of them said it would have helped them to have a letter with encouraging words and news from home.

Annaveta stood up and made her way past the nurses and doctors toward her aunt. She saw Aunt Esther talking to some ladies she recognized from last week's luncheon. She remembered talking to the blonde girl, who was Sacha Yudin's sister. Her name was Dinah. Beside her was a taller girl with dark brown hair. She had come to the last luncheon with her father. If her memory was right, her name was Jarena.

"Ah, there is my favourite niece." Aunt Esther put her hand out and Annaveta clung to it like a lifeline. She was unsure of herself around these cultured and refined girls, who had grown up used to having whatever they wanted. The thought that weighed heavily on her mind was what they would say if they knew where she had come from? Would they run away from her as fast as they could if they knew she had grown up with a drunk father, living in poverty with only two pieces of clothing to her name?

She was afraid of the answer.

Her aunt interrupted the negative chatter in her head. "Annaveta, you remember Mrs. Yudin, her daughter Dinah, and her friend Jarena from last week's luncheon?"

"Yes." Annaveta did her best to put on a gracious smile despite her quivering nerves. "I'm happy to see you again so soon."

"Mrs. Yudin was inviting us to a dinner party they are hosting in their home soon."

"Sounds enjoyable, Mrs. Yudin." Annaveta gave the customary smile, but on the inside she worried about being in the company of Mrs. Yudin's son for an evening. However, there was nothing to be done. Maybe Alex would come with them. Although he had not been at the last two dinner parties they had gone to. It seemed like Uncle Roman usually had some new job he needed Alex to do last minute when they went out. Hopefully this time would be different.

It was late afternoon by the time they left the hospital.

They sat across from each other in the carriage. Aunt Esther looked at her for a long time before she spoke.

"I know this wasn't easy. I felt sick to my stomach the first time I went and saw all those men and the pain they endure because of this wretched war."

Annaveta was still a little shaken by the pain she saw in those men's eyes and the stories they shared with her.

"I feel so helpless as I talk with them, Aunt. I see their pain as I look in their eyes, and I don't know what to do." She raised a hand to smooth her hair, a force of habit when her nerves had been frayed at the edge. "What is being done for these men and their families?"

"I don't believe their families are taken care of, but the soldiers themselves are looked after here in the hospital. And then our group of women send socks and practical clothing and food to the men who are fighting. We're doing our duty to help the war effort." Aunt Esther looked at her, a grim smile on her face. "But let's not go on about soldiers or this cursed war. Not when we have something much more interesting to talk about. I'm glad Mrs. Yudin is giving a dinner party. I think this night will be big. It's sort of a send off for Sacha who, she tells me, has been assigned to his regiment. Since the Yudins are quite wealthy, they put on the biggest and most lavish dinners. So it will be a nice change. Don't you think?"

"Yes, Aunt." Annaveta nodded and gave a slight smile to her Aunt, even though she was frustrated. How could she talk about dinner parties when these soldiers and their families needed so much help? She decided she would need to think about all that she had learned as she listened to their stories. Maybe there was something she could do to help make the conditions of the wounded soldiers a little better.

The week seemed to fly by. In Annaveta's mind, the day they were to have dinner at the Yudin Estate came much too soon.

She woke up early in the morning from a horrible dream. Baron Yakov, Misha, and Monsieur Arnaud had been talking together. She saw them whispering, looking over at her, and then they put their heads together to whisper again, but she couldn't hear what they said. All she knew was that it seemed like they were conspiring to get even with her. She ran to escape from them, but they started chasing her.

That's when the dream ended.

She rubbed her forehead and was surprised when she found her hand wet and shaking. She needed to talk to Alex.

Jumping out of bed, she hurried to put on the old brown dress she had when she arrived at her aunt and uncle's home. It was the easiest dress to put on because the neck was scooped wide. Normally she wore an insert in the top, but she didn't bother trying to find it. With quick footsteps, she went down the hallway and out the back toward the garden. A reddish glimmer of dawn just began to creep over the tops of the trees above the guest house where Alex lived. She looked around, hoping no one was watching her. The guest house was surrounded by trees and was quite a distance from the main house. Still, she knew she shouldn't be knocking on his door at any time unless she had a chaperone with her.

But as she saw it, she was desperate.

Her three quick raps on the door must have awakened him, because she heard rustling and then footsteps.

"Ja, what is it?" Alex's eyes widened when he saw who stood on his front porch. "Annaveta what's wrong? Did something happen?"

Annaveta just stared at him, his suspenders looped loosely over his bare shoulders. Her face flamed, and she looked away to gather her thoughts.

"You can tell me." Alex put his hands on her shoulders and put his hand under her chin so she would look up into his eyes. This was even worse for her to resist. Now he was so close to her, she could see the dark stubble on his chin.

She found herself swaying toward him, and she rested her head on his shoulder.

"I needed to see you. I had a bad dream about the Black Hand, and I just needed to feel safe and loved again. That's how I feel when I'm with you. That's why I came here."

Annaveta moved her head to look up at him. He ran his fingers through the length of her hair and pulled a lock of it up to his lips and kissed it. Annaveta shivered at the intimate gesture.

"It's just a dream. You're safe here." Alex looked into her eyes, as if willing her to believe his words. "Have you seen anyone or anything that seems suspicious?" His two calloused hands gently caressed the sides of her face, and he looked deep into her eyes. "You'd tell me, right?"

"I would tell you. And I don't think I've seen anyone suspicious."

"Did you recognize that older dark haired man at the dinner party the other night? He was with Jarena."

"I do remember meeting Jarena. The man with her was her father. When I looked at him, I had a weird creepy feeling, but I can't say I remember knowing him." Annaveta shuddered as she remembered. "But that dream I had terrified me." Tears filled her eyes as memories flooded her of the last time she had experienced the twisted and evil minds of men that were part of the Black Hand.

"I know. But you're safe here. With me." He put his arms around her waist and held her in a loose grip. She could see a small vein pulsing in the corner of his forehead. She ran her hands down the muscles in his arms, drawing strength from his warmth. He tilted her head back and ran his fingers through her waist length hair. Suddenly he pulled her close to him and kissed her, gently at first, then he trailed kisses over her face and back to her lips as if he couldn't get enough of her.

"Alex, we need to slow down." She pushed on his chest and stepped back from him. "Besides, I have something else I need to talk to you about."

She watched as he closed his eyes and ran his hand through his hair. She could tell he was frustrated, but they both needed to listen to the voice of reason. He went over to sit on the bench on the deck of his house and patted the seat beside him, urging her to sit down.

"Okay," He winked at her and grinned. "Tell me what's on your mind."

"Well, you aren't going to like it, but I want to tell you because above all I want you to trust me." Annaveta sat on the bench opposite him and watched as his muscles bunched and the smile left his face.

"Is this about you being busy again tonight? Is this the same reason why your uncle asked me to design and build another bedroom set? He told me if I got it done faster, there would be a big bonus in it for me. So what is it you're doing tonight?" He stood up and paced for awhile before stopping in front of her. When he crossed his arms, she worried.

"Alex, don't be upset with me. I can't help it if my aunt plans these parties. I need to go with them. I wish they would've asked you to join us." Annaveta stood, imploring him with her eyes.

"Well, we all know why they didn't ask me to come with you. So which man are they parading you in front of this time?" Even in the early dawn, she could see his cheeks flush red with anger.

"We're going to the Yudin Estate." His hands bunched into fists. Annaveta took one of his hands in hers and kissed it. "I know you're not happy about that, but it's only for tonight, and then Aunt Esther said many of the men are being transferred to their regiment this coming week. Besides, there will be a lot of people there, so there's nothing to worry about."

"I don't like it, Annaveta. I don't trust Sacha to be within ten feet of you." Alex glared at her and crossed his arms. "If he or any other man touches you, I'll kill them."

"Alex, I hear you. Unfortunately so does the rest of the world." She turned her head when she heard a door slam. The cook stepped outside to dump out some water, and she looked through the trees right at them. "I need to go. Everyone is starting to wake up for the day. I didn't come here to fight. But I would appreciate if you would answer me one question."

He looked at her, his jaw clenched just as hard as his fists, without saying a word.

"Do you trust me, Alex?" Annaveta stared at him as the silence went on for what seemed like minutes. "Because I think you need to know the answer to that question first, before you worry about anything else."

Annaveta turned and ran off the porch, her feet stumbling through the trees on her way to the main house. Questions about their relationship flooded her mind. She didn't understand how Alex could be passionate and tell her how much he loved her in one moment and not say anything about trusting her in the next? How could he love her and not trust her?

Sometimes he made her mad and confused all at the same time. Annaveta decided this night she was going to go and enjoy herself anyway, no matter what.

She stared at herself in the floor length mirror. Again her image was foreign to her. Tatyana had twisted her reddish-brown hair into a loose bun with ringlets framing her face. Her green satin gown shimmered in the dimming light.

"You look so beautiful, miss." Her maid picked off imaginary lint from the back of her dress. "The hue of this dress brings out the green in your eyes."

"Thank you, Tatyana." She was grateful for the new clothes Aunt Esther's modiste had delivered earlier this week. She hoped she would have fun tonight, and that tonight's adventure would help her to forget that Alex couldn't answer the one question she needed him to.

She hurried down the hallway to where her aunt and uncle were just putting on their wraps.

"Oh, my dear. You'll be the most beautiful young lady there tonight. Won't she, Roman?" Aunt Esther walked around her, looking at the dress.

"Every young man will be vying for his chance to dance with you." Uncle Roman put the matching wrap around her shoulders.

Annaveta tried to shake off the guilt that flooded her as she stepped into the carriage. She peered out the window toward the guest house and saw the dim light of a lantern. She felt guilty going to dinner knowing men would be there, hoping to court her. She knew Alex hated that she would dance with them to appease her aunt and uncle, but she felt like she needed to respect their wishes.

The whole thing confused her.

Deep inside she knew she craved the approval of both Alex and her aunt and uncle, but right now it looked like she needed to pick sides.

That was impossible.

All three of them had shown her different sides of love that she had never known before. All three of them had helped her understand who she was. All three of them meant the world to her.

She had to remind herself to smile as they walked up the ornate staircase toward the massive doors of the Yudin mansion. The butler took their wraps as they entered, then a maid led them toward the dining room.

After they introduced themselves to their hosts, Sacha came, bowed and kissed her hand, and talked with Uncle Roman and Aunt Esther. Annaveta realized what a smooth talker he was. He was definitely used to mingling with the gentlemen and ladies of the upper class. Some of the other young men she had met at her ball came to talk to them.

She remembered Anton with his red hair and lisp, and the way he was so easily embarrassed. The black-haired man, Judge Saratov's oldest son. Sacha called him David and said he was serious most of the time, much like his father. Then there was Yuri, who was by far the funniest of all of them. Always making jokes and running his hand through his wild, curly brown hair whenever he had to think seriously about anything. His father was a General in the Army. Sacha told her he was constantly trying to get his father upset at him because he was tired of living under strict rules. And she also saw many other men and women her age whom she hadn't met yet. The guest list appeared much larger than that of any other gathering she'd been to.

Soon dinner was announced, and Annaveta discovered Mrs. Yudin had seated her on Sacha's right hand side. Annaveta was surprised that in his own home, when he could choose any one of the beautiful women to sit with, he chose her. On his other side was the tall, raven-haired beauty, Nadia Berkovitz. She wore a red, low-cut gown that hugged her voluptuous figure and increased the male glances aimed in her direction.

Annaveta noticed Sacha drank three glasses of wine in between bites of food and the many questions he asked her.

After talking about what she thought of Odessa and living with her aunt and uncle, he finally began to ask her deeper questions that made her somewhat uncomfortable.

"That guy that I met at the ball, he seems very protective of you. Do you two have an understanding?" Sacha's brown eyes turned dark as he looked intently at the expressions that crossed her face.

"Nothing formal has been spoken, but we understand each other." Annaveta gave him a small smile and hoped her words would discourage his attention.

The strains of the orchestra began to softly play in the background.

"Well, I'd like the chance for us to understand each other better." He stood up beside her chair and sketched a bow. "Would you dance with me?

"I would be honoured." Annaveta said what was expected of her even though she didn't want to encourage his affections.

She glanced over at Aunt Esther, who beamed at her. She knew that her being chosen by the rich heir to the Yudin fortune—and the fact that he was also Jewish—would tip the scales in Sacha's favour, because those things were important to her aunt and uncle.

When she would tell them about Alex, she didn't know.

She danced with Sacha, and his dark brown eyes looked mischievous as he pulled her closer to him. She blushed and turned her head to the side. He moved his head down and rested it against hers.

"You're so beautiful." His breath warmed her ear. She tried to move back, to put a little distance between herself and his invitation to come nearer. Soon the last notes of the waltz lingered in the air, and she was claimed by David Saratov for the next one. She had fun dancing with all the other men, each one a unique personality.

At one point, she looked up and saw another young lady her age, Jarena, dancing with her father. She remembered Alex asking about him, and now that she had a closer look, he did look vaguely familiar, but she couldn't quite place where she had seen him before. She smiled at Jarena and hoped she would be able to talk to her new friend at some point during the evening.

After the last dance set, she felt very warm—like she wouldn't make it another minute unless she got some air. She spied a door that led out into the back garden and quietly made her way outside. It was such a relief to breathe in the cool air. She walked toward the tree shrubs, keeping the house in her view.

"This is one of Mother's favourite places to sit on a summer evening." She tensed and turned around at the sound of Sacha's low baritone voice. "I'm happy you appreciate it, too."

"I do. It's beautiful. But it's starting to get chilly. I should go back inside. My aunt is probably wondering where I am by now." Annaveta turned to go past him, but he grabbed her hands and held them tight.

"I know you don't know me very well, Annaveta. But I'm telling you I want to change that." His low voice turned sultry, and Annaveta felt very uncomfortable being close to him out here in the shadows of the garden.

"Sacha, I told you. Alex and I have an understanding. I don't know what else to say." She peered up at him, unsure of her next move, of his intentions. He tucked a tendril of her hair behind her ear. And before she could move away, he pulled her to close to him and kissed her until she felt like all the breath had gone out of her.

She shoved away from him. "Why did you do that?"

"I needed to take a little taste of you with me when I leave for the war. I know there will be days when your sweet kiss will be all I have to remember of anything good." The wistfulness she heard in his tone turned her own anger upside down, and her heart softened. She couldn't stay mad at him, just when he was about to go to war. Who knew if he would ever come home again?

"God go with you, Sacha." She moved past him, and he grabbed her hand and kissed it. Then she walked back to the crowded dance floor, searching for Aunt Esther.

Annaveta thought of Sacha's kiss and the heat of embarrassment flooded her face. How could she face Alex?

She hoped he wouldn't find out about tonight.

Chapter Four

The knot of uncertainty that sat at the bottom of Alex's stomach like Oma's day-old porridge wouldn't go away.

He sat on the deck recalling the angry words they threw back and forth at each other. In the end, Annaveta had run back to the main house. He should have told her so many things.

Like how much he loved her. That he trusted her. And he did, but for some reason the words wouldn't come when she asked. Part of the reason was because he was so frustrated with her. Why did she feel like she needed to please her Aunt and Uncle? And why did that include not telling them about their love for each other?

He didn't know what he could do to get Roman and Esther Levinson to like him. He wasn't pleased with how he had been excluded from their dinner parties in the past couple of weeks, usually with the excuse that there was so much work for him. He liked the extra money he made, but he knew they didn't think he was good enough for their niece. They did their best to keep him as far away from Annaveta as possible.

He didn't know what he could do to get them to like him more. Of course, it would please Annaveta's uncle if he joined the army, which he would need to do anyway by his twentieth birthday in November. Why couldn't he do something now to help them to see him in a positive light? It was something he prayed for. Now he asked also for a way to make things right with Annaveta. An idea struck him.

Maybe a visit from Mama and Papa right now would be a good thing. Annaveta got along well with them, and it had been too long since he'd seen them. He decided he would ask them to come to Odessa right after the fall butchering and Oktoberfest in Pleve colony. He longed to hear their wisdom and just be with them again.

Alex sat down to pen the letter he hoped would help him win the heart of the only girl he ever loved.

He was the first of the family to enter the breakfast room the next morning. He wasn't surprised the family wasn't there yet. They were probably all trying to catch up on sleep from their dinner the night before. There was a constant inner voice nagging him with questions—like how many men Annaveta had danced with at the Yudin Estate.

Alex felt an invisible fist punch his chest, tightening and twisting things.

He walked to the sidebar where coffee was already made and poured himself a cup. The Odessa newspaper had been brought in, and he picked it up before taking his seat. He sipped his coffee, opened the paper, and nearly choked on the hot drink as he read the headlines.

The Black Hand to Undergo Heavy Investigation. He read further—*The the police were searching for the role the Black Hand played in the Assassination of Archduke Franz Ferdinand.* Alex saw the picture of the Sarajevo police capturing Gavrilo Princip right after he had shot the Archduke. Knots of tension formed in his belly as he remembered that day.

Images flitted through his mind, and he relived the horrible event he'd witnessed. He read on. More Black Hand members were involved than the police had originally thought. Also, the ones who were in jail right now would be behind bars for a long time. And others were implicated and were under investigation.

Alex closed his eyes and rubbed his forehead.

"Good morning." Annaveta seemed to float when she entered a room. He didn't even hear her footsteps. He folded the paper and got up from the table, taking his cup with him.

"Good morning. Can I get you a coffee?" Alex hid the newspaper on the sideboard where hopefully Annaveta wouldn't find it. He poured both of them a cup.

"Listen, Annaveta. I'm sorry for getting mad yesterday. I had no right to take out my anger on you. Do you forgive me?" Alex looked into the green eyes he loved best and saw hurt and anguish there.

"I do forgive you." Annaveta sighed just as Aunt Esther and Uncle Roman entered the room.

"Good morning, Alex. Happy you're up so soon, Annaveta." Aunt Esther motioned for the maids to bring their food and pour more coffee. They bowed their heads for the blessing.

"Well, it looks like another good day for getting work done." Roman eyed Alex from across the table. "How are the bedroom sets looking?"

"I'm almost finished with the first set, and I'm halfway through the second. It looks like all I need is the wood oil to finish them."

Mr. Levinson seemed surprised. "Well, that is good to hear. Esther you'll be getting those bedroom sets sooner than you thought." Roman nodded at Alex as he spoke to his wife.

"Alex, that is so good. If you're almost done with them, I'd like you to make us another dining room set. One much larger than the last." Mrs. Levinson's eyes sparkled. "We might have more dinner parties here in the future, and we could always use a bigger table that would seat more people. Right Roman?"

"Whatever you want my dear." Roman Levinson ate his food, glancing through the newspaper. "Looks like we're off to a good start with the war effort. Many young men are volunteering even before they are conscripted."

Alex tightened his grip on his fork as Mr. Levinson peered at him over the top of his newspaper.

"When are you going to sign up to help, Alex? At the dinner party last night, there were many young men who were being shipped out to their first regiment. Don't you think it's time you stood up for the country you live in?" Roman's neck and cheeks turned to a mottled red.

"I promise sir, I have been giving it all some serious thought.

It's hard to think of fighting against my own relatives—my cousins and uncles. If I'm honest, I admit I struggle with that. That and the fact that I don't turn twenty, the age of conscription, until November." Alex looked at Roman, trying to do his best to put sincerity in his words.

"Well, son, you need to decide soon. I can't have a non-supporter living beneath my roof." Roman Levinson stood and kissed his wife on the forehead. "I have an appointment this morning with a farmer from the Volga region. I might not be back in time for lunch."

Alex watched Roman Levinson's retreating back with misgiving. No matter what he said, he never measured up in the eyes of Annaveta's uncle. With other men trying to court Annaveta, and the fact that he didn't see her very often, he felt like he was growing apart from her. And didn't know what to do about it. He thought about what Roman said as he left the room. He had an appointment to talk to a farmer from the Volga area.

All of a sudden, an idea came to him. Maybe there was something he could help with after all. He knew the people in the Volga region. It might be a way to get into Roman Levinson's good books. He needed to try.

"Excuse me, I need to go. Thank you for the breakfast." He nodded at Annaveta and her aunt.

Mrs. Levinson raised one eyebrow as if wondering why he was suddenly leaving, but rather than speaking, she just nodded.

He walked down the hallway past the library to the large office Mr. and Mrs. Levinson shared. He raised his hand to knock on the door, but stopped when he heard voices.

"The crops this past year in the Volga area were excellent. It seemed like the sun shone at the right time and the rains came down just when we needed them. So the grain I have to offer you for export is some of the best you've ever seen." The man spoke Russian with a heavy German accent.

"What area in the Volga region are you from?" Mr. Levinson's question mirrored Alex's own thoughts.

"I'm from Katherinestadt, not far from Frank colony. We have many really good farmers out there and a lot of good grain to export. For the right price, of course." The man's voice sounded almost cocky, like he was sure he had the better product.

Alex stood outside thinking about the letters he had received from his dad and mom. They were full of worry because of all the rain they had in this year's growing season. His dad's crops had turned out only half as good in comparison to last year's crops.

He knocked on the door, hoping to stop the deal before Roman Levinson went any further with it.

"Come." Roman's booming and clearly frustrated voice called out.

He walked into the office, much to Mr. Levinson's surprise.

"Alex. This isn't a good time, maybe we can talk later." Mr. Levinson's voice was a clear dismissal.

"I'm afraid not, Mr. Levinson." Alex interrupted him to look at the man from the Volga German area. "I have a few questions I'd like to ask this man."

"Alex, we can talk about this later. Whatever is so important can wait until after this meeting." Annaveta's uncle stood up to escort Alex out of the room.

"I have information that you really need to understand before you continue this meeting, Mr. Levinson." Alex stood still and looked at Annaveta's uncle who now stood waiting for him at the door.

"Make it quick, Alex." Mr. Levinson gave a reluctant nod. Pointing to Alex, he introduced the two men. "Peter Bauer, this is Alex Wagner. Alex comes from a German colony not far from yours, I think."

"Ah, good to meet you." Alex nodded. "I overheard a little of your conversation before I knocked on the door." Alex admitted as he looked at Annaveta's uncle and then back at the man in front of him. He looked to be only a few years older than himself. "I thought I heard you say that your region had excellent crops this past year. Is that right?"

"Ja, that's what happened. That's why I am here to see Mr. Levinson about exporting my grain." His hands toyed with suspenders hidden under a thread bare black jacket. Alex noticed his eyes kept darting back and forth between him and Roman Levinson.

Alex hesitated. The two men in the room watched him. His hands started to sweat. This wasn't the kind of questioning a person did on a whim. But he knew much of what Peter was saying wasn't the truth. So even though he felt a certain kind of loyalty toward someone from the German colonies, he had more of a loyalty to the truth. It was the reminder he needed.

"Did you remember having heavy rainfall in May of this year just as you had seeded your crops?" When Peter nodded,

Alex continued his line of questioning. "And how about the end of June, didn't your colony have a big storm then, too? August when it was supposed to be sunny, it hailed so that a third of the crops in Pleve colony failed." Alex looked in the man's gray eyes, trying to get to the truth of the matter. "So my question is, how could your crops be excellent when your weather is not all that different as my father's in Pleve colony? Wouldn't you have had very similar weather?"

The man's face turned red and his lips started moving, but no words came out.

"I propose you sell your grain for half of what the usual rate would be for what is considered above grade grain." Alex watched as the man frowned. He grabbed his hat and Alex thought he would hurry out the door. Instead he turned to face Roman Levinson.

"Your man drives a hard bargain, sir. But we'll go three-quarters the usual rate."

Roman looked at Alex, who shook his head. "My man says no. Your crops aren't worth it."

"Your man! He's Volga German!" Bauer's face contorted as violently as the hat in his hand as he looked between Alex and Roman. When neither responded to him, he sputtered then yelled, "Fine! I'll take half the usual rate. Not a penny less."

"You have a deal," Roman said. "I'll have the contracts ready for you tomorrow, noon."

Bauer shook Roman's hand, then he walked to the door. Before leaving, he turned to Alex. "It's sad to see one colony member not standing up for another. I'm sure your father

wouldn't be pleased. Good day to you." With that, he walked
out the door and slammed it behind him.

Alex stood there staring at the closed door for the longest
time, wondering how he could have chosen his words better.
It needed to be said though. And Peter was wrong, he knew
his father would have been proud of him for standing up
for truth instead of cowering under pressure from anyone. If
anyone's father wouldn't be happy, it would be Peter's. He'd
be ashamed of what his son had tried to do.

"Well, it looks like I owe you my thanks, Alex. I didn't have
any idea he was about to swindle me." Roman Levinson
reached a hand across the desk.

Alex shook his hand, appreciating the gesture.

"I'm surprised you would go against a man from your own
German colonies. What if he goes back home and speaks
against you to all your friends, and all the neighbouring
towns start to think badly of you?"

"Then I guess they weren't really my friends in the first place,
were they?" Alex looked at Roman, and with a surety that
came from the depths of his soul, said, "I was taught to be
honest and forthright in all my dealings, Mr. Levinson. And
even if people are related to me or come from a similar cul-
tural background, if they aren't honest, then I have to speak
up."

Annaveta's uncle stared at him for a long time without saying a word. Alex shifted uncomfortably, not knowing what
else to say.

"It seems I might have misjudged you, Alex. Not just about
your willingness to stand for your principles, although that's

really important." Roman walked around his desk, put his hand on Alex's shoulder, and walked toward the door. "I didn't realize the skills you have in negotiating new business or in your understanding of farmers and their crops. If I need your skills again in the future, can I count on your help?"

Alex reached the door and looked back at Roman Levinson. This powerful businessman was asking for his help. He never thought the day would come when Annaveta's proud uncle would ask for his advice.

"Of course. I'll do what I can." Alex was still dazed by this change of attitude.

"Good, then." He clapped him on the shoulder, the echo of his laughter following Alex as he left the office.

Alex felt more lighthearted than he had since they had first arrived. Maybe there was still hope that his relationship with Roman Levinson would get better.

He whistled while he walked back to the old carriage house. Even watching Annaveta and her Aunt leave for another afternoon excursion didn't dampen his spirits.

They were probably out shopping again, or more likely, Annaveta was meeting more of her Aunt's society friends. He shook off a laugh. He knew how much she didn't like the primping. Especially because she grew up poor and then worked as a nanny. She felt out of place with all the society functions that Mrs. Levinson asked her to attend. Well, it was better here than in St. Petersburg, where they had been hunted and chased like animals by the Black Hand.

Alex looked up toward the tree line on the edge of the Levinson estate before he rounded the corner to walk toward the carriage house. He thought he saw a figure dart in between the trees. He ran toward the person, but when he reached the place where he had seen him last, the man had disappeared.

Alex walked among the trees listening for footsteps, but he couldn't see him anywhere. His nerves were on full alert as he made his way back to the guest house.

Fear gnawed at his stomach as images and vivid details of his and Annaveta's last encounter with the Black Hand sprang to his memory. The horror of what Annaveta had gone through with Misha, Baron Yakov, and Monsieur Arnaud caused his imagination to go wild with ideas of what could happen. From reading the newspaper, he assumed the Black Hand members would be behind bars for a long time. So how could it be members of the Black Hand?

They made sure they only told Annaveta's trusted friend at the hospital that they were coming to Annaveta's aunt and uncle's place. No one else in St. Petersburg or Pleve colony knew they had escaped to Odessa. Maybe he shouldn't be worried, it could've been someone hunting deer. Annaveta's uncle had said before that sometimes hunters came close to the estate. He would need to talk to Mr. Levinson before he said anything to Annaveta.

It could be that he was worrying over nothing.

Misha sat in his cell, waiting for the prison guard to come to the door. He had asked for the guard known as Namuth and expected him at any moment. Misha recalled that Apis, the leader of the Black Hand, had mentioned his name, and that Namuth was dedicated to helping the Black Hand members escape from prison or whenever they were in trouble. Well, he needed him now.

Whispers and comments rushed through the prison cells like wind from an oncoming thunderstorm. Heavy footsteps stopped in front of the cell door.

"What do you want?" Namuth's gruff voice broke through the chatter. Misha stood up and strained his neck to see his tall form. He was impressed by the guard's massive upper body, his shoulders nearly the width of the cell door. "I don't have all day."

"I need your help." Misha looked at him, his confidence wavering as the burly man stared him down.

"Why would I want to help you?" He sneered through the metal bars of his cage like prison.

"Because of this." Misha pushed the sleeve of his shirt up to his shoulder. He hoped the Black Hand symbol of the skull would turn him around.

"So, you survived Craven." Namuth stared at Misha's seared flesh where the skull and crossbones had been forever imprinted. Misha could see the light of recognition come to his eyes. "You got off easy. Here's mine." He lifted his sleeve. The deep branding looked like it had been done twice. The skin was so wrinkled and burned around the skull, it was almost unrecognizable.

"That's fairly unsightly." Misha looked closer at the ugly branding before he rolled down his sleeve. "So, will you help?"

"All for one and one for all." Namuth surprised him by the reference to Alexandre Dumas' book, *The Three Musketeers*.

"Good, then." Misha peered through the bars, and seeing no other guards nearby, he spoke. "I've two other friends and myself that need to get out of here. I can pay you handsomely for your efforts." He looked up at the burly man, convinced he was on his side now.

"I'll work out the details. You just see to it that I get paid." The guard left as quickly as he had come.

Misha paced his cell, excitement filling his body. *Now I'll be able to find those two and pay them back for all the trouble they've brought into my life. They'll finally get what's coming to them.*

Chapter Five

"I want to do something useful." Annaveta and Aunt Esther had just finished another luncheon and were on their way back home. Annaveta smoothed out her blue dress, another new one Aunt Esther had commissioned the modiste to make for her. She thought about how her life had changed since she got here. Quite suddenly, she had become the treasured niece of her wealthy aunt and uncle. She wore the newest fashions, attended many parties, and lived a life of ease.

It was so opposite her childhood.

She was treated with respect here, whereas growing up she was treated like her life had no value. When she was the nanny for Countess Tashkova, and then later when she worked as a nurse at the hospital in St. Petersburg, she felt useful because she was caring for people and helping them. But it was still hard work.

Since she got here five weeks ago, all she had been doing was going from one party to another, wearing the latest fashions. Today's outing had been the third luncheon this week. Most of the time when she talked with the other women, all they wanted to talk about was the latest fashions. She did love to wear the pretty clothes, but she felt as productive as a limp dishrag, being around these wealthy people and doing things for appearances sake only. Many of them only did charity work as a duty, not because they wanted to make a difference. She was one of the few who wanted to do more for others. And to become a better person. More than ever she felt unsure of who she was and the part she played in the world.

"What would you like to do?" Aunt Esther busied herself writing some notes as she sat across from her in the carriage.

"I could help out at the hospital, as a midwife and a nurse, like I did in St. Petersburg. What do you think of that?"

Frown lines appeared on her Aunt's face.

"No, that wouldn't be a good idea. It's much too unsafe." Aunt Esther shook her head, ruling out that possibility. "I know. We need help in our business. It would only be a few days a week for right now, but we do need help organizing our paperwork and making new files for incoming customers. Especially now that your uncle has added farm equipment to the import-export business."

"I wouldn't know where to start or what to do, Aunt Esther. I've never done anything like that before." Annaveta had never considered that as something she could do, but maybe if her Aunt showed her, it might be interesting. And she would be helping out Uncle Roman and Aunt Esther, who she owed so much. "But I'm willing to learn."

"Well, that settles it, then. You will be our secretary. I can't wait to tell your uncle." Her aunt clasped both of her hands tightly, a big smile on her face. "He'll be as pleased as I am, wait and see."

"Okay, then. I'm looking forward to learning all I can about your business and helping you." Annaveta was happy she pleased them, but she couldn't help but think that something was missing. She wanted to be able to do something to help those wives of the soldiers who were wounded, the children who might be left without anyone to take care of them, and people who had been in some way ravaged by the high price of war.

"Do you think I could start a Junior Red Cross Society? Something for teenagers and young adults who would help families who are victims the war? I was thinking we could give clothes and other necessities to people who have been hurt or have gone through loss in some way because of the war." She glanced up at her Aunt and saw her big smile.

"Of course you should start a Russian Junior Red Cross." Her aunt clapped her neatly gloved hands. "What a great way to help the war effort. I'll make a list of the girls you've already met from the society functions, and then as you grow, you can add more members to the group."

Annaveta looked forward to these new beginnings. Not everyone would be excited with what she was doing. How would Alex respond to her doing a man's work in her uncle's business?

Annaveta had asked Tatyana to help put on her most practical gown. Today was a day of firsts. She needed to show her aunt and uncle that she could do this job well. She walked quickly down the hallway. She didn't want to be late. Aunt Esther said she was to meet her in the small room attached to Uncle Roman's office.

"Aunt Esther?" The door was ajar, so she walked into the room.

Her aunt had already sorted many papers and put them on the large desk in front of her. And from the boxes on the floor, there were many more papers that she needed to go through.

"Come in, my dear. Now that I've looked at all this paper-work, I realize just what a job this will be to get it all organized. But I'll help you get started the best I can." Aunt Esther began giving out instructions as to how to make different file names and have a file for each separate part of the import-export business.

"Last year, we started importing farm equipment. So that's another separate side of this business." Aunt Esther explained different aspects of what they did as they worked to organizes the boxes of paperwork. It seemed to take hours to get through one box, but Annaveta was quick to catch on to how her aunt and uncle liked things organized.

"You've been the one who has kept the books and ordered supplies and kept the business going, haven't you?" Annaveta suddenly had a new appreciation for her aunt.

Besides her role as a wife, mom, and society lady, Annaveta now saw the efficient and confident business woman her aunt was. Annaveta wanted to grow in confidence with who she was made to be and to learn all she could from her aunt.

"Yes, I've needed to. Uncle Roman is much too busy meeting with important clients. But it's something that can be learned." Aunt Esther finished sorting through the last box and stood up. "Well, I'll leave you to get the rest done."

Annaveta heard her aunt's footsteps echo down the hallway.

It was a few hours later when at last she found the end of all the paperwork. Without warning, the door swung open.

"Just bringing back the other file—oh."

Annaveta turned around at the sound of Alex's voice. She stood up, rubbing her sore back.

"I thought your aunt was in here." She watched his expression go from shock to amazement all in a moment. "Are you organizing your uncle's business files?"

She nodded. His tone was both teasing and cynical at the same time. "I'm surprised you're doing this type of work, Annaveta. I didn't think this would be quite as exciting as all the parties you've been going to." Alex stood in the doorway, his muscled arms folded across his chest, looking every inch like a swarthy pirate. His blue eyes held a challenge that made Annaveta bristle.

"It's good to know I can still surprise you." She busied herself with organizing the last of the papers on the desk, not wanting to look him in the eye for fear of what she might see there. It was her own insecurities that made her believe he would think she wasn't smart or good enough to help out in her uncle and aunt's business. "Aunt Esther mentioned they could use the help, so here I am. Anyway, I thought you'd see this as a step up from all the frivolous dinner parties and luncheons."

"Well, even though I do like how you look in those beautiful, daring gowns, I would prefer it if you would stay closer to home. You'll be safer here." She wondered at the brief flash of fear that flittered across Alex's face.

"It looks like you'll get your wish, then. All this work will keep me at home more often. Not so many parties for me anymore." She toyed with her hair, trying to put the stray tendrils back into place.

"Well, I'm glad to hear it. I know I would feel much better knowing you were safe under your aunt's watchful eye." Alex's grin appeared. "Not that you haven't managed to escape from other places when you wanted to."

"Those little escapes, as you put it, were necessary. Now that I'm here, I plan on honouring my uncle and aunt. I just hope they decide I'm a help and not a hindrance when it comes to their business." Annaveta sighed and then changed the subject to avoid his sympathy.

"How are your woodworking projects coming along?"

"The first bedroom set will be done by the end of this week." He looked at her for a long time before he continued. "I think you'll be a big help to them, Annaveta. You're smart, and you have good instincts."

She blushed, but was secretly pleased by his compliments.

"Here, I'll put these files your uncle gave me onto the desk and then I'll get out of your way." Alex stepped toward the desk. She took a step backward to make more room for him. "Why are you being so overly polite to me lately?"

His face was right next to hers, and she suddenly felt cornered. She backed up some more and tripped on one of the boxes behind her. She started falling over, but Alex reached out and grabbed her around the waist, pulling her to him. She reached behind his neck, to hang onto something solid.

"I caught you just in time." Alex looked down at her, his hand reaching over to put the file on the desk. Annaveta watched as his eyes turned darker. His warm breath tickled her skin. "I know I should let you get back to your work, Annaveta, but I don't like this air of politeness that's between us. You have to know by now that I need you like a man needs air to breathe." His strong arms pulled her closer and his lips kissed hers in an urgency that left no doubt as to his feelings for her. Annaveta tightened her arms around his shoulders, her fingers weaving into his thick hair. Desire flared in her belly and she moved even closer to him, longing for more of him. Their breath seemed to meld together until she couldn't tell if she was breathing heavy or if it was Alex.

"Oh, Alex. I love your kisses. I love you…" Annaveta sighed and boldly kissed him again.

Without warning, he pulled his lips from hers, steadying her for a moment before he stepped back. His mouth was set in a tight line as if he warred with his emotions.

"I'm sorry, Annaveta. We need to stop now, or I won't be able to." Alex ran a hand through his thick blond hair and the curl on his forehead sprang back into place. She moved her hand to push back the stray curl, but the hard expression on his face caused her pull her hand back to her side.

"I'll let you get back to work then." He left just as quickly as he came in.

Annaveta had wanted to have a few more kisses, but knew Alex was wise to stop. She didn't understand why he seemed so angry at her lately. There never seemed to be enough time for them to talk. She had to put it out of her mind, so she continued to work until Aunt Esther came into the office.

"Oh, dear girl. You've done so much for one day—too much, really. I never intended for you to work this long. It's time to be done for the day." Aunt Esther walked her out of the office and ran the bell for her maid. "Tatyana will take you to your room and help you dress for dinner. Later I'll order a hot bath for you to soothe your sore muscles."

It didn't take long to dress for dinner. She put on a pale green day dress, which made her feel like a princess. She sighed as she walked to the dining room. It was nice to be home in the evening for a change.

Surprise stopped her in her tracks when she saw Alex at the table.

"Good evening." She spoke to everyone, but Alex only nodded at her, his face brooding as he looked at her with a serious expression. They talked around the table, and for the first time since they had come here, Uncle Roman didn't berate Alex about not joining the army. She was surprised at the turn of conversation.

"So, did you assist your father with negotiating better prices for your seeds when you helped him on the farm?" Uncle Roman asked Alex about his life in Pleve colony.

Annaveta was surprised. She thought her uncle didn't want anything to do with knowing about Alex's German background since the start of the war.

"Yes, until I left to go to St. Petersburg, for three years I had done the buying and selling for what we needed and also for some of the others in the colony. My father was pleased with my efforts."

Alex's confidence in his skills was good to hear.

"Good, then, because I have someone coming next week who wants to sell me some grain, and I'd like you to be there. To listen in, to be an extra set of eyes and ears. Would you do that for me?"

Uncle Roman's request shocked Annaveta. What had happened to the dislike her uncle seemed to have for Alex?

"Sure, sir. I'd be happy to help." Alex nodded to the maid to pour more tea. Annaveta looked between the two men in her life, confused but happy with the change.

"Oh, and I wanted to let you know that the first bedroom set is now finished. Just let me know where you want it, and I'll set it all up for you." Alex looked at Aunt Esther and was rewarded by her big smile.

"Wonderful. It's to go in Annaveta's room. This will add more beauty to her room, so maybe she'll stay with us a long time." Aunt Esther winked at her niece.

Annaveta reached over and squeezed her hand. "Thanks, Aunt Esther. I've never had a bed of my own before. I know I'll love it." Annaveta was excited to have something that Alex made with his own hands.

"Have you had any word from your parents, Alex? I wonder how it is going for them now that Russia is at war with Germany." Aunt Esther asked the question that Annaveta wished she would have asked earlier.

"I sent them a letter a few weeks ago, and yesterday I got

one back. They are planning to come for a visit at the end of October. Right after my sister Clara's wedding." Alex seemed pleased at the news.

"Oh, that is good news. Too bad it has to come at such a terrible time with the war going on. Your parents can stay here for their visit. You tell them to plan on it. We have lots of room." Aunt Esther looked at her husband, whose shrug seemed to indicate that it was her decision.

"That's very kind of you. I'll let them know of your invitation."

Annaveta thought about her best friend getting married. She couldn't believe it. Her friend—Alex's sister—whom she met in the meadow a year and a half ago, was getting married. Together they had worked the fields, milked the cows, done the laundry at the creek, and shared their dreams of marriage and life.

Now her friend had found love. Of course, it was this time of year when marriages took place in the German colonies. They celebrated right after harvest and butchering, during Oktoberfest. Annaveta wondered who she was marrying. She would have to ask Alex later. What could she send Clara for a present? She would have to think about that. And Papa and Mama Wagner, at least that's how she still thought of them, were coming here to Odessa. It would be good to see them again.

Soon dinner was finished. They left the maids to clean up the dishes, and they all went to the parlour. Annaveta was surprised because they had only been in the parlour once before on the day of their arrival. It was nice to talk about some of the new people they had met in the week.

Annaveta was pleased when Uncle Roman and Alex decided to play a game of chess. She spoke of how she had fallen in love with Roman and about ballets and operas they had enjoyed. Annaveta loved hearing of her aunt's interesting life and was surprised how quickly the evening ended.

"Well, service at the synagogue starts early tomorrow." Aunt Esther stood and everyone else followed suit, taking the hint. "It would be good for you to come, Annaveta, and of course you are welcome to join us, Alex."

"I've always wanted to go to the Synagogue ever since I first came to visit Bubbeh and Zaydeh's home here when I was five-years-old." Annaveta couldn't hold back a smile. She had good memories of visiting her grandparents.

As she went to bed, she lay there for a long time thinking about what it had been like when she had come with her mama and papa to Odessa all those years ago. It had felt like a new kind of life—spending time at the table reading through the Torah, and Bubbeh asking the blessing before each meal. They had stayed for a month, because it was such a long way to visit. Papa had seemed mad at everyone the whole time, and more often than not he didn't do things with the family. Mama, on the other hand, enjoyed her visit. She was with her family, and Annaveta remembered how happy everyone—other than her father—had been.

Every Sabbath they went to the Synagogue to repeat the words the Cantor said and to listen to the Rabbi speak. She sat beside Bubbeh, her mama, and Aunt Esther. All the men sat separately on the other side of the assembly. It was all very solemn until they got back to her grandparents' home, then there were all kinds of delicious foods, and they played hide and seek along with other games.

And they had so many books, too. Zaydeh said they learned how to live with wisdom from the reading they did.

That was the last time she had seen them. The next year, everyone in the family had been murdered in a pogrom in Odessa. Everyone except her Aunt Esther.

Tears filled Annaveta's eyes as she thought back to that awful day when she heard the news. Annaveta remembered her mama sobbing when she heard what happened. It didn't seem to bother her papa at all—he had been so carefree the day they heard the news. She had been troubled by that, but in her mama's despair and her own sadness, she forgot about it. She didn't think about it again until Misha told her that her father had been involved in the Jewish massacre in October 1905.

The idea that her own father had been involved in killing her mama's family was too much to take in.

She cried herself to sleep as she thought of the people in her life that were now gone. She was grateful she and Alex had come to her aunt and uncle's place. Maybe this was a place for her to heal from all the losses. She hoped so.

Morning came fast, and Tatyana helped her dress. It didn't take her long to choose her most simple clothes for the Sabbath. A modest skirt and blouse were required. When she got downstairs, her aunt and uncle were already waiting. Alex was there too, much to her surprise.

They all rode in the carriage to one of seven synagogues in the city. It was a solemn place to worship and later to mingle with people. All her memories came back to her as the sights, sounds, and smells of the candles were so familiar. She couldn't help but smile as she thought of the happy times she had with her grandparents and mama back then. She sat with her aunt on the women's side and stared at Alex sitting beside her uncle. He seemed interested, even though the Cantor said everything in Hebrew.

The sight of the star of David hanging on a flag behind the Cantor shook her to her core.

She raised a shaky hand up to smooth her hair.

 Mama had given that star to her as a lasting reminder of who she was and where she came from. She had found it in the ashes of their burned *izba*.

Yet Misha had taken the star away from her. Taunted her with it when he imprisoned her in Baron Yakov's basement. Annaveta wiped the tears that sprinkled down her cheeks and looked up at the star again.

Her mama would say there's hope in that star. That the star had a way of leading her home to where she belonged.

Chapter Six

All afternoon, since they got home from the service at the synagogue, Alex thought about how somber Annaveta appeared. He took a little walk around the perimeter of the estate to check for intruders, as had become his habit. Seeing no one, he walked back to the old carriage house where he began working on the next bedroom set. He measured, cut, and began sanding down the edges of the headboard, then a shadow appeared in the doorway.

"Hi." Annaveta stood there, beautiful but sad. She held a piece of paper.

"Out for a walk?" Alex put down his sandpaper and took his gloves off, using a cloth to wipe the sawdust from his hands and clothes. He looked at Annaveta, wondering at the sadness in her eyes. "Did you get bad news?" He pointed to the letter.

"Malina wrote to me. Aunt Esther said it came yesterday, but we were so busy in the office, she forgot. I just read it." Annaveta's hand shook as she held up the letter. "I knew it wouldn't be good news, because she promised she would only write if there was something serious she needed to tell me."

"Well, what is it?" Alex could feel fear trying edge its way up his throat.

"She said Eliana had rushed to the hospital yesterday to tell her news she heard from a friend who keeps her informed of Baron Yakov's whereabouts." Annaveta's hand shook as she retold what was in the letter. "It seems one of his house staff was joking one day that soon they'd see the master home. That he was planning on surprising them all."

Alex stepped forward and held her hands to stop the shaking. He wanted to calm her fears.

"I probably should have told you sooner, but a couple of times I've seen a man on the outer perimeter of your aunt and uncle's estate. He didn't do anything that I know of, he was just watching. I was trying to protect you from worry." Alex squeezed her hand, but she pulled away.

"I'm not a child who needs to only be told good things about the world, Alex. I'm an adult and want to be treated with respect. You can tell me what's going on, especially if it concerns me." Annaveta began to pace. "I mean, we're living in a time of war. People are dying all around us. I've been to the hospital and I've seen men who are blinded, whose hands and legs have been blown off by grenades, whose bodies have been basically torn apart. I know a little bit about the real world. So would you please just tell me when there's a situation that concerns me, even if it is scary?"

Alex knew she was right. He should have told her what happened. She was no long the skittish young girl he had met in the meadow. She had matured and grown into a beautiful woman.

Her reddish brown hair had loosened and fell in waves to her waist. She faced him with her hands on her hips, looking like the mature adult she claimed to be. Still, her eyes held a hint of fear.

"You're right," he said. "I'm sorry I didn't say anything. Next time I'll tell you."

Her hands dropped from her waist. She looked down at the letter.

"Do you think the Black Hand knows we're here? I know none of our friends would have told them, but they seem to have their ways of finding out information." Annaveta bit her lip and tucked a stray hair behind her ear. When she fidgeted with her hands, it was a sure sign she was worried.

"I think for right now we're safe, but I think we need to take extra measures to see to your safety. Some good safeguards would be only leaving the house when you absolutely have to be somewhere. And always telling someone, like your aunt or uncle or me if you are going somewhere, so that someone is with you." Alex's voice sounded still as death. "I don't want to take any chances with your life. I care about you way too much to let anything bad happen to you."

"I appreciate the way you protect me, Alex. I'm glad we can look out for each other." Annaveta twisted the bracelet on her wrist. It was the three corded arm band Alex had made himself and given her months ago when he had first spoke of love. She never took it off her wrist. She looked up at him with a wistful look on her face, wishing there was less tension between them. She decided to change the subject. "So Clara is getting married. I'm happy for her. Who is she marrying? Is it John Koch?"

"Yes, that's what Mama wrote in the letter. This Sunday

after services, there will be a few couples getting married, as usual." Alex grinned. "She seems so young. But I'm happy for her. John's a good man."

"I wish I could be there. That we could both be there. But writing to her is the next best thing. So that's what I'll do, and I'll send her a present. Some lace that I just finished. She always liked the delicate French lace. So this will be a good gift for her." She paced again, thinking out loud. "What do you think?"

"Sounds like a good idea. Clara will love that you thought of her. We can package it up along with my letter I'm sending to my parents. They should get it all about a week before they come here by train." Alex smiled at the thought. He hadn't realized until now how much he needed to see his parents again.

"Good. I'll write a letter tonight and give it and the lace to you to package tomorrow. I'm glad your parents are coming. I've missed talking with your mama." Annaveta got up and paced, stopping every so often to look at him. She usually started pacing when she was thinking deeply about something.

"I had a dream last night about them." She took her time before continuing. "It started with three huge ships coming closer and closer to Odessa's port. They didn't look like Russian ships. As soon as they were close enough, I heard shots being fired and saw many of the houses and businesses along the beach and on the hillside burning. People were being killed, and I saw your mama and papa lying on the sand by the beach. I'm not sure if they were injured or something worse." She rubbed a shaking hand on her forehead as if to wipe away the vivid pictures that tortured her mind. "I don't know what it all means, Alex. But I feel like it might be a warning of some kind."

"Not all of your dreams come true." Alex spoke his denial, even though fear gripped his heart that her words might be true.

"I know, but there have been many, you remember, that have come true. Maybe we can help protect your parents, so nothing bad happens to them."

"Well, I'll tell them the dream when they get here, then. But they will decide for themselves whether they need to take it seriously or not, you know that." Alex brushed off more sawdust from his shirt. All of a sudden, he had the need to fix something. To make things right in the world around him. Annaveta's dreams always had a big affect on him. He needed to pray, his mama would say. Well, that was true too.

"Show me what you have made so far."

He nodded, happy to get his mind off the topics that wrecked his emotions. He was proud to show her the wood he crafted with his own hands. It had always been something he loved to do, and he was good at it. He wanted Annaveta to know, respect, and love all that he was. He showed her the chairs he had started to work on for her aunt's dining room set, and desk that he started on.

"You really are talented, Alex. Since we've come here, you've had a lot of opportunity to do your woodwork. Are you glad we came?" Her question took him off guard. He took a minute before he answered.

"I am glad I came with you so that you could get to know your aunt and uncle better." Alex rubbed his hand on the table in front of him. "I think I'm just struggling to understand the changes I see in you, me and all around us with the war."

"What changes do you see in me?" Annaveta looked puzzled.

"I think you've adjusted nicely to all the beautiful clothes and society functions that your aunt has introduced you to. Also, you seem to have enjoyed the list of eligible men from wealthy families she's lined up for you. That includes kissing Sacha in his mother's garden at the Yudin's dinner. Yes, Nadia Berkovitz happened to also been in the garden and saw you two. How could you Annaveta?" Alex couldn't seem to stop the harsh tone that came out of his mouth.

"I'm sorry Alex." Annaveta sighed deeply. She didn't know how she was going to explain the incident to Alex in a way that he would understand. "SI didn't kiss Sacha. He kissed me before I even knew what was happening." Tears glistened in Annaveta's eyes. She crossed her arms over her chest and tapped her right foot, suddenly feeling angry for his lack of belief in her character.

Alex looked at her, his knuckles white as he gripped the edge of the table.

"Alright, I'm sorry about criticizing you about Sacha. If you say that's what happened, I believe you." Alex's blue eyes pierced hers.

"Thank you." Annaveta stopped tapping her foot.

   "But I need to know. Are you doing whatever your aunt tells you, to please them no matter if it's something you don't like, or even if it goes against your commitment to another?"

"Alex, stop it!" Annaveta did not so much as glance at Alex, but her eyes were bright with unshed tears after digesting the words that flew out of his mouth. She closed her eyes and took a deep breath, then looked at him. "Is that really what you think of me? You believe that I'm just following blindly along to everything they tell me?"

"Not blindly, Annaveta. I just think it's all so new to you, and you've been enjoying all the things that money can buy. I sort of understand it, given what you've had to endure in your life."

Annaveta's cheeks got red and her lips tightened. "I'm sorry you feel that way, Alex. I am trying to change. I'm even learning about how to help run a business now." Her quiet dignity was his undoing.

"I'm sorry, Annaveta, I don't know what came over me." He looked down at his shoes. What had come over him? He was jealous of the men her Aunt Esther kept parading in front of her. "I hope you can forgive me for saying such mean things." He walked over to her and kissed her hands. He tried to meet her gaze, but her eyes were squeezed closed. When she finally looked up at him, her neck looked blotchy, and she had a glassy look in her eyes.

"I need to be going. I told Aunt Esther I would come back after a short walk, and I've been gone much longer than that. She'll be expecting me." She pulled away from him and walked out of the carriage house.

He watched her leave knowing she was angry. He wanted to go after her but stopped himself. He didn't trust his emotions, or the words that might come out of his mouth. He was angry, too. It just finally came out in words today, almost like he couldn't help himself.

There was a big gap of misunderstanding between them.

Maybe it was a wide canyon neither of them could cross.

Alex waited on the wooden platform, watching as the first passengers exited the train from Saratov. He was so happy his parents were here. The last three weeks had been torture. Annaveta had barely spoken to him, and if he were honest, he hadn't done much talking, either. He had told her his frustrations, and maybe that had been a mistake. He knew she didn't believe in herself very much and didn't feel she had much value to offer to people, so his words probably did more harm than good. He didn't know how to make things better between them. He needed Mama's wisdom.

Finally he saw her tall, slim form step down the steps on the train. Her brown kerchief tied under her chin, hiding most of her graying brown hair, reminded him of home. It was comforting. Papa followed right behind her, his brown trousers held up by his black suspenders, and underneath those the red and brown plaid shirt mama had made him last Christmas. He put his arm up and walked quickly toward them.

"I'm glad you're here." Alex wrapped his mama in a hug and soaked in the love and comfort he always found in her arms. Then he gave his papa a quick hug. Papa had never been one for many hugs. He was more serious than Mama, but he was honest and faithful. That was something Alex appreciated even more now that he had experienced the lies and abuse of members of the Black Hand. And since he had been around the some of the false fronts put on in the society of Odessa. He realized that way of thinking was everywhere – even with that Volga German farmer - and he was even more grateful for parents who were faithful and trustworthy.

"Ach Son, it's so good to see you safe and sound." A stray tear rolled down Mama's cheek. "We have been worried about you, with all that you wrote about a few problems in St. Petersburg and then your sudden move to Odessa. We've prayed Gott's protection for you."

"Danke, Mama." Alex's thumb wiped away the stray tear, and he kissed her cheek. "Let me take your bags. Mr. and Mrs. Levinson asked their driver to bring the large carriage." He picked up the two bags they had with them and led the way to the street where the driver waited.

"Thanks, Vassily." Alex spoke to the driver who held the door open for everyone to get settled inside.

"So, how is everyone at home?" Alex looked at his Mama, knowing she could talk for hours about her family.

"Helmut and Inga are are expecting their second child by Christmas time. Clara and John's wedding was wonderful, along with the eight other couples that joined in. Of course, Katarina and Erica loved all the attention at the wedding feast. Oh, and we got a letter from Ernest saying that they are enjoying living in Canada. And you, Alex? How are you doing?" Mama looked at him in that knowing way that had always made him talk.

"Ach, Mama. You know me. Most of the time I'm doing good."

"And right now?" She probed for more answers.

"I'm having trouble right now with a few things. Annaveta

and I are kind of at odds and not really understanding each other. Her uncle and aunt are happy to have their only niece living them, but she's changed a lot because of it. She's grown used to all the nice clothes, all the attention, and her aunt has invited all these men from wealthy families to meet her. I feel like I can't compete with that. And it just feels to me like its all too much." Alex ran a hand through his hair. "I guess I would be grateful for any advice you could give me."

"Sounds to me like you're jealous, Alex." The truth of Mama's words hit home. He knew he was jealous. And on top of that he was mad because Annaveta still hadn't let her aunt know she loved him. Because of it, he doubted her. Was she embarrassed of him? Did one of those men she had met make her wish they weren't in a relationship? Or with all the changes happening in her, maybe she didn't need him anymore?

"Ja, what you say is true. I guess I have some changing to do, too." Alex's papa laughed. "Son, that will be true for the rest of your life. There are always ways we men need to change." A teasing twinkle lingered in Papa's eyes. "Don't fight it. And don't wait too long to talk things out, either."

"Ja. That sounds about right. Danke, Papa." Alex was grateful to have parents who had so much experience at working through the hardships of marriage and other relationships.

The carriage slowed, then stopped in front of the front doors of the mansion. His mama's eyes widened as she peered up at the stately home. Soon, the door opened, and Mrs. Levinson came out to meet them.

"Ah, Alex you've brought your parents here. You must be Mr. and Mrs. Wagner. So good to have you in our home." Mrs. Levinson shook their hands and brought her husband over to meet them.

His parents were very kind and gracious, as usual. The Levin-sons invited them into the parlour for some evening tea and some biscuits.

Annaveta joined them a few minutes later. Her face flushed pink, her normal reaction to nerves. Her eyes looked only briefly in his direction before they landed on his parents.

"Annaveta, oh my darling girl, it is so gut to see you." His mama stood up and gave her a hug. Annaveta clung to her for a few moments, stepping back only to have to wipe tears from her eyes. "I'm so glad you are doing good. Papa and I were so glad Alex wrote us so we could come to see our son and you. You are like our very own daughter."

"Oh, Mama Wagner, thank you. I've missed you." Alex's heart felt lighter than it had for a long time when he heard the love in her voice. "And Papa Wagner, I'm so happy you came to visit, even though right now it's such unhappy times."

"Gott knows, my daughter. We can trust Him to see us through." Papa's faith was stronger than ever. Despite all that was going on in the world. Alex wished his was as strong.

They talked until the sun began to set.

"Well, the maid will take you to your room for the night, and then tomorrow you can choose whether you'd like to stay with us or in the cottage we have down by the beach." Esther Levinson stood up and so did everyone else in the room. "But for now we'll each have a earlier night. You both have had a long journey already today, and I'm sure you must be very tired."

Soon they all went their separate ways. Even Annaveta had

left with her maid. Alex walked back to his guest cottage thinking about how good it was that his parents had come to visit.

In the morning, after breakfast, they talked as they walked toward his guest cottage and the carriage house.

"Alex, your Papa and I have decided that we would like to stay in the cottage down by the beach. We've never had time just to ourselves, and this would be perfect." Mama sounded excited at the idea.

"Mama, I don't think that would be a good idea. Why don't you just stay here with us, instead of being by yourself down there." Alex was trying to think how he could convince them to say at the estate without mentioning the dream. But after his mama kept insisting, he had to tell all.

"If you insist on staying there, I have to tell you about a dream Annaveta had not too long ago." Both his parents stopped and waited. He knew they had a deep respect for Annaveta's dreams, as many of them had come true. "She dreamed there were German ships coming to harbor, and they began shooting at the people on land. Many who were on the beach were killed, and even some houses burned to the ground. Your bodies were lying on the beach. Annaveta is scared for you. And frankly, so am I. Please, Mama, Papa, stay here."

Alex pleaded with his parents, but they were insistent.

"Please, Alex. We go home in five days, let's enjoy the short time we have together."

"I'd like that, Mama."

Over the next few days, Alex enjoyed taking his parents to see a few sights in Odessa. They listened to the Orchestra, stopped by the hospital, and went to the German Lutheran church in Odessa where his Mama made friends. The rest of the time, they talked with Annaveta or himself. He knew that because on the last day before they were to leave, his Mama had a long talk with him in his woodshop.

"I believe Annaveta loves you, Alex, and yet I can tell you're frustrated with her." His Mama put her hand on his shoulder.

He gave a weak laugh. "Well, I've had moments of frustration with her before."

"Yes, but both of you are changing. Annaveta right now is trying to find her own way. She's wanting the approval of her aunt and uncle, wanting to do what makes them happy. But she also wants to please you." Mama thought for a minute. "She's the one in the middle, and she's confused. Also, when I talked to her, I could tell she is trying to find who she is. I believe this next year she's really going to find more of who she is. That she's going to discover she is stronger and has more talent and ability than she ever knew was in her. But Alex, she needs someone, like you, who will continue to love her no matter what. To keep believing in her and standing by her side. Can you do that, Alex?"

He thought long and hard about her words, then he nodded.

"In the end, I believe she will make a beautiful wife for you. She is your match in every way."

"I'm going to try to be more patient and to understand her, Mama. I really am."

"I know you are. You have a big heart." Mama found her husband coming out of the guest house. "Papa and I are going to enjoy our last night in our honeymoon suite, and then we'll say our goodbyes in the morning. Don't lose sleep over any of this. There's a much bigger design to your life than what you can see right now. Trust the process you're in."

The three of them exchanged hugs, and his parents headed down to their cottage.

After everyone had gone to bed, Alex was in his own place, feeling very restless. He fell asleep much later. He woke with a start to loud blasts and shots being fired. He got up and ran outside to see what was going on. The glow of orange-red firelight rose above the tops of the trees surrounding the Levinson estate. He ran until he could see what had happened, just through the trees. To his horror, he saw three ships in the water shooting at the merchant ships and war ships in the harbour. They had also raised their guns to shoot at the houses all along the beach.

He looked down below to where his mama and papa's cottage was located. Red flames exploded into the blackness, flickering outwards like the vicious tongue of a snake devouring everything in it's path. It stole his breath and his heart hurt in his chest. What once was beautiful, now cracked and wilted. There was no escaping the bright red famished beast who doled out pain and death to the young and old, guilty or innocent, that lay in it's path.

"Mama! Papa!" He ran through the trees down the hill, his heart sinking with each step.

Annaveta's dream had turned into a real life nightmare, right before his eyes.

Chapter Seven

As the pastor of Odessa's Lutheran Church droned on about the recent tragedy in Odessa, Annaveta squeezed her gloves in a white-knuckled grip. She quietly looked up at Alex beside her, the shock of his parents' sudden death etched across his white face and clenched jaw.

Three days ago, everyone was happy. Life was good, and there was laughter. Now the war had truly hit home. For all of them, but most especially for Alex. German ships had shot down Odessa's Navy ships and then turned their guns on Odessa's innocent women and children. Her aunt and uncle's cottage down by the beach was destroyed, along with Alex's parents. She remembered vividly what had happened that day.

She heard shots fire in the distance and ran outside to see what had happened. She could see the reddish glow in night sky and wondered what was going on. She ran to Alex's house, but he wasn't there. He must have gone to check on his parents. She ran down the hill, wondering if she could help in some way. Nearing the beach, she saw two ships bearing the flag of the Ottoman Empire leaving the harbour. They had done their damage. One of the Navy ships was on fire, and the merchant ships in port were badly damaged.

Annaveta saw the raging inferno that used to be her aunt and uncle's cottage. People yelled and ran all along the beach. The port was a hive of activity at the wee hours of the morning.

The sound of heavy sobs coming from the direction of the burning building quickened her steps. She neared the building and saw Alex on his knees, his head in his hands. His shoulders shook as he cried. Each spasm that jerked his muscles, felt like a knife stabbing her own heart. Tears slipped down her own cheeks as she approached him and went down on her knees to touch his hands. He moved his hands away from his face to look at her.

"Alex. I'm sorry. So desperately sorry." She rubbed her hand along his back as he continued to sob.

"Why?" He threw his arms around her. "Why did my parents have to die?" He spoke between sobs that wracked his body. Annaveta just held him until he was exhausted. "It's all my fault. If I would have insisted that papa and mama stay at your aunt and uncle's place, they would be alive now."

"Shh. That's not true. It's not your fault they died. And you did what you could to get them to stay on the hill instead of coming down here." Annaveta continued to speak encouraging words to soothe him. "You were a good son, Alex." She looked deeply into his eyes, hoping he would believe her words.

After a long while Alex stood, and Annaveta stood with him, her arms around his waist. They stared at what used to be her aunt and uncle's small cottage. It had been reduced to a mountain of small fires and embers.

After some time had passed, Annaveta spoke. "We should let

Aunt Esther and Uncle Roman know what happened."

"Ja." Alex face looked like it was set. There was no expression, only empty eyes as he walked away from the place he had found his parent's dead bodies.

She grabbed his hand and together they walked up the hill. They found Annaveta's aunt and uncle in the breakfast room.

"There you are, Annaveta. I was worried sick." Aunt Esther looked her over and then saw Alex. "Good heavens. You both look awful. What has happened? And where are your parents, Alex?"

"That's what we came to tell you, Aunt Esther." She walked over to the empty chairs and pulled one out for Alex. He slumped down without saying a word. "Alex's parents were killed last night."

"What? Oh Alex, we're so sorry." Aunt Esther sat beside him and Uncle Roman followed soon after. Annaveta held Alex's shaking hand, unsure of how to help him.

"How did this happen?" Uncle Roman ran his hands through his hair.

"Didn't you hear the shots fired early this morning?"

"We just assumed it was our navy ships shooting at the German ones trying to sink them." Uncle Roman spoke, the frown line getting deeper in his forehead.

"No. It was the German ships shooting at us. They not only sunk a few of our Navy ships, they damaged merchant ships as well. Then they shot at civilians and the houses in range. It was a cruel slaughter of innocent lives." Annaveta shifted her gaze to Alex, who was clenching his jaw. She ran her fingers over one of his fisted hands, hoping to soothe his frayed nerves. She looked back at Aunt Esther.

"We're so sorry to hear about your parents, Alex." Aunt Esther's eyes filled with unshed tears. "Please let us know if there's anything at all we can do for you."

"Ja, danke." Annaveta knew Alex was at his wit's end, because he lapsed easily into German. "Right now, I need to be alone. I need to write to the rest of the family and I just need time to think… about everything." He got up from the table and retreated from them.

"I'm worried about him," Annaveta said.

"He'll heal in time, Annaveta. Just continue to be his friend and pray for him. We'll all do what we can to help him. That will get him through."

Annaveta knew Aunt Esther spoke from the experience of having lost her whole family, except her sister, to a pogrom when she was newly married. Uncle Roman didn't say anything at all. He just sat at the end of the table, frowning.

"I need to clean up and get properly dressed. I'll see you at luncheon." Annaveta still had on the coat she had thrown over her nightgown when she left in a hurry this morning. When she got to her room, her maid was already there and announced that a bath was being prepared at that moment. Annaveta cleaned herself up but was too tense to relax. It wasn't long before she got out, and with Tatyana's help, put on a morning dress.

She quickened her pace as she left and hurried toward the guest house. She didn't trust Alex to not do anything stupid right then.

He opened the door after her quick knock and let her come in. Right away she noticed the wide open door to his bedroom, its unmade bed, a bag on the floor. The dishes were stacked in a dirty mess beside the sink, and on the table were a few handwritten letters.

He motioned her to a chair at the table, and he sat down beside her.

"Alex, I see you have your travel bag open. Where are you going?"

"I'll tell you about that in a minute. But first I wanted to ask you something." Alex looked so serious. He got up off his chair and got on one knee in front of her. He grabbed her hand he held it between both of his.

"You'll probably think I'm crazy, but I love you, Annaveta. And I really want to marry you. This week. It would be better if we could go to the preacher right now and get it done today. I want you by my side. I'm tired of waiting to live life to the fullest. As we learned today, you never know which day will be your last day on earth. So will you marry me?" Alex looked up at her, hope shimmering bright in his eyes.

"Alex, you know I love you, too. And someday I want to marry you. But I really don't think right now is the best time for us to do this. You just lost your parents." He got up, pacing back and forth.

"You think I'm rushing this, don't you?" His words were angry. "You know I wanted to marry you when we lived in St. Petersburg, but I didn't think that was the right time. Now I think it is. I love you. I think its time we married. Then we could move somewhere where I can keep you safe."

"Alex, I love you, too. I really do. But I really think we need to wait with this. I gave my word to my aunt that I would help them with this next phase of their business. I can't go back on my word. It doesn't feel right." Annaveta stood and reached for his hand, but he walked away. "Besides, what about being here for the memorial for your parents."

"Don't you understand? It doesn't matter about the memorial for my parents. They are gone. Dead." Alex ran a shaky hand through his hair and sighed. "If you're so set on keeping your word to your aunt and uncle, then you've made your choice." He turned around and looked at her. His jaw clenched tight in anger. "I'm packing to enlist in the Navy. So I guess this is it for us, too. I hope you have a good life, Annaveta. Good-bye."

"Oh, Alex. Do you really want to do this now?" Annaveta felt scared for him. His handsome face tightened in scarcely controlled rage. "I don't want us to end." Tears slipped unheeded down her cheeks.

"I don't want us to end, either, but you made your choice. So now's as good a time as any for me to join the Navy. Really good, in fact, because now I'm angry enough at the Germans to kill them all. I'll be leaving today." Alex walked to the door and opened it for her.

She couldn't believe this was it. First he asked her to marry him, then because she wanted to wait, he was going off to war. His last words rang in her ears like a funeral dirge. She walked to the door and looked up at him, thinking any moment he would change his mind about everything.

"I'm sad to see you go, Alex. I'll miss you. I'll pray that you come back safe." She looked up at him, hoping he would change his mind. But he stood there silent, back stiff and jaw clenched.

"Goodbye, Alex."

She walked through the door and down the stairs before she turned around. He still stood there, staring at her. She waved a little and, after a slight hesitation, he turned and closed the door. It seemed like he had cut her out of his life. Would she ever see him again? She didn't know. Tears pooled in her eyes and ran down her cheeks.

No longer would she have her friend to talk to. No longer would there be someone who would look out for her and protect her.

Her life, as of that moment, had changed forever.

It had been almost a week since Alex had left to join the Navy. Annaveta spent almost all of her time in the office, working as the secretary for Uncle Roman and Aunt Esther's business. She tried her best to get over the sadness and confusion she had about Alex's abrupt departure and their last conversation. She hadn't heard anything, and the worst part was she didn't expect she would. When she left, his words sounded final.

She dabbed her eyes with the end of her sleeve.

"Annaveta?" Aunt Esther poked her head in the doorway. "Oh, there you are." Her aunt looked around the room.

She looked at Annaveta, and her brow creased in concern. "What's wrong?"

"I miss him, Aunt Esther." She bit her lip until it hurt, hoping the pain would be greater than the ache she had in her heart. "I can't seem to stop thinking about Alex. I'm worried about him. The worst part is that he left angry. At me, at God, and at the Germans who killed his parents. I'm unsure of what he'll do when he's this angry."

Aunt Esther patted her shoulder.

"Well, the first thing to remember is that you can't hold yourself responsible for Alex's emotions or actions." Aunt Esther pulled up the extra chair to the desk. "It's understandable that you're unsure of yourself and maybe you even feel insecure right now, but you can't allow yourself to wallow in self-pity and confusion. That won't help you at all. What you need is something that will help you get your mind off yourself and onto other people." She drummed her fingers on top of the desk as if in deep thought. "I know, you could start what you mentioned a few weeks ago. Helping those families who have men fighting the war and who don't have clothing and the help they need. You could enlist some of the other girls you've met recently to help get the clothes and deliver them."

"You're right, Aunt Esther. It would be better for me to focus on helping others. And thanks for your advice about Alex." Annaveta got up and paced a little, wondering if she should tell her aunt all of it. "There's one other thing I should mention. The big reason Alex was mad at me is because I said we needed to wait when he asked me to marry him."

Annaveta stood still and watched the look of surprise followed by worry that crossed her Aunt's face.

"Do you love him?"

"I do. I guess I've loved him for a long time already, but I don't believe now is the right time for marriage. Not when his parents were just killed and he's full of such anger." Annaveta toyed with stray strands of hair in her nervousness. "And your words are true, Aunt. Both of us still have so much growing up to do."

"Well, I think that was a wise decision. Waiting for something that you really want shows that you are growing into a very responsible woman." Aunt Esther got up and gave her a hug. "You will be okay, you'll see, and so will Alex. You both just need time to sort things through. Meanwhile, get started on that Junior Red Cross idea. Make up a list of young ladies your age to help you, and then we'll take the next steps from there." She winked at her before she walked out the door.

Annaveta started pacing the large office again, from the bookshelves on one side of the room to those on the other. It had been helpful to talk to Aunt Esther. She knew Alex was angry at her, but what she had difficulty admitting was her own anger at Alex. The way he talked to her, his angry tones and meanness, reminded her of her own father. His anger had caused her to trust him less. She didn't want to turn back into who she had been when she was under her papa's roof. Someone scared of everything around her and fearful of doing new things. She had decided she wasn't going to live like that, ever again.

She walked over to the desk, sat down, and on fresh paper made a list of everything she would need to get started on her new venture.

Annaveta smoothed her hands over her dark green morning dress. She deliberately chose one of the more practical dresses she had for this morning's first gathering of those ladies joining the Junior Red Cross.

The first person that Larson announced in the parlour was Jarena Barinov. She remembered seeing her at the last dinner ball at the Yudin Estate. She had a small group of friends. Anastasia, Ekaterina, and Dinah were the young ladies that she had hung around with at the ball. She was happy she had already met these girls so they could dispense with formalities.

"Hello, Jarena. I'm happy you could come." Annaveta tried to remember all that Aunt Esther had taught her of proper etiquette. "Please, won't you sit down?" She settled Jarena on a couch not far from her. She liked this quiet girl with the dark brown eyes and hair. "Would you like some tea?"

"Yes, please." Jarena's quiet voice was barely heard above the sound of the door opening and closing again. Someone else had arrived.

"Miss Dinah Yudin and Miss Anastasia Borovitz." Larson announced the newcomers with a flourish.

"Larson." Annaveta found her aunt's butler waiting in the corner for further instructions. "Could you ask Cook to send some tea and cakes into the parlour? Thank you." Annaveta waved her hand to Dinah and Anastasia to sit on the other settee facing her and Jarena. Hopefully the other two girls she had invited would be here soon, as well.

"Miss Yudin and Miss Borovitz, it is good that you could come. I'm so happy you found the time in your schedule to help with the war effort." They sat across from her and nodded. They looked bored already, and the meeting hadn't even started.

"Miss Moriah Lapin and Miss Svetlana Borodin." Larson nodded to her and took his leave as these last two young ladies found another couch to sit on.

"Ah, so good to have everyone here. I thought we would first have tea and chat, and then we could talk about how to go about helping the war effort." Annaveta smiled and wiped her palms discretely on her skirt. She just didn't fit in with these high society ladies, and she prayed she'd get through the meeting without making a mistake that would embarrass herself, or even worse, her aunt.

A kitchen maid, Yana, pushed a cart into the room. It was loaded with tea, cakes, and biscuits. She prepared the service and left. Annaveta gestured to everyone to help themselves. Meanwhile, she struggled to find a way to start a conversation. Thankfully, one of the girls saved her.

"What do you girls think of the new guard over at my father's bank?" Dinah giggled, followed soon by Anastasia and Svetlana. "He has the bluest eyes and is ever so tall. Of course, Papa has forbidden me to have anything to do with him, but what if I trip as I go up the stairs at the bank, then I'd suddenly find myself in his arms? That would be perfect." More giggles erupted. Annaveta smiled, then she looked at Jarena and Moriah, who also smiled slightly.

"It's so sad that a lot of the handsome men had to go off to war." Annaveta quickly got tired of their frivolous chatter and sought to turn the conversation in a new direction. "But even though they are gone, we can still help them here. And some of the older men have wives and children that could use some help here, too." Encouraged by their attentiveness, she went on. "That's why I asked you all to come here today. I thought maybe we could start a Junior Red Cross Society. Our goal would be to help give out clothes and food to those affected by the war in some way here in Odessa. From talking to the men in the hospital, I realized many of them are worried about their wives and children, who have hardly any money and very little food. I thought that's something we could help with. That's why I asked you to gather old towels and clothes. I thought we could start by distributing what we have, and then go about securing more from others."

"It sounds like a very good thing to do, Annaveta." Jarena soft voice spoke out in agreement after no one said anything.

"Well, I asked my maid to gather up some old clothes and to put them in bags to give away. I wasn't about to do a servant's job." Anastasia spoke in disgust. "My driver brought them here. I hope it's what you were looking for." She waved her hand into the air as she didn't care one way or the other.

"I agree with Anastasia. It seems so… lower class to do all these dirty jobs. I'd much rather just get together and let our maids take care of the other things." Dinah looked over at Anastasia and the two giggled.

"It's okay if you don't want to be part of it." Annaveta smiled at the two of them. "I just thought I'd ask. There are so many families that could use our help, and I'd like to do something for them. So for those who are willing, I thought we could start sorting through the old towels and clothes."

Jarena, Moriah and Annaveta ended up being the only three to work their way through the bags organizing everything in to separate piles. The other three girls sat, talking and giggling together. They had only two bags to go, when Moriah found a note in one of the pants pockets.

"Look, Annaveta, your name is on the outside of this note. I wonder how it got here?" Moriah handed the note to her. Surprised, she opened the note and started reading: *Find those two troublemakers—Annaveta and her German friend. They've interfered with the plans of the Black Hand one too many times. Time is running out.*

Annaveta's shaking hand closed the note and put it into the pocket of her dress.

"Well, was it from someone you knew?" Jarena asked. "That note came from the bag from my house, so I don't know how you could have a note from anyone there, do you?"

"I don't know, Jarena. Don't worry, it wasn't about anything important." Annaveta did her best to put a smile on, even though fear had a chokehold on her throat. "Let's finish up, okay?"

While they worked Annaveta's mind whirled with questions. *Who could have written that note? Why would it have been in the bag Jarena brought from home? Does Jarena know someone from the Black Hand? This person from the Black Hand, it sounded like they had plans to get rid of her and Alex. What could she do?*

The questions kept coming even after the meeting ended. *I need to write Alex, even though I don't want to. My aunt and uncle don't know much about the Black Hand, and I don't want to worry them. I think Alex knows more than he's telling me. I need to know who is behind this threat and do what I can to stop it, before they hurt more people I love.*

Chapter Eight

Alex couldn't sleep. His orders stated he shipped out to-morrow. It seemed like he waited forever for his turn. But the letter from Annaveta bothered him. He almost hadn't opened it. He was still so mad at her for rejecting his offer of marriage, anger that almost equaled the rage in him over what happened to his parents.

In the end, he decided to see what she had to say. And it chilled him to his core. Someone wanted to find both him and Annaveta. Called them troublemakers. He believed it must have been someone from the Black Hand, but who? Had someone managed to get Misha, Baron Yakov, and Monsieur Arnaud out of prison?

He felt a chill on the back of his neck. He quickly wrote a letter to Annaveta, asking her to also check out the people in the home where the note had come from. Maybe that would lead them to clues. He hoped so.

Morning came too quickly, and Alex was exhausted. He

dressed in uniform and went to his commanding officer.

"You get to start from the bottom up, Seaman, Second Grade. Are you ready for your first assignment?"

"Yes, sir." Alex saluted Quartermaster Vassily Yurlov. His training camp had only been for two weeks. He didn't feel like he knew all the safety or military procedures. But each new seaman for the Navy had two weeks in base camp and then was assigned to a ship.

He had to swallow his fear of the unknown and just do his duty. Quitting at this point wasn't an option. One new recruit had been so scared that he tried to run away on the first day of training. Lieutenant Kornilov summarily shot him to death. All of the new recruits, Alex included, took that as a warning of what would happen to whoever dared to try the same thing. Besides, he wanted to go to war. He wanted to make the enemy pay for his parents' deaths.

"You will start by swabbing the deck, Seaman. Understood?"

"Yes, sir." Alex had gotten used to replying quickly and listening closely, but he didn't like it. He walked to where the supplies were kept, got out the brisk brush, and filled the pail with water and disinfectant soap. He started in the corner. All seamen got an opportunity, at least that's what the quartermaster called it, to swab the deck, help the cook, clean out their quarters, or the worst job of all—to clean out the military guns on the ship and refill the ammunition. Alex had heard of a seaman on another of the Baltic Sea Russian Navy ships who had been cleaning the guns and one went off, killing him. By far, that job was the most worrisome.

Soon another seaman joined him in scrubbing the deck.

"I heard you are from the Volga German colonies, too. My name is Otto Schultz. What's yours?" He was scrubbing really close to where he was working. Alex knew they would get in trouble if they talked to each other. He needed to do what he could to try to shut him up.

"I'm Alex Wagner and yes, I'm from the Volga German colonies. We're not supposed to talk while working, remember? We can talk later." Alex gave him only a sideways glance before moving a little ways away from him, pushing his brush even harder.

The rest of the afternoon, they worked until the deck was completely finished. It shone clean, like a bright new penny. Alex got up and brought the supplies back to the small supply closet. Seaman Schultz followed behind with his supplies.

Lieutenant Adrik Kornilov stood on the main deck with his quartermaster, and he looked up as Alex passed. "Seaman Wagner!"

Alex stopped. "Yes, sir!"

"Your words have a German accent to them, Seaman. Are you sure you're fighting for the right side?" Lieutenant Kornilov's words came out with a bite.

"Yes, sir!" Even though Alex responded with a confident tone, he still felt the sting of his words.

"Keep an eye on him, Quartermaster Yurlov." He spoke in derisive tone that showed his contempt for all things German, including people who were Russian but spoke with a German accent. "Seaman Wagner might decide to switch sides unexpectedly."

Lieutenant Kornilov glared one last time at Alex and walked away, arrogance in his every step.

"Yes, sir." The Quartermaster saluted his superior. As soon as the Lieutenant was out of sight, he turned to Alex. "Watch yourself around the Lieutenant, Seaman Wagner. You don't want him on your bad side, because he can really make your life miserable."

At Alex's nod, the Quartermaster gave him new orders to begin cleaning the guns below deck.

He started the much hated job and carefully cleaned like he was taught in base camp training. He was extra careful to double check each gun barrel for gun powder and to empty out the old cartridges. It took quite awhile, but when he was finally finished, he was relieved.

He reported to the Quartermaster to let him know he'd finished his duties.

"Well, if you want your rations, Seaman, you best hurry to mess hall."

Alex hurried to sit with his other shipmates. He had already lost weight because of the hard work and missing a few meals already.

He was just in time. Alex sat beside some new recruits. Boris Olenev was from St. Petersburg, but he had been assigned to the Black Sea Russian Navy Fleet. He was a fast talker with red hair, much like Alex's friend Oskar, whose family he had stayed with in St. Petersburg.

Moeshe Abramovitz sat beside him, cleaning up his plate. He was another Jewish man who was skinny and more of a scholar than fighter. He was from Odessa. Of course Otto Schultz, the blond haired one with all the jokes, was there to keep them all laughing. Alex listened as Boris told his stories of surviving on the streets of St. Petersburg, gathering food for his mom and two sisters ever since his papa was killed on Bloody Sunday in 1905. Understandably, he didn't like Tsar Nicholas II very much. He was desperate for change in Russia.

"So what happens when we win this war over the Germans?" Seaman Olenev was very confident of the outcome, even though it had been only three months since the war began.

"What makes you think we're going to win? Already the Germans under Commander Graf von Spree have cut off the communications cable of the British squadron in the Far East. And just a few weeks ago, it was the Ottoman Empire who joined forces with the German ships to shell our Russian port of Odessa. With many thousands of casualties, I might add. That's the reason we had to declare war on Turkey, too." Moeshe seemed to be keeping a running tally of which country had won this and lost that. He didn't seem convinced that Russia would win this war.

"Whose side are you on, anyway? It kind of feels like we're having our own 'massacre of innocents' like when Germany sent young boys into battle. Except in this case, you're attacking our hope." Otto Schultz frowned and shook his head at Moeshe.

"I'm just being realistic and trying to look at all the angles." Moeshe pushed his wire rim glasses up his nose. "It's not like each of you weren't thinking the same thing."

Alex nodded. Moeshe was only speaking aloud what they all thought but were too scared to say.

"I still say we'll win. Especially if our Navy has anything to do with it." Seaman Olenev winked at him. "Besides, we really need this win. Maybe somehow the leaders in our government will realize it's time for Tsar Nicholas II to step down. Our country is desperate for change. I think Bloody Sunday proved that our Tsar isn't the 'great father' that our parents tried to convince us he was. I, for one, can't wait until that day comes."

They had been assigned to the large dreadnought *Ekaterina*, which held two hundred sailors, most of whom were spoiling for a fight because of what Germany and Turkey had already done to them. It was a little worrisome since the Germans had just sunk two large British ships during a sea battle in the Pacific. There were no survivors. However just recently they heard that France and Britain declared war on the Ottoman Empire. That had encouraged all of them, because it stung all the sailors that Turkey had a hand in helping the German ships destroy all their ships in Odessa and kill the innocent people there.

Soon the Quartermaster came to announce it was time for all seamen to go to their quarters. The morning came early for men in the Navy, so Alex had learned.

For the next week, life on the Imperial Navy Ship was much the same. Taking different shifts, cleaning and repairing, shifts with other seamen, and practicing emergency drills. Alex tried to write a few lines everyday in his journal about what he had done or seen that day. If he survived this, maybe his future children might want to read it, and if he died in this crazy war, then at the very least it helped him clear his head each day.

One day, one of the sailors got his his leg caught in the rigging. Somehow it pulled him up, and he flew overboard.

The waves were really high around them and soon the man was farther out at sea. Alex tied a long rope around his waist, fastened the other end to an iron pole, then he jumped overboard. The force of the water against his body was like that of hitting a brick wall. He swam against the waves until he reached the sailor. He was one of the youngest men on the ship. Seaman Cruschev had lived in the city of Odessa up until he volunteered. He told the other sailors that he lied about his age. In fact, he was only seventeen and proud of it. Here in these wild waters, Alex thought he might change his mind about being eager to go to war.

He finally reached the young man, who was yelling and flailing his arms wildly in the water. Alex was exhausted from fighting the deep waters. He didn't want to fight both the water and Seaman Cruschev.

"I've got you now. You need to relax and just hold onto me." Alex spoke to him, trying to calm him. He didn't listen. His arms kept flailing, hitting Alex a few times in the face. Finally, Alex knocked him out so he could swim back to the ship. He made his way back slowly, keeping the man's head above water and just letting him float beside him. When they were back at the ship, the men on the deck tugged Alex's rope tight so he didn't drift away. Then they lowered a rope ladder. A man climbed down, grabbed the limp seaman from Alex, and carried him up the ladder. Then Alex made his way up the ladder, limbs leaden from exhaustion. Once he was at the top, men helped him over the edge, while others stood back and gave him a cheer. He slid to the deck, dripping wet and panting with exhaustion.

"I don't know if that was foolhardy or brave, but you did save a man's life." Captain Yakubovich stood there, shaking his head at him. He stared at him for awhile, his hands on his hips. "Quartermaster, help this man to sickbay along with the seaman who nearly drowned. See to it that they're taken care of."

"Yes, sir." Quartermaster Yurlov commanded two seamen to help. It didn't take long before Alex was dry and rested. The man he saved however, had swallowed too much water, they were watching him. In the mess hall that night, Otto teased him about not doing all the hero stuff. To leave some of that for the rest of them. Maybe the Captain would actually notice them, too. Moeshe wondered if he had a death wish with all the risks he took. Alex just laughed it all off.

The next day, Alex and twenty other sailors took turns learning how to operate each of the four, forty-calibre guns mounted in the turrets in the fore and aft of the ship. Alex took his turn learning how to load and fire. These were the biggest guns on the ship and took a couple of minutes between each loading and firing to repeat the process.

Alex stood beside Otto, as they tried to improve their speed and precision with each shot. They had just finished training and were waiting for the others, when Alex heard Lieutenant Kornilov's loud voice booming behind him. He turned his head, ready to follow new orders.

"I don't care if they were just cleaned, Quartermaster Yurlov. I want all the guns in the barbettes cleaned today! And I want this German Kraut to be the one to do it." Lieutenant Kornilov pointed at Seaman Shultz. Otto pressed his lips together, and his face looked pained, pleading.

Alex held his breath, biting his tongue. He understood the paralyzing fear of working with gunpowder. His hands had shook last week when it had been his turn. There was nothing he could do to help Otto, not without being locked up in the hold… or worse.

"Yes, sir." Quartermaster Yurlov took Seaman Schultz to the large circular and well-armoured guns mounted in the fore of the ship. Every new sailor was required to take a turn. Since they were training on the large gun turrets, Alex glanced at Seaman Schultz every once in awhile. Schultz's hands shook. Alex wished there was something he could do. He turned to see Lieutenant Kornilov watching Otto closely. The smirk on his face suggested that he hoped the new German recruit would make a mistake.

Alex turned away from watching Otto, to pay attention to his commander.

"Good, Seaman. Now you're ready to start sending some fireworks to blow those German flatfoots out of the water." Commander Lukin laughed and talked some more about the drill they would have the next day.

Alex cleaned up the guns at his station and every now and then glanced at Otto. Suddenly, Alex heard a loud scream shatter the air. Somehow the deck around where Otto was working, was on fire.

His heart stopped. It was like seeing everything in slow motion around him.

Gunpowder must have accidentally fallen to the wooden floor. He saw an electric wire that had fallen onto the deck and shot sparks near Otto's heels. Fire wrapped it's slithering tongue around his friend, flames licking at his uniform and neck.

 Alex ran to the nearest water bucket and splashed it all over his friend. It took a few pails full of water, until the fire died down. Otto collapsed on the deck, moving slowly, vomiting and spewing loud moans. His arms, legs and neck a picture of red and blackened meat. Alex heaved what little food was in his stomach over the side of the ship.

Hurried footsteps sounded and Alex moved out of the way. Medics ran up to Otto and gently put him on a carrier to take him to sickbay.

Alex stared in shock as he watched his friend carried away. His loud moans of pain were heard long after he was out of sight.

Alex could hardly focus the rest of the afternoon. When supper time came, no one at his table talked in mess hall. Men at the other tables around them talked, but the three of them stared at Schultz's empty chair with the awkwardness of a fish out of water.

"I've got to try one more time to see if I can see Otto." Alex stood up, more determined than ever.

"I hope the doctor lets you talk to him. Tell him… tell him we miss his jokes." Moeshe, the quiet one, spoke up. Alex nodded and made his way down to sick bay. Knocking quietly on the door, he was soon ushered into the small office that stood as a barrier to the sick beds.

"I really need to see Seaman Schultz. Please." Alex was desperate now. He didn't mind doing a little begging if that's what it took.

"You can go in and talk to him. But I must warn you, even though we've treated him, the burns cover most of his body. He won't live long." The medic opened the door.

Alex walked into sick bay, his stomach knotted in fear for what he'd find. He saw Otto lying there, unmoving. Black charred skin was outlined with red blisters that covered most of his body. Only the faint movement of his lips assured Alex he was still alive.

He walked up to the bed and forced a smile. Looking at his face up close, Alex nearly lost the few bites of food he'd eaten. Blue eyes created contrast on the red, scabbed face. His eyebrows and hair were singed off his head. Alex took a deep breath before he spoke.

"Hey, friend." Alex leaned over the bed slightly so Otto could see his face. "The guys were saying how they missed you and your great jokes. How are you feeling?"

"Pain…" Otto had to take long wheezing breaths between each word. "I don't… have long."

"Don't say that…" Alex stopped speaking when he saw that Otto tried to raise his hand to stop him.

"Don't worry… about…me." Otto had to stop for words.

"I hate the Germans for the war, for killing my parents." Alex clenched his jaw and took a breath. "I'm sorry, Otto…"

"No. Don't be… sorry. I needed you to say it…" He paused and took another painful breath. "I want you to promise me…"

"Anything Otto, you know that." Alex assured his friend. He would do all he could to help his friend die in peace.

"…you will let go of anger… not let it fester inside you." Otto wheezed again. "Forgive Lieutenant Kornilov. Remember the Germans… just doing their duty, like us." Otto looked drained from talking.

"I don't know how I can forgive, Otto. But I promise I will do my best." Alex was taken aback by his friend's request and didn't think he'd be able to do as he asked. But he promised he would try.

"You will, somehow I know you will." Otto sounded so sure. "And… could you tell my family I love them?"

"I will do that, my friend. You should rest now." Alex wanted to hug him, but knew that was impossible. So he looked into Otto's eyes. "Thank you for being my friend, Otto."

"Thanks for being mine, too." His eyes glistened with moisture, and he looked at Alex for a long time before he closed his eyes.

Alex wiped his eyes with the edge of his sleeve, knowing this was the last time he'd see him alive. He reached for the door handle with a trembling hand, squared his shoulders, and left.

It took a few days for Alex to process everything. By that time the captain had said his few words over Seaman Schultz and dumped his body in the sea. On the outside, it seemed like everything had returned to normal, but even the few skirmishes they had with some smaller Turkish ships didn't help to get his mind off what Otto had told him. No one had asked so much of him as Otto had. His heart and mind warred over what he had promised, and he didn't know how he would come to a place of peace.

At the end of the week, they landed again in Sevastopol for a few minor repairs and to restock the ship with coal and food supplies. It was also the time of the ship's mail delivery. He had mailed his letter to Annaveta just a few weeks ago, so he wasn't sure if there would be another one from her. When the mail was finally delivered, he was excited to see her familiar handwriting. He sat down to read it.

Dear Alex,

I hope this letter finds you safe and well.

I am well, but busy. Lately, I've been helping my uncle and aunt in their business. I never thought was smart enough to understand how a business worked, but I am learning. Thanks to Aunt Esther, who is a good teacher.

It's been so good to help those wives and children whose lives have been shattered by this awful war. The Junior Red Cross Society is thriving and many more women and children have been able to get the clothes and food they desperately need. Some women have even chosen to start a soup kitchen for those who don't have enough food. It feels so good to be able to help those in need rather than just going to dinner parties.

So far, I haven't learned any more information of the whereabouts of the BH. If you know anything, it would really be helpful if you would let me know.

Aunt Esther and Uncle Roman don't know anything so far. I don't know how long I can keep things hidden from them. I struggle daily with fear about the BH and safety for my aunt and uncle and you.

Please keep safe.

Annaveta

Alex could tell Annaveta was no longer the girl he first met. Now she was a mature woman doing important work. But, in this letter her words held emotions that were cool and reserved. He had hurt her, badly. Even though they said their goodbyes, Alex realized he had been too angry and too rash with her when he left.

He felt an invisible fist punch into his chest and hold there, squeezing his heart. He had ruined his relationship with one of the most important people in his life. Face to face with his past, he was determined not to be as ignorant now as he had been then.

It was time to win her back.

Chapter Nine

Annaveta walked up the steps of the massive country home of Jarena Barinov's family.

Her hands and knees shook. It wasn't the grandeur of the home that had her in such a jumpy state. It was the note that Moriah found two weeks ago in the bag of used clothes that came from Jarena's house that worried Annaveta. She wondered who could have written it. It was a definitely a member of the Black Hand, but who could it have been? Someone she had met? Someone she knew and liked? Or maybe a stranger to her, a hidden threat? Annaveta knew she had to find out who penned the letter.

She knocked on the door. A maid answered her knock and led her to the parlour.

"Annaveta, I'm so happy you're here." Jarena came forward and took her hands. "I brought all these bags down from the attic. Since Moriah came early, we started sorting through things already."

"That's good of you to do so much to help the war effort, Jarena." Annaveta wondered how anything sinister could come from the home of such a kind girl. Maybe she'd find out this was all a horrible mistake. She willed herself to calm down and followed Jarena into the house.

"Hello, Moriah. I'm glad you could come and help us." Annaveta saw Moriah separating the shirts, pants, and dresses and laying them over the back of the couch. "I'm sorry to tell you that the other three girls only wanted to come to our monthly meetings, but they didn't want to help sorting through the clothes. So it looks like it will be just the three of us."

"I'm happy about that." Moriah didn't often say much. She seemed glad that she was included in what they were doing for the war effort.

"I hope we're not disturbing your parents, Jarena." Annaveta hoped to learn more about her papa and mama.

"Oh, my dad and step-mom went to a small village on a mission for one of his students from years ago. So they won't be back for a couple of days." Jarena handed Annaveta a large stack of mismatched old clothes, rags, towels, and bed sheets. "Here you can work on sorting those."

"Your papa is a teacher then? I thought he was an investor in real estate?" Annaveta was confused by this new information.

"He used to teach students in military intelligence and strategy, but he's been retired from that for a few years. Since then, he's been investing in real estate or something like that. I think that's how papa was able to get such a good deal when he bought this estate." Jarena shrugged. "Anyway, I'm happy it can be just us girls for today. My father doesn't let me have my friends over to the house very often."

"I agree. It's nice that it's just us today." Annaveta, Moriah, and Jarena organized all the old clothes and put them into piles—men, women, children, and household. Once they had it all sorted into baskets to take to Annaveta's house, they put the baskets by the back door for the Levinsons' carriage driver, Vassily, to pick up from the Barinov Estate. They had been using the guest house as the place where they stored all the clothes and other things to give away. From there they planned to deliver the items to the different homes that needed the help.

"Well, it's getting late. I should be going. I promised Mama I'd be home by dinner. She invited guests." Moriah got up, and Jarena saw her out. Annaveta stood up and walked around, looking closer at the paintings on the wall. One was by Claude Monet, another a storm at sea – a famous painting called *The Ninth Wave* - by Russian artist Ivan Aivazovsky, and a third painting by Vincent Van Gogh of thunderclouds over a wheat field. It seemed like the general themes were of life filled with storms.

She walked to a desk along the far wall. A few pictures sat on it. She had first seen cameras used at Count and Countess Tashkova's estate, but the mechanics of how it worked fascinated her. She picked up the first framed photo. In it, Jarena stood behind an older woman who was seated, her long gown pooling into silky lines. Behind her stood a man who Annaveta recognized as the man from the train. The photo was black and white and a little grainy, but she'd recognize that man and the skull and crossbones that was uncovered from a sleeve that had been scrunched up.

She jumped when she heard a voice behind her.

"Sorry, I didn't mean to shock you. That's my step-mama. I don't have a picture of my birth mama. She died when I was born." Jarena's wistful tones were hardly more than a whisper.

"Of course, the man behind her is my papa."

Annaveta swallowed a few times, trying to rid herself of the fingers of fear tightening on her throat. The symbol of the Black Hand was the same as the one she saw on the man's hand on the train. Her hand gripped the side of the desk to steady herself.

Jarena's papa is involved with the Black Hand.

"Oh, you were curious about my papa and what he did. These are some of his friends and business partners in this picture." Jarena picked up the other black and white photograph which showed four men standing side by side with freshly caught fish in their hands.

"On the far right is Captain Yakubovich, who is in the Russian Navy. Beside him is a peer of the realm that my papa knows. I think he's a baron, but I can't think of his name. Next to him is a former student. Papa had to go talk to him about some business ideas. And then at the far left is my papa. So that's all of the family pictures we have. You probably saw the paintings. My papa loves the impressionist art. I like it too, but I wish we had some Renaissance art like Da Vinci or Michelangelo. Papa said, if I really want one, he would see what he could do to get me one of my own."

Annaveta's mind scrambled as she looked at three people she knew in the picture. She leaned against the desk, her fingers gripping it tightly.

"Sorry, Annaveta, most likely I'm boring you." Jarena stopped pointing out the paintings and walked back to the desk.

"No. Not at all." Annaveta's voice wavered. She looked at Jarena and forced a shaky smile.

"You look kind of pale. Are you not feeling well?" Jarena touched her arm with a light touch, concern in her eyes.

"It's true. Suddenly I don't feel very well. Would you ask your driver if he would take me home?" It was the truth. She was too

shaken to stay in the Barinov home any longer.

"Of course. You must go home and rest. I'll take care of it." Jarena smiled at her and left the parlour.

Annaveta closed her eyes and breathed deep before opening her eyes again. The picture of the four men together seemed to mock her, as if it was telling her she wouldn't get away from them no matter where she went or what she did. She started to think of the many unanswered questions that plagued her.

I know two of them, Baron Yakov and Jarena's father. If Mr. Belinkski and Baron Yakov were friends, then they were part of the Black Hand. When Jarena talked, it sounded like her papa had gone to visit a former student out in one of the villages near where she grew up. Did he know Misha? Had he escaped from prison? What does that mean for me and Alex? I have to find out more about their plans.

She looked at the desk before her and saw two drawers. Opening up the first drawer, she saw a few books and some pencils and pens. She looked in the books. It was just re-search on weapons and ammunition. Not of much interest to Annaveta. Opening the second drawer, she saw blank writing paper. It looked like that was all it was until she saw the crumpled edge of an older piece of paper sticking out from under it.

"Papa. Mama. You're home." Annaveta heard Jarena's surprised voice ring out from the parlour.

"We thought we'd surprise you and come home early. I saw the driver bring the carriage around. Are you going somewhere, my dear?" Mr. Barinov's cultured Russian voice surprised Annaveta.

"No, I had a friend visiting today and she's on her way home. Would you like to meet her?" Annaveta heard Jarena's question and panicked. Grabbing the letter she found under the writing paper, she folded it into her skirt pocket and hurried out the side door of the parlour. She walked in the opposite direction of the where the voices were coming from until she found a door that led to the outdoors. Annaveta ran outside, walking close to the side of the house, so she wouldn't be seen. Her heart beat like a loud drum, hoping against hope that Jarena or her parents wouldn't see her. Soon she saw the carriage and the driver, who was checking the harnesses.

"Jarena said I should ask you for a ride home. I'm not feeling well." She walked up to the driver.

"Of course." The driver opened the carriage door and helped her inside its luxurious interior. Soon the carriage was moving down the Belinkski driveway and out onto the road that led to Odessa and to the Eastern hill where her aunt and uncle lived. Annaveta breathed a sigh of relief that she was almost home and safe once again.

Hopefully Jarena wouldn't be too angry at her for leaving unexpectedly. The next time she saw her she would just explain that she wasn't feeling well. Annaveta knew there was no way she could have stayed. She couldn't take the risk of Mr. Barinov recognizing her as the same woman from the train. By now, he might have talked to Misha, who she knew would never give up seeking to destroy her life and Alex's.

She stepped out of the carriage and sent the driver on his way. Walking into the Levinson's home, she nodded to Larson and asked if he would let her aunt know she was home, but that she wasn't feeling well. She went to her bedroom, and when her maid came, she asked for a hot bath. She needed to calm her nerves. While Tatyana was busy, Annaveta took out the crumpled letter. Her hands shook as she opened it up and read it.

Boris,

It took some scheming to rid myself and our two other friends of the confines of those horrible walls around us. But now we are closer than ever. It's time to move on.

By now you know our mutual friend and leader, Apis, has decided that our group needs to back off for awhile from our duties. It seems we're all being investigated for other so-called crimes, so he said we should keep a low profile for awhile.

But that's a point I don't agree on. I believe now is the time to take even stronger measures against those who oppose us. Not just in matters of politics, but also in matters of silencing a race of people who controls the money we need. I helped this effort in Odessa in 1905, but now it is needed more than ever.

I also mean to avenge all those who put me in this awful place. Like that little red-haired skazka.

But for now, I'll see you soon, and we'll make plans for a lucrative future for both of us.

Annaveta wiped the tears from her cheeks. Even though the letter was unsigned, she worried it might be Misha. According to the letter from Malina – her friend in St. Petersburg - all three of them planned to escape from prison. She remembered when he had imprisoned her, he had laughed about his part in the 1905 Pogrom in Odessa where her family had been murdered. As she thought back to what she and Alex both had endured at his hands, as well as at Baron Yakov's and Monsieur Arnaud's hands, she wasn't really that surprised at his frenzied search for vengeance.

Fear filled her. What was she going to do? For once she was happy that Alex was in the Navy. Maybe he would be safer there than here in Odessa. She decided she would write to Alex, tell him what she had discovered so far, and ask him what she should do next.

"Annaveta?" The knock at her door had her scrambling to hide the letter. She just put it under her pillow when Aunt Esther walked in her room. "Oh, you are here. Have you been crying? Tell me what happened."

"Oh, Aunt Esther, I probably should have told you the moment Alex and I came to your doorstep, but I didn't want to frighten you."

Aunt Esther listened closely as Annaveta told her all that had happened since she had escaped from her village – and a forced marriage to Misha – to the Wagner home.

"Alex saw those men get arrested, then he escaped from a policeman who was actually a member of the Black Hand. He came back to me in St. Petersburg and we came as fast as we could to you and Uncle. So far, I am fairly certain no one from the Black Hand knows that Alex and I are here, but today when I read something that forced me to recognize they will never give up." Annaveta had tears in her eyes. "I'm so sorry. I didn't want you to be in danger because of me."

"Listen to me." Aunt Esther put her hands on either side of her cheeks. "Your uncle and I, we can take care of ourselves. We've done that for years." She stroked Annaveta's hair like her mama used to when she was upset as a little girl. Annaveta closed her eyes and relaxed. "I'm more concerned about you." Her hand stopped moving through her hair. "I didn't realize all the danger you've been in. You've carried a heavy weight, haven't you? Well, you don't have to carry it alone anymore. We're here to help you now."

"Thank you." Annaveta wiped more tears. She couldn't seem to stop crying. To have family that was willing to help take the load from her shoulders felt so good. So freeing. Some of the pressure had been lifted from her shoulders.

"I will need to tell Uncle Roman about this. He'll want to know so he can prepare for how he can better protect everyone in his family." Aunt Esther spoke with unshakable calm. "Thank you for telling me, Annaveta. You are growing into such a mature and responsible woman. Alex will hardly recognize you the next time he sees you."

Aunt Esther's voice held a teasing note which surprised Annaveta. She had done what she could to introduce Annaveta to different men in their social circle. Maybe realizing how much Alex had protected her made her aunt soften a little toward Alex. Annaveta liked the thought of that. It might keep the matchmaking at bay. Aunt Esther had told her that Sacha would be home on leave for the weekend, and he had invited their family over for dinner. Maybe this time Aunt Esther wouldn't insist that Annaveta talk to Sacha for most of the night. That would be a relief.

"I think it would be better if you always had someone with you when you leave the house from now on. We just don't know when someone will be watching and waiting to harm you. We can't take that chance." Aunt Esther hugged her and stood up. "I'll have your maid bring you a light supper. You look tired."

"Thanks. For everything." Annaveta gave her aunt a tired smile.

Her aunt blew her a kiss and clicked the door shut.

Minutes later she drifted off to sleep.

The morning came too fast. She had more secretarial work to do for her uncle. He had a meeting with a client, and he wanted her to sit in the room and take dictation.

She dressed in her serviceable dark blue skirt and cream-coloured blouse. She pinned the cameo Aunt Esther gave her—the one with the young woman with the angelic face and upswept hair—to the high neck collar of her blouse.

She took her notepad and pen and knocked on Uncle Roman's office door.

"Come." He waved her inside and continued talking to the man who sat across from his desk.

"How did he die?"

"In his letter, Alex told us that the lieutenant had ordered Otto to clean the guns in the barbettes. But something went wrong and the gun powder got on him and somehow it caught fire. He sustained burns over most of his body."

Annaveta sat still, her heart breaking at the sound of this man's sobs. She found the extra handkerchiefs and put them in front of the man.

Once he had calmed, the man continued. "So I'm here because Otto told us in his letters how good Alex had been to him. He said, 'Next time you sell your grain, Papa, you go to Roman Levinson in Odessa. Alex says he's honest and will do his best by you.'" The man swallowed and wiped his nose again. "So that's why I'm here."

"So sorry to hear about your son. War is a terrible thing." Uncle Roman shook his head. "From the sound of things, it seems like I owe Alex my thanks that you came to do business with me, Mr. Schultz. I'll do my best to live up to the honour you've given me by trusting us to export your grain."

"I want to do all I can to honour my son's memory." Mr. Schultz dabbed at his eyes with the handkerchief. "So should we talk specifics about the grain?"

"Yes." Roman nodded at her. "My niece will take notes so we have all the details."

"Ja, ja. Gut."

The meeting went longer than Annaveta expected, but her notes were thorough. It looked like because of Otto's friendship with Alex, Uncle Roman and Aunt Esther would get one of the biggest contracts not only with Herr Schultz, but with many people in his German colony. Her biggest concern was over what Herr Schultz had said about the death of his son Otto, and how Alex had been a faithful friend. She wasn't surprised by that. Alex was a good friend. She had just received a letter from him where he had told her he was sorry about all the mean words he had said the last time they saw each other. He said he had been angry at his parents' senseless deaths and about going off to war, and he had taken it out on her. He asked her forgiveness.

Could they begin again together? Annaveta did forgive him, but maybe it was better if they began again as friends. Now she feared Alex a little, which hadn't happened before. In that moment, he had reminded her of her papa who had abused her all her life. It would just take a little bit of time for her to see if Alex was trustworthy.

In his letter, he told her of some of the other sailors and what they ate, but he never talked about Otto's death. She wondered what else he wasn't telling her?

Weeks had gone by without any word from Namuth. Misha was angry. He'd said a few words to his cousin, Monsieur Arnaud, and to Baron Yakov the few times they had whispered to each other on their work days outside their hateful prison cell. They said they hadn't talked to Namuth. Misha told them not to worry about trying to contact him, he would handle the guard. He just finished his small supper of rice, bread, and a small portion of meat when he heard the rattle of keys.

He stood up when he saw the massive form of Namuth squeeze through the small door. He backed up, a little scared of the giant before him.

"What took you so long?" He couldn't seem to stop the angry words that popped out of his mouth.

"Don't tell me you're actually surprised that I came back?" The burly man grunted and shook his head in disgust. "This kind of planning takes more than a few days. It's a lot of trouble, arranging this for you and your two friends. A little thanks wouldn't hurt you." He stood there with his hands on hips, glaring at him.

"All right, sorry." Misha grumbled out a reluctant apology. "So what's the plan?"

"Shh. Keep your voice down. Do you want all the guards to come running?" Namuth growled at him.

Misha backed away. He couldn't show his fear.

"Here. Take this." Namuth pulled some bundled clothes out from under his vest and handed it to him. "Put this under your mattress until it's completely dark. Then change into them. We leave tonight. I'll come for you, so be ready."

The guard left as suddenly as he came in.

Misha hurried to put the dark clothes under the mattress. Finally, they would be out of this loathsome hell hole and he could move onto more important things.

Chapter Ten

The battleship, the dreadnought *Ekaterina,* slowly pulled into dock at Sevastopol for refilling of coal and food.

"We're docking for four days at Sevastopol." Quartermaster Yurlov spoke. "You've been given permission to visit who you wish, but you must be back here at the base in four days' time."

Alex thought this would be a perfect time to go to Odessa to see Annaveta. He was desperate to see her. Because he only heard little tidbits of news in her letters, he wondered how she was really doing.

He used the little pay he had received to purchase a two-way ticket by train. The whole way there he had questions about so many things. He wondered if Annaveta had received his last letter and if she was willing to forgive him, or had he gone so far out of line that she didn't want anything to do with him anymore? And what about Mr. and Mrs. Levinson? How would they receive him now that he was in the Navy? Roman Levinson believed Alex needed to serve his country. Maybe now Alex would be in Annaveta's uncle's good books.

Of course, he would never measure up to their son, Lieutenant Jude Levinson. He had heard his name mentioned with fierce pride by his father at every discussion where the Imperial Navy or war was discussed. The lieutenant was obviously a man of character and discipline. Alex thought that at some point he would like to meet this amazing paragon of all things that made a great man.

Alex didn't think he measured up the way he was, and he feared he never would. So far he hadn't been able to let go of his anger. It was like a quiet poison affecting his whole body. Otto had wanted Alex to forgive Lieutenant Kornilov for putting Otto in harm's way and for his comments against against Germans. Otto had also encouraged him to forgive the Germans who had killed his parents. Right now that was impossible. How was he supposed to do that? Mama's last words to him had been, "There's a much bigger hand guiding you than your own, son. Trust the process."

Right now, all he knew was that it seemed like he needed to start by asking Annaveta's forgiveness. He knew that on this earth, she was the one person he needed more than anyone else. She saw his mistakes and flaws and loved him anyway.

Or at least, she had loved him.

The train let loose a low whistle as it chugged into Odessa in the early morning hours. He stepped down onto the platform, and not seeing anyone he knew, started walking. It would be a long walk from the train station up the hill, but it was worth it. He had just made it beyond the outskirts of the city when he heard a wagon behind him. He spotted old Boris Rusnak with his horse and wagon.

"Let me give you a ride, son. I'm going to the Levinson Estate to deliver milk. You can ride along and tell me about your days in the Navy so far." Mr. Rusnak clucked to the horses to bring them up the hill.

"I only have a couple days leave." Alex told him some of the things he was doing on the dreadnought *Ekaterina*. The old man nodded his interest. Boris Rusnak was one of the few Russians in Odessa who had been kind to him since the war started. Most people were suspicious of anything German. The German minority were called the *enemy within.*

"The ship needed to be refitted with a new boiler, too, so they gave us leave. I'm grateful. I made some big mistakes before I left, and I needed to come back and set some things right." Mr. Rusnak smiled his toothless smile, and that comforted Alex. "Have you needed to do that, Mr. Rusnak?"

"Ah, son, in my long lifetime I've made many mistakes that I've need to go back and fix, and even some that I waited too long to fix at all. Be grateful you're not too late." He slowed the horses to a stop in front of the Levinsons' house.

"Thanks for the ride and advice." Alex nodded at the old farmer who touched the brim of his straw hat. He jumped off the wagon and headed toward the front door. It was very cold this November morning, and his hand ached when he knocked on the door.

He was surprised when Esther opened the door. "Alex!" Esther Levinson's jaw dropped. "Come in, come in. It's freezing outside." Larsen stepped in and took his jacket and gloves. "We just finished breakfast, but I'll ask Cook to fill you up."

He followed her into the breakfast room, where Roman read his daily newspaper. Annaveta sat there talking with some man he had never met. When they shared a laugh, he pushed down the jealous thoughts that threatened to spill over.

Esther Levinson asked for more coffee and food be brought and then sat down again. "Well, Alex, I'm glad you're here. Besides seeing everyone again, you can meet our son, Jude."

"Nice to meet you, sir." Alex nodded at the muscular man who sat beside Esther. He relaxed his stance.

"It's always good to meet another Navy man, Alex." Jude stood and shook his hand, his firm grasp lingering. Steady gray eyes met his. Jude's exacting gaze seemed to take in the measure of a man that he was. After a moment he spoke again. "I understand you've put the glow in my young cousin's cheeks, again."

Alex felt heat burn his neck and cheeks at the not-so-subtle reference to their romance. "I'm just glad Annaveta's safe and happy with her family again."

"Spoken like a true gentleman." Jude grinned and clapped him on the back. "You'll do." A smile lingered on his face as he sat down at the table once more.

Alex smiled, glad to discover that Mr. Levinson's son was easy going and just an ordinary man after all.

"It's good to see you again too, Mr. Levinson." Alex nodded at Jude's father, who peeked up at him above his newspaper with a quick nod and continued reading.

"Annaveta, you're looking beautiful, as usual." Alex's gaze lingered, starved for the sight of her. She glanced up at him once, before looking down. Her unsmiling face spoke louder than words. He had his work cut out for him.

Soon the maid brought coffee and a plate overflowing with steaming eggs, bacon, and toast.

"So, Alex, what brings you back? Not absent without leave, are you?" Roman Levinson put his paper and glasses down on the table, a crease deepening between his brows.

"No, sir. The captain and some of the crew are refitting the ship with a new boiler, and they are filling up on supplies. He gave us four days leave."

"Oh?" Jude asked. "And what ship is that?"

"The dreadnought *Ekaterina*," Alex answered.

"Isn't that the ship you've been transferred to, Jude?" Roman looked at his son.

"Yes, it is." Jude looked back at Alex with a raised eyebrow. "Looks like I'll be one of your new commanding officers. I heard of the recent fire. That's tough. How many wounded?"

"Two wounded and two dead. One of them a good friend." Alex lowered his eyes as tears formed in his eyes. "It shouldn't have happened." A muscle jerked along his jaw as he remembered. He wasn't going to go on and on about the faults of his commanding officers, especially not now that Jude would be one of them.

"Well, maybe there needs to be new safety procedures in place. I'll look into it." Jude's assurances were good to hear, but too late for Otto. Alex didn't think it was safety procedures that were lacking, but rather their leader.

"So, have you read the news?" Roman eyed both his son and Alex over top of his newspaper. "They've officially changed the name of St. Petersburg to Petrograd. Because of the war with Germany, they wanted a name for the city that doesn't sound German."

Alex thought that it likely wouldn't have much of an effect.

Roman continued. "Ever since the Germans solidly defeated our troops in the battle of Tannenberg, the country has doubted the effectiveness of the leadership of Tsar Nicholas II. Our troops have suffered terrible loss on our own western front."

"There is much change in the air." Jude nodded at his father's words, the muscles around his lips tightening. The atmosphere at the table gained the weight of molten lead, the stifling intensity known only to those who had lived through the ravages of war.

They talked a little more about the latest news.

Alex hadn't heard some of the most recent reports. France and Britain just declared war on the Ottoman Empire, and the British Empire invaded Mesopotamia to protect the oil pipeline from Persia. Only two weeks later, they captured the city of Basra. It looked like the German Naval base at Tsingtao was captured by the Japanese with help from a British and Indian battalion.

"Oh, let's not talk about war." Esther laid her hand on Roman's arm. "I'd much rather talk about how well our Annaveta is doing as secretary in the import-export business. She has even met many of our clients and inspired more business."

"Thank you, Aunt Esther. I'm happy to hear I've helped in some way. I've really enjoyed learning about buying and selling grain and farm equipment from both you and Uncle Roman."

Alex was cheered somewhat the knowledge that Annaveta

seemed to be doing what she loved. It was quite the opposite in his case. He didn't feel any freedom at all. Rather, he felt more bound. Part of the reason was because his German heritage caused people to doubt him and suspect his motives all the time. However, since the death of his parents, his anger raged against both Germany and anyone who mocked other Germans' heritage, like Lieutenant Kornilov had with Otto.

Alex wanted to live each day with the kind of peace that he saw in Annaveta. He hoped, while he was at the Levinsons', it would help him gain a better perspective.

"Alex, I had Larson put your bag in the guest house. Let us know if there's anything else you need." Esther stood up from the table, a sign to everyone that breakfast was over.

"Well, Jude, are you ready to come with me to inspect those ships? Maybe you can look over our two merchant ships that were shattered in the German attack. You can let me know if you see places where they could be fortified better." Roman Levinson spoke to his son as they stood to their feet.

"I'll see you when you get back, son." Esther patted her son's arm and then turned to look at Annaveta and Alex. "Oh, go on, you two. You need to talk. We'll see you for lunch."

Alex followed Annaveta.

"Wait here. I need to get something." Annaveta hurried down the hall to her room and retrieved the letter she had discovered at Jarena's house. She hurried back, putting it into the pocket of her skirt.

They walked toward the grove of trees on their small mountain that overlooked Odessa and sat down to watch the early activity there.

He turned his head to look at her. His interest caught on how the wind reached its long fingers through her reddish-brown hair, loosening long strands of it and lifting it in the breeze. The freckles dotting her nose glistened in the morning sun.

"Alex, I had no idea you were coming home." She pulled her knees up to her chest and leaned her forehead to them. Her body created an invisible wall between them.

"I didn't realize I was coming home, either, until Captain Yakubovich told us we were stopping in Sevastopol. I'm glad we did, because I really needed to see you again." His gut clenched in fear that she might reject his next words. "I wanted to tell you in person how sorry I am for the things I said before I left. It was wrong of me. I shouldn't have attacked your character like that. You are the most honest and trustworthy person I know. I was being petty and jealous and I'm so sorry. Can you find it in your heart to forgive me?"

"I got your letter, where you said much the same thing." Annaveta wiped tears from her eyes. She shifted so her legs were stretched out. "I forgave you then, and I forgive you now. Like you said, I would like us to start over, too. I really think starting from the beginning is what it is going to take. I'll be honest. I don't think I've seen you quite that angry before, and it's left me a little wary."

Her words felt like someone punched him in the gut.

"You really scared me. I felt like I was back with my father, uncertain of when he would attack me next. I don't want our relationship to become like that. I've always liked how honest, caring, and respectful we were with each other. I really don't want to lose that."

"Oh, Annaveta. I'm so sorry. The last thing I want to do is scare you." Alex touched a strand of her long hair, fingering its silkiness. "And you're right, our relationship has always been so much more. I'm sorry my anger brought that down to a low level. Thank you for forgiving me and giving me another chance."

Annaveta squeezed his hand, and she looked back out over the city. "I'm very happy you came home, even if it is only for a few days, Alex."

Alex held her hand and kissed the tips of her fingers. Then he winked at her and turned the conversation to a lighter topic. "Tell me more about the wonderful job you're doing as a secretary. The way your aunt tells it, you're a miracle worker with a natural understanding of business."

"Ah, well, she's being overly kind." Annaveta bumped her shoulder against his. "I don't know if I've done that much. But I do feel like I'm learning so much about business. I never thought I'd hear myself say that, growing up so poor in the peasant village of Noltava." She looked at him and frowned. "My parents would be surprised if they could see me working as a secretary as well as helping with the Junior Red Cross Society, I think."

"Your mama would be proud of you. I know my mama was as proud of you as she was her own daughters." Alex swallowed the lump in his throat as he thought of his parents and how much he missed them. "It's good then, that you are learning, growing, and doing things you like. And helping others at the same time."

"Yes, it's been good to help many people who have struggled to have enough food to eat or to have the warm clothes they need especially now that cold weather is coming." Annaveta's face lit up as she talked about the different people that the Junior Red Cross had helped. "But, even with the good we're trying to do, trouble still seems to find us. Not too long ago, we were helping Jarena sort through clothes she wanted to give away, and that's how Moriah found the note in clothes. Then when I was at Jarena's home, I—"

"You went to her home? Annaveta, that's like going into a hungry lion's den. You could have been hurt. Or worse." Alex was shocked at the risks she took sometimes. It reminded him of when she lived at his parents' home and was constantly being threatened by notes and even gun shots. This time was slightly different, because Annaveta was no longer willing to just sit back and let the terrorists scare her. Now it seemed she was choosing to go after them and do what she could stop them. Even though he admired her courage, he feared for her. "You should go to the police."

"Only to find that some of the police had joined forces with the Black Hand, like what happened to you in Sarajevo? I don't trust them, Alex." Annaveta shook her head as if to say that was the last thing she would do. "I was careful. Besides, if I was hurt, then it would involve you and my aunt and uncle, and I'm not willing to put any of you at risk because of me."

Alex nodded. Annaveta was very protective of the people she loved. She had lost too many in people already. "So, did you find anything at Jarena's home?"

Annaveta nodded and looked around as if to double check that no one was listening. "Yes. First I saw a picture of Jarena's father, Boris Barinov, standing with Baron Yakov, and there was a faded picture of two other men, one of whom she called Captain or Admiral or something. I think they are all members of the Black Hand. I was desperate to see if there was anything that would give me more information. I looked around, and in one of the drawers in the drawing desk I found an old letter. Her parents came home then, unexpectedly, so I stole it and hurried home." She took a shaky breath.

"You know what kind of trouble you could be in if you're caught, don't you?" Alex grit his teeth, letting out a frustrated groan.

"Yes I know, Alex. But I need to get to the bottom of this. Here read it for yourself." Annaveta stood up, gave him the letter and paced. "So what do we do?"

"Well, we keep our eyes open and don't try to put ourselves in harm's way." Alex responded to the fire he saw in her eyes.

"I can't just sit around and wait. I did too much of that the last time we were terrorized by the Black Hand, remember?"

Annaveta had her hands on her hips. She looked like a *Russian rusallka*—a water nymph rising up out of the water—ready to stake claim to what was hers.

Alex raised one eyebrow. His memories were of running away, not really sitting around. Later, after they returned to St. Petersburg from Sarajevo, they investigated who was behind the threats. However, he understood her need to uncover the truth.

"I just don't like you taking all these risks, and I'm so far away and can't be here to keep you safe."

"I'll be careful. But don't you see? I need to do this. They played God with our lives when we were in Pleve colony, as well as when we were in St. Petersburg, and this time I want to know what the Black Hand are doing before they get a chance to hurt us any more than they already have." Annaveta put both hands on her hips and held her head high. "I talked to Aunt Esther about it, and she is worried. She made me promise I would stay close to home. So I will, unless I really need to go somewhere."

Alex laughed. "Wow, you really have changed. I don't know that I've ever seen the determined adventurer before. I like the new confident you." He stood up, grabbed both of her hands, and kissed them. "Promise me you'll keep writing to me to let me know what you find out? I'm really curious about the name of that captain who was also in the picture."

"I'll try to find out." Annaveta moved just out of his reach, still deep in thought. "I plan on going back again to Jarena's house to return the stolen letter. And maybe I'll find more clues."

"What?"

"Before you get too worried, you need to know that I have to get that letter back before Jarena's father finds it missing and gets suspicious. He may be already, given the way I rushed off."

Her words made sense, but he didn't have to like it. In fact, he feared what would happen to her.

Alex was able spend time a little more time with Annaveta over the following two days. He also wrote to his brother Helmut and asked about news from home. And he wrote to his brother Ernest, who lived in Canada. Too soon, it was time for him to leave. He said goodbye to Annaveta the evening before he had to board the train. He knew he had to earn her trust again, so he only kissed her hand even though he wanted to do much more. Heavy-hearted, he followed

Lieutenant Jude Levinson onto the train.

Misha rode the train, happy to be out of that vermin-infested prison. He didn't feel bad that he, Baron Yakov, and his cousin escaped while none of his other inmates did. They deserved to be there. He didn't. It was that simple.

He had to tell his cousin to be quiet a few times, but other than that, things had gone smoothly. Namuth had paid off some of the guards to look the other way as they drove the vehicle through the prison gates.

He had been stuck in one of the cars in the back of the train for a couple of days now. It would be good to finally see the light of day.

Misha stepped off the train, moving quickly toward a waiting carriage, hoping no one, specifically any authority figures, would recognize him. Getting into the carriage, he closed the door and looked out the window, double-checking that no one had followed him. Suddenly he spotted two uniformed men walking across the platform. He saw both of them take off their hats as the conductor checked their tickets. He pulled his hat lower onto his head to hide his face. It wouldn't do to be caught when he'd just barely escaped.

He would ask his friend Boris to find out from his contacts if they had seen either Alex or Annaveta. Then he would track them both down.

Misha got out of the wagon that had taken him to the man that was his teacher and taught him the ways and rules of the Black Hand. It had been three days train ride from Sarajevo and hiding in the cargo car of the train, to come here to Odessa. The prison guard who had worked it out for all three of them to escape had connections to get them hidden on the train. Monsieur Arnaud had taken the train to Saratov to get to his home, and Baron Yakov had taken the train to St. Petersburg. But Misha wanted to see his teacher. So he had come to this city.

He had hoped that somehow Boris Barinov would have advice that he needed. He wouldn't rest until he found Annaveta and Alex. They managed to wreck his plans and ruin his life. They needed to pay for what they had done to him. He would need to check Pleve colony and her old Russian village to see if anyone had seen her. He planned to do that soon. Meanwhile, he wanted to see what his old teacher was doing.

Misha looked at the large brick house on the sprawling estate and realized his teacher must be doing something right. His teacher met him at the door and invited him inside. His daughter, a young lady with big expressive brown eyes and dark brown hair, took his coat led him into her father's office. In a few minutes, she was back with tea and biscuits. He could get used to this. Looking around the room, he spotted a photograph of him, Baron Yakov, the teacher, and their common friend, Captain Yakubovich. He was glad he was given a place of respect and honour here on the desk.

"Ah, my friend. So you managed to break out of your jail cell, did you?" His mentor's loud laugh seemed to boom off the walls in his office.

"Of course, Boris. What else would someone as resourceful as me do?" Misha laughed with him. He was proud of what he did. He told Boris how he had managed to discover

140

which of the guards in that horrible prison in Sarajevo were members of the Black Hand. A few well placed questions and it didn't take long before he knew who he could work with. Namuth was one guard who was desperate to get back at the Sarajevo police, and he would do whatever he could to make them look bad. Misha got him to organize their escape.

"So, you decided to find me." Boris handed him a box of cigars and lit a match. "As long as you weren't followed, we have nothing to worry about, do we?" Boris puffed on his cigar and exhaled a long row of curly smoke rings into the air. "You obviously have something on your mind to come all this way. What is it you want?"

Misha took his time, drawing a long exhale from his cigar. "Hmm, these are good." He could tell Boris grew impatient, so he got on with it. "I was hoping you could help me find someone, if they are in this area. Actually two people. A beautiful redhead and a blond German fellow. It seems I owe them my thanks for the part they played in putting me in prison."

"Ah, revenge is sweet." Boris got up and poured them each a small glass of Russian vodka. "I could probably help you with that. Right now I have two men who work for me. Their job is to scout out residences here in Odessa. They report on who lives there, who works there, how the people make their income, and if they have anything worth stealing." Boris gave a little laugh. "Around here, they all think I make my money from investing in real estate. No one suspects I'm behind the thefts and property destruction. It's funny how easily people are fooled, isn't it?"

"Well, I'm happy your men can help out. It's all to be very discreet, of course. At the first sign anyone is looking for them, they'll disappear again, and they might be even harder, if not impossible, to find next time." Misha hoped he wasn't being a fool, asking Boris to do this for him.

"Of course. My men haven't let me down yet." Boris smoked his cigar down to the nub and ground it in the hand-carved ashtray on the edge of his desk. "However, if I do this for you, there's a favour I'd like in return."

Misha tilted his head and waited.

"I want my daughter to go to finishing school. It was her Mama's dream for her, and I want to see that she gets it. But it will take connections like yours and your father's for that to happen. So what do you say?" Boris stood up and walked around to the front of his desk.

"That shouldn't be a problem." Misha was proud of his family connections. His father knew many powerful men in Parliament, and other wealthy landowners like himself. Many of whom owed him favors. A few greased palms and he could get his teacher's daughter into any finishing school in the country. He could get one named after her, for the right price.

"Good, then. I'll keep you informed."

"Messages for me can be sent for now to my father's farm. I'm planning on finding my cousin, and we'll be searching around there as well as Pleve colony to try to find them."

He shook Boris' hand, happy that part of his search was taken care of. Now he would spend a little bit of time looking around a few different German colonies as well as in Noltava, the village Annaveta grew up in. When he found them, he would make them sorry they had ever tried to get in his way.

Chapter Eleven

"Thanks for coming ladies." Annaveta spoke to a group of women ranging in age from sixteen to late twenties. The group had grown to fourteen women, and they were starting to let people in the small villages around Odessa know they would come once a month to bring used clothes and help with food. "I'm happy the Junior Red Cross Society is growing. Now we can help more people in the surrounding villages, too. They are very grateful for your generosity."

After the meeting, when the ladies filed out into the parlour, Annaveta said, "Remember next Thursday is our day to volunteer at the hospital." She followed them to the door, where Larson handed them their overcoats.

Aunt Esther had sent Vassily to their homes to bring them to the Levinsons' for this monthly meeting.

Annaveta sighed. She wished those other girls were more like Jarena. Trying to get them to help was as difficult as a visit to the doctor.

Annaveta hurried to the office where Aunt Esther reviewed some papers with Uncle Roman. She had promised to work this afternoon with them. She got a lot done even though she struggled to focus on her work, with thoughts of Alex barging her mind. She was happy that he had apologized and she did forgive him, but she needed some time to see that she could trust him. She needed to know for certain that he didn't have an uncontrollable temper like her papa had. That he wasn't happy one minute and angry the next. She didn't need him to be perfect, but she did need to be able to trust him.

She prayed he would be safe on the ship. Uncle Roman would mention things he read the newspaper, and it didn't sound like Russia was doing very well in the war. She didn't know what she would do if Alex was taken from her life, too. She had faced too much grief already.

The next morning after they had mid-morning tea, she reminded Aunt Esther of what she had asked her a few days ago.

"I just wanted to remind you that I'll be going today to Miss Barinov's home. Tatyana has agreed to come with me." Annaveta worried a little at the brooding look her Aunt gave her. Maybe she'd stop her from going. She clenched her fists at her side.

"I never really liked Boris Barinov. He says he's done well in real estate, but it seems strange that no one in our social circles has invested in property with him. Besides, I don't like a man who has shifty eyes and hardly smiles." Aunt Esther looked at Uncle Roman, who shrugged behind his newspaper.

"Jarena's papa and mama aren't going to be at home. It will just be Jarena and me and the servants." Annaveta hoped that would ease her mind.

"I'm still unsure about you going there. But if it's just going to be you girls, then I'll agree. Only if you promise you won't stay overlong."

"We'll only stay a short while. Thanks, Aunt Esther." Annaveta kissed her cheek and hurried to get ready to go. She wanted to find a hat that would hide most of her hair and a little of her face, just in case Jarena's father and step-mother came home early. She couldn't take the chance that Mr. Barinov might recognize her.

Tucking the letter into her skirt pocket, she hurried from her room. She was having a late luncheon with Jarena. Annaveta also hoped sometime during their visit she would be able to return the letter back to the desk in the parlour. Knots formed in her stomach at the thought of going through other people's stuff. But she needed to search the Barinov home to see if she could uncover the threat to Alex and herself.

Tatyana waited for her by the front door, holding Annaveta's shawl. "Where are we going today, miss?"

"To my friend Jarena Barinov's house. Do you remember her?"

"Yes, miss." Tatyana frowned and looked down at her clasped hands in her lap.

"What is it, Tatyana? Is something wrong?" Annaveta wondered why her maid would frown over visiting the Barinov home.

"Well, I don't like to speak ill of other people, miss."

"I know you don't, Tatyana. But if this is something that concerns me, I should know about it, don't you think?" Annaveta leaned forward and gave an encouraging smile.

"I just heard from some workers at the Barinov estate. He's doing something over there that he doesn't want anyone to know about. He and that other man who has started to visit him regularly. They are hauling things into an underground tunnel." Tatyana shivered as she spoke. "One of my friends works in the kitchen there, and she hears about things, miss. She says they never ask for any of the help to carry whatever it is into the tunnel. And they always do their work in the blackest of nights. I think all kinds of evil happens on their property, especially on the southern side of their land, where the land is cursed."

"What do you mean, the land is cursed?"

Tatyana took a deep breath and crossed herself. "Back in 1905, a bad thing happened here in Odessa. Over eight hundred Jews were killed, and several more thousand were wounded. Many people's houses were burned to the ground. Mr. Barinov is the one that bought most of the land where the houses burned. That's why the land is cursed. Some of the workers who work at that estate say their family is cursed because of it."

"My grandparents died in that attack. I remember my mama talking about that day." Tears pricked Annaveta's eyes as she thought of her own dear Zaydeh and Bubbeh and her aunts, uncles, and cousins dying in the Pogrom nine years ago. "I didn't realize that Jarena's father had bought up most of that land."

"That's all I know, miss. I just get scared going over to that house, is all." Tatyana peered up at her, her bottom lip quivering.

"Thanks for telling me, Tatyana. Don't worry. You'll be all right. I won't let anything happen to you." She wondered what Mr. Barinov hid in his tunnel. If the workers had noticed two men, who helped him? She wanted answers to all her questions.

Soon the carriage wound its way up the dirt road to the Barinov Estate on the northwest hill of Odessa. Annaveta looked through the carriage window down the tree-lined driveway to the white three-story mansion and all its surrounding buildings. She was amazed at the opulence of their home and not for the first time wondered if all that wealth had been gained through legal methods.

Annaveta was ushered into the large entryway by the maid. While she waited for Jarena, the sound of the letter crinkling in her right pocket unnerved her, and she tensed.

"Ah, there you are." Jarena came to meet her just as the maid took her wrap. She followed Jarena to the dining room where the table was set for two. The room had large windows which overlooked all of Odessa. It was a pretty picture. They sat down, just the two of them and a light salad and soup was served.

"I'm happy you came, Annaveta. I wasn't sure if you would." Jarena's small smile didn't reach her eyes as she looked across at her. Her dark hair, combined with light gray eyes, made her look like her father, and it reminded Annaveta of the cold stare of the man from the train. It gave her a chill. She shook her head as if she could shake off the bad thoughts. She had to remind herself that the girl across from her wasn't her father. This girl didn't have a cruel bone in her body. This girl was kind. And by the looks of her, vulnerable.

"Why did you think I wouldn't come?" It surprised her to

think Jarena didn't think she would come to her home.

"Oh, come now, Annaveta. I might be naïve, but I still know when I'm being shut out of activities." Jarena sipped on her iced lemon water then stared into the glass as if it held some new secrets that would magically change things. "It's been that way ever since my father bought up property here some years ago. It certainly propelled him upward in the social strata of the adult population of Odessa—at least on the surface of things—but the same can't be said of our generation. Despite his constant efforts to insert me into certain social circles, I'm clearly not welcomed. Before the ink was dry on the property deeds, he insisted we get to know what he called 'the more influential citizens' of Odessa. But girls our age from proper families—like Dinah, Anastasia, and Svetlana—don't invite me to their events. I've heard them whisper behind my back that my family is too common, and my father's activities too erratic. So you must understand I could only assume that a family like the Levinsons would surely steer you away from socializing with the likes of me."

"Jarena, I haven't shut you out of anything. And I never would. I can't say anything about your father's business dealings, but I wouldn't judge you on his merits. Nor would my aunt and uncle. I'm happy you're my friend. But I understand it hurts when people speak badly of people you love. It wasn't that long ago that I was pushed out of a group of girls my age in my old village. They didn't want me to be their friend and called me hateful names. I was grateful to have one good friend who stayed by my side."

She looked at her friend now, who was living through something similar. Her heart ached for her, but there was also anger at those other girls who were so mean. She reached across the table and squeezed Jarena's hand. "I'm going to be that friend for you. So don't worry about them. We'll have fun without them."

"Thank you. I'm so relieved." The sadness left Jarena's eyes and they finished their meal. "I forgot to tell you. My stepbrother, Anton, just got out of the hospital and is recuperating here. He was a soldier in the army and was badly wounded. You won't see him much. He keeps mostly in his room." Jarena spoke about her stepbrother as if he were a stranger. "He's six years older than me, and I don't really remember seeing him much during my growing up years. Anyway, I thought I'd let you know so you aren't shocked if you see a strange man wandering around this house." Jarena shrugged and stood. "Come, let's go riding. I want to show you my private special place where I go to think and just be."

"But, Jarena, I only have this dress." Annaveta walked quickly behind her friend, down the wide and long hallway in the west wing.

"I have a riding habit you can wear."

Annaveta hurried behind her friend, but stopped suddenly when she saw the paintings on the walls. One was a portrait of Jarena wearing a white dress standing beside her favourite horse. Another was a painting of her with her parents and her stepbrother. It looked like it was done not long ago, during happier times. Before the war. Aunt Esther had said she planned for Annaveta's portrait to be painted sometime soon. She didn't know if that was a good idea because of the war, but her aunt was insistent. She looked at the pictures again, loving how regal Jarena looked. Maybe getting her portrait done would be fun.

"That was done earlier this year. I think the artist is a friend of my father." Jarena tugged at her hand and pulled her to the only room at the end of the hall. "My parents' room is in the other wing. I have this one to myself most of the time, unless we have guests."

"This is beautiful." Annaveta walked into a suite of rooms which included a bathing room, a bedroom, and a few couches in a sitting area. But the best part was the two large picture windows which made the room so bright and cheery. "What a peaceful place you have all to yourself."

"Well, it is beautiful, but not so peaceful." Jarena's muffled voice came from a large room where Annaveta could see many dresses and beautiful clothes hanging.

"What do you mean?" Annaveta walked toward the sound of rustling clothes. Jarena made piles on the floor.

"It's my father. He had this beautiful home built, but he's always tense or gone. It's like he's constantly worried and stressed. And he suddenly has become so strict about where I go." Jarena handed her a beautiful jade green riding outfit with gold buttons down the front. "When he finally finished the house and we moved in, he told me there were certain places on the estate he wanted me to stay away from. He didn't really give a reason, except he told me life would be much simpler if I did what he asked." She shook her head as if to get rid of the negative thoughts.

"Maybe he just wants to keep you safe. Sorry it's been hard. Maybe things will change for your papa." Annaveta hoped that was true, even at the same time her conscience forced her to admit the truth of who she believed her father was. Her conscience warred within her. Should she tell Jarena who she thought her father was involved with? No, not yet. That would only hurt her. Jarena needed a friend. And so did she. But if the right time ever came, she would tell her.

"Let's go riding. It's a beautiful day, and I feel the most peaceful outside."

They both changed into the riding habits. Annaveta slid the letter into the side pocket. She couldn't leave it lying around. She followed Jarena down the hallway toward the kitchen entrance.

"Wait here for a moment. I want to ask Cook to make a little snack to have ready for when we come back." Jarena walked toward the kitchen, and Annaveta realized this was her chance to return the letter. She hurried to the library and rushed to the desk. She slid open the drawer where she had found the letter. The same old leather-bound journal still sat inside, but the other letter she had seen there before was gone.

Someone took it out. Did they notice the other letter was missing? Maybe they are waiting to find out who took the other one.

That thought sent shivers up Annaveta's spine. She quickly reached for the letter in her skirt and tucked it inside the journal where she had found it the first time. Closing the drawer, she wondered if there were other places she could find the answers to her questions.

Who were all the people Mr. Barinov was involved with? What were their plans?

Letting her curiosity lead her, she wondered over to the books that Jarena said her papa read all the time. She said he read about military strategy, weapons, and he even other cultures, like Germans and Jews. Annaveta's mind flashed back to the man who had stared at her on the train and shivered. She pulled out one book after another, searching for something that might reveal clues to what Mr. Barinov was after.

Opening the books on Jewish background she found a page that had been marked and underlined and began reading.

The Jewish people, on average, make more money and seem to have more connections than any other group of people. Stricter measures must be taken against them so that the people in this country have more of the jobs, money, and influence. Pogroms have been tried and failed in the past, perhaps something more radical that touches the heart and soul of where they live—perhaps their synagogues? Or maybe some act that might cause dissension in their tight-knit communities? These are the kinds of ruinous acts that must be done to bring down a group of people that has the potential to overthrow us, which they almost did in 1905. We have to subdue them by whatever means possible.

Annaveta felt a cold shiver up and down her spine as she read these words. That they were underlined made it all the more real, all the more vile.

A loud thump sounded behind her. Annaveta jumped nervously and looked behind her. A stranger stood behind her, and he'd dropped his crutch.

"Do you not like what you're reading?" A man stood behind her, his hands on crutches. One leg was wrapped, and his weight rested on the other.

She jumped in surprise. "What?" The book slipped from her hands and fell with a thud to the floor. She turned her head just as the man leaned down to retrieve it.

"Ah, another book about the state of the Jews in Russia." He looked at the title before he held it out for her to take. "You're not like my father, are you? Another person hoping for the unexpected demise of all the Jews?" His eyebrow went up as he stared at her. His disheveled black hair added playfulness to his question. Dark brown eyes held her glued in place.

"No." Annaveta wished she could sink through the floor. Little did he know he was talking with someone who not only was a Jew, but was spying on his own father. His intense scrutiny suddenly ended in a small laugh.

"Good then." Annaveta heard her name being called, it sounded like it was from far away. "Ah, you're my little sister's friend."

"Who are you?" Annaveta backed up a little as he leaned closer to her. He was handsome and a little too sure of himself.

"I'm Anton. Jarena's stepbrother." He winced and stumbled as too much weight fell on his bad leg.

"Let me help." She picked his crutch up from the floor and helped put it under his arm. She heard his whisper. "My little sister has never brought someone home as beautiful as you."

Annaveta flushed and stood up straight. Then she put the book back into its spot on the shelf. She didn't want to look at him. His smile held a rakish glint that made her nervous.

"Annaveta, where are you?"

She sighed in relief as she heard her name being called. "Your sister is waiting for me. I must go." Annaveta nodded at him and hurried from the room. Down the hallway, she saw Jarena.

"There you are. I wondered where you'd gone. You didn't get lost, did you?"

"Ah, I was looking for the washroom and got lost." Annaveta felt heat rising in her face at the lie. "I met your brother, too."

"Ah, yes. He's wandering around the house. And he likes to talk, especially to pretty women." Jarena winked at her. "Next time just ask where the room is that you're looking for, and it'll save us time."

Annaveta looked sheepish when she realized the room in question had been only a few steps away from where she had been standing before. She slipped inside to carry out her ruse.

Soon they were outside and on their way to the largest set of stables Annaveta had ever seen.

As soon as the groom saddled up a black mare and a bay gelding, Jarena handed the reins of the bay to Annaveta.

"You have Apollo, and this mare is Zeus." Jarena got onto the back of her horse like she'd been doing it forever. Even though the groom held the reins, Annaveta was nervous as she got on. She had been riding her aunt's horse, since that first week she got there, but she was no expert.

"Apollo's gentle for a gelding, Annaveta. You can trust him."

Soon they were riding around the estate. Annaveta savoured the earthen scent of packed undergrowth and the crackle of leaves under the horse's hooves. She urged Apollo onward and they caught up with Jarena. At the top of a hill, the sound of a nearby waterfall grew louder as she approached. She and Jarena sat there, feeling the cool mist fall gently on their faces.

"This is my oasis. My special place where I come to think."

They sat there in companionable silence for a few minutes until some loud birds spooked Zeus. "Well, I know you can't stay long, so we should get back. I just wanted you to feel the peace I feel when I come here."

"It's beautiful." Annaveta loved the nature sounds and smells. It brought her back to her walks in the meadow when she first met Clara and Alex.

"Meet you at the stables." Jarena spurred her horse, and she took off like a flash. Annaveta urged Apollo to follow, and soon they were back at the stables. They handed the reins to the groom and started walking toward the house.

"Wait. I want to show you something." Jarena grabbed her hand and led her to the northeast part of the estate. "This is the place my father told me to avoid. I don't really understand why. All he has here are some piles of really old burnt wood, and then over there is an old underground tunnel." Jarena turned to Annaveta and shook her head.

Annaveta couldn't seem to shake the dark, cold feeling that swept over her as she stood in this place. "Maybe your father has some chemicals or something here that are unsafe, and he doesn't want you to get hurt."

"Maybe." Jarena shrugged her shoulders and tucked her arm in Annaveta's as they walked along the edge of the hill. "It's not just that. It's other things he says that trouble me. Like when I overheard him talking to another man just this past week. The other man said, 'If we could kill many of both groups of people at one time, that would really be something that would help the cause.' Then I heard my father say, 'Well, they have a few large buildings where many of them gather during the week. Some of the buildings are so old, they'd never realize it wasn't an accident.' It sounded awful to hear my own father talk that way, Annaveta. I didn't know what to do or what it all means, so I'm telling you. I'm scared."

Annaveta hugged her friend to calm her. "I know you are. It scares me, too." She stood there wondering what it all meant. Who were they planning to hurt and what building did these people meet in? "Your father wouldn't let anything happen to you, Jarena."

"I know. But what about those other people? Who's going to save them?" Jarena's words rang in the air like the clang a funeral bell.

"I don't know." Annaveta felt a wave of panic hit her. Who were these people the Black Hand planned to strike? Did that book she found in the Barinov library, the one that was dog eared, have anything to do with what Jarena had overheard her father say?

Fear crept up her spine and she shivered.

She couldn't just sit idly by and wait for something to happen. Somehow she needed to find out more.

Chapter Twelve

"Our orders are to launch an attack on Trebizond. We start early in the morning. Make sure all the weapons and ammunition are in order." Admiral Eberhardt spoke to the entire nine-hundred-member crew, standing on the massive deck of one of the newly made dreadnought battleships, the *Ekaterina II*. "We'll be a large fleet of five ships and three cruisers, escorted by three destroyers and eleven torpedo boats. We should take over that small city in no time."

Alex stood at attention, listening to the Admiral along with the rest of the crew. He knew Trebizond was the capital city of Trabzon Province, which was on the Black Sea on the coast of northeastern Turkey. Ever since Russia had declared war with the Ottoman Empire a few months ago, they had begun to spy on the all the Turkish cities along the coast. With all the ships that would be part of this mission, he didn't see how it could fail. He didn't like the thought of innocent people dying. He'd seen enough of that already.

He thought of Annaveta. Another innocent he wanted to protect but couldn't. It had been so long since he had seen her. It seemed like this war would never end.

For him, the real war had begun with the German attack on

Odessa. That day would be forever etched in his memory. He had a hatred that burned inside him, spurred him to avenge the deaths of his parents. It wasn't fair that he lost Papa and Mama to a war he didn't want any part of in the first place.

He focused forward, trying not to look at Lieutenant Commander Kornilov, whose gaze roamed the long line of crew members. It seemed the Lieutenant Commander was always on the lookout for subordinate crew members or for any new way he could discredit seamen of German or Jewish ancestry. Lieutenant Levinson stood next to the Lieutenant Commander, his attention focused on the captain's words. Since his train ride together with Annaveta's cousin, he noticed that Lieutenant Levinson did his best to be fair to him and to the other crew members. Alex respected that, especially on a ship where many of the leaders used their ranks to strengthen their own positions and to achieve their own agendas.

Alex's thoughts were on Annaveta and her latest letter, which he had received in their stop in port last week.

She had written about the talk she had with Jarena and that Jarena's father was the same man they saw on the train. Annaveta wrote of what Jarena had overheard her father saying about the people they were planning to kill, making it seem like an accident. It sounded like he was a madman, much like Misha. Alex worried about Annaveta and had written her back, telling her she should back off from trying to uncover details of the plot. He warned her there might be more people involved than she expected. He feared she might get in trouble or someone would try to harm her. He was grateful that Misha, his awful cousin, and Baron Yakov were in prison.

"Stop your daydreaming." The burly sailor to his right whispered with a sharp elbow to his ribs. Alex winced and moved slightly away. It looked like he had missed most of that speech. Well, he could always ask his other friends what had been said.

"Our goal is for the takeover to be quick and efficient so we can head back to Sevastopol. If we meet up with the enemy, we will be able to chase them out of the Black Sea like we've done the last two times. Get ready. We leave early in the morning."

For the rest of the day, Alex found himself working beside quite a few other seamen, including his friend Boris Olenov and Moeshe Abramovitz. They double-checked that all the extra equipment onboard was tied down and that what they needed for emergency was in place. It took all the strength Alex had in him not to run away from checking the ammunition.

It was the same place Otto had died.

Alex stumbled to the mess hall along with another few hundred seamen.

He had only taken three bites of his oatmeal when the alarm sounded.

The men around him all stood. Some of the men, like him, were still chewing the few bites they'd been able to eat.

"All hands on deck." The loudspeaker boomed, and each sailor made a beeline for one of the four stairways that led to the top of the ship. Alex followed the rest of the crew as they made their way onto the deck.

He knew his position. He was responsible to keep the guns loaded with ammunition. His step quickened as he heard the bell ring again. Seaman Onipchenko, his team mate, was a few steps ahead of him. They were both assigned to the same gunnery, so Alex knew he needed to hurry.

He looked across the white caps on the blue-gray waves of the Black Sea, and saw the city of Trebizond through the sunrise that cast an orange-red glow over the tops of the buildings. Alex watched as they drew closer to the ships that lined the harbour. They were about to attack those six ships, their hulls swaying peacefully in a gentle rocking motion. Somehow it disturbed Alex that they were about to ruin the peace.

"We're not on this ship for a holiday, Seaman Wagner. If you haven't noticed, we're at war." Quartermaster Yudinov's eyes flashed with anger. "Next time, hurry it up."

"Yes, sir. Sorry, sir." Alex saluted and got to work. Seaman Onipchenko walked beside him, puffing as he carried heavy ammunition-filled containers from storage. The four sea-men who manned the artillery closest to him had enough shells piled up behind them. At least that would hold them until real aggressive action began. Alex hurried down the line where the seamen stood ready at the guns and saw that the other munitions lacked enough lead. Calls were being made through the voice pipe from the officers manning the weaponry about what was needed for their gunnery units. He hurried down the hull to the large storage room and found the materials he needed. He carried the heavy wood boxes up to the deck and quickly divided what was needed between all the guns topside.

"Ready positions." Quartermaster Yudinov's booming voice was barely heard over the deafening sounds of all the other men getting their ammunitions in place.

"Fire." Out of the corner of his eye, Alex saw a bright red explosion light up the night sky. He hurried down to get more ammunition, wondering how long it would take before all the Turkish ships were destroyed.

Hurrying back topside, he brought the heavy boxes of ammunition to the men who were loading the guns. He did this three more times.

"Cease fire!" Quartermaster Yudinov used the voice pipe so all the sailors manning the guns heard him. Suddenly everything stopped. The silence was deafening. Alex peered over the shoulders of many of the sailors who stood in front of him, trying to see what happened. He finally caught a glimpse of the pieces of wood and metal that had spewed into the sea from their volley of fire. The ships that belonged to the city of Trebizond were completely destroyed.

"Well done, sailors." Admiral Eberhardt's praise brought a surge of pleasure to Alex. He admitted to himself that it felt good to be part of a team. "Now we can set course back to port."

It would be good to get back to Sevastopol where they could take a break and focus on mundane things like fixing the ships. Hopefully they would find their way back in spite of the thick fog that surrounded them.

"Clean up the ammunition, and then you two can swab the deck." Quartermaster Yudinov pointed at Seaman Onipchenko and himself. They hurried to carry the ammo down to the storage room below ship.

"I'm glad that's over with," Seaman Onipchenko whispered with a wry grin. "Now we can get back to port, and I can write a letter to my girlfriend in Moscow. She says she's worried about me. I'll need to reassure her that I'll come back to marry her yet." He winked at Alex, his green eyes dancing mischievously.

"I know what you mean." Alex winked at his comrade as they finished the final trip unloading the ammunition.

"Where's your girl?"

"Odessa. What I wouldn't give to see her again." He frowned. That was impossible for a long time to come.

"I know the feeling. Letters will have to do for now, until we can see our girls again." Seaman Onipchenko hurried ahead of him to pick up scrub brushes and soap for washing the deck. He handed Alex his pail and brush. "Don't worry, it will happen sooner than you think."

They each started on opposites ends of the deck, scrubbing the dirt and gun powder away. They didn't want an accidental fire on the deck, so seamen like Alex and many others had scrub duty everyday. He had been at it for only a little while when a sudden commotion from the aft deck alerted him that something was wrong.

"All hands to battle stations!" The unexpected announcement blared over the voice pipe. Alex stood. He wondered what had caused the Admiral to sound the alarm.

"Sailors, we've spotted the German battlecruiser *Goeben* and the light cruiser beside it, *SMS Breslau.*" This time it was Lieutenant Commander Kornilov's voice that boomed over the voice pipe. "Repeat. All hands to battle stations!"

Alex put his bucket between two unused wood panels on the top deck. He hurried to his place on the broadside of their ship. He looked out over the water, but all he could see was fog everywhere. There were two dark spots that looked like they could be enemy ships. He hurried down to the holding area to bring up more ammunition. Seaman Onipchenko followed him, each of them hurrying to bring what they needed to the sailors who manned the guns.

He heard the shots ring out from one of the fleet ships beside them, and then he heard the gunnery commands being shouted. The *Ekaterina II* opened fire. The shots hit one of the enemy ships and the sight of red flames broke through the fog.

"We hit the *Goeben!*" One of the Sailors hollered out. "It looks like we hit them even at this distance."

To Alex, it looked like the German ships were about three or four miles away.

"They're turning to fire their broadside!" Quartermaster Yudinov yelled out. "Everyone get down." Alex ducked behind one of the gunners. He looked over and saw Seaman Onipchenko standing beside the last gunner toward the middle of the boat.

"Seaman Kolchuck, get out of the way!" Alex saw Seaman Onipchenko's head turn to look at him, when a shell detonated in the middle of the ship. He saw his friend fall face down to the deck along with many other men, hit by shards of metal and debris from the explosion. Fear gripped his stomach, and nausea threatened to bring up all his breakfast as many men were wounded or killed by the chaos around him.

Another shell hit their broadside. They kept up their own rapid fire against the enemy ships until just as suddenly as it started, all the shooting stopped.

Without waiting for any command, Alex rushed over to where his friend lay face first on the bloody deck. He touched his neck searching for a pulse. There was none. He turned him over and saw a large shard of metal had struck him in the heart. Alex flinched at the sight of Onipchenko's lifeless green eyes.

"I'll write your girlfriend to let her know your last thoughts were of her. And tell her she doesn't need to worry about you anymore." Alex put his hands on his eyelids and closed them one last time.

He hated war. It had already taken his parents, and now two of his friends.

On top of it all, he was starting to hate the man he was becoming because of the part he played in it.

War was a fierce oppressor.

The Admiral said final words over the last of thirty men killed in battle. As Alex watched the body slide into the sea, he was taken aback by the rage that welled up inside of him. He could hardly think. Suddenly he found it hard to breathe, and he had to force himself to concentrate on slow steady breaths. He was so angry at what the Germans had done to his parents, and now to two of his friends and many others who had died in this cursed war.

He attacked his duties onboard with a vengeance, not knowing what to do about all the feelings inside of him. He remembered Otto's words to him before he died. "Let it go, my friend. Promise me you'll forgive."

I can't. I don't even know how.

Anger filled him at the continual pain and death that lay thick and heavy in the air around them.

This misery was like a new form of punishment. The unforgiven in an unforgiving world.

Chapter Thirteen

Annaveta grabbed the letter off the table by the door. She was always grateful when another missive arrived. It had been three months since Alex's last message and she worried that one of these days, his short handwritten notes would stop coming. Fear gnawed at her. Even reading the Torah with Aunt Esther and Uncle Roman at the breakfast table only helped for a couple hours, and then she started to worry again. Ripping open the envelope, she started reading before she got to her room.

Annaveta,

Another friend died today. Remember when I told you about my friend Seaman Onipchenko and how I wrote a letter to his girl-friend and his parents? Now, many months later, I had to write a similar letter for another fallen friend, only to a wife instead of a girlfriend. I can't tell you any details about what happened, but I just had to tell you that I am so sick and tired of this war. I get so mad at so many senseless deaths. I blame it all on the Germans. So many people died too early, people who had loved ones waiting for their safe return. Needless to say, I didn't really know what to write. But someone needed to let her know. I'd want someone to do that for me—to write you a letter—if something happened to me.

Well, enough about that. Thanks for your letter. I know you worry about my safety. I appreciate your prayers, but from your last letter, I'm thinking you need my prayers more. What are you thinking, going to Jarena's house, especially if you're not sure about her father and what he's involved with? It sounds fairly sinister to me. You shouldn't be trying to find out what's going on all by yourself. Especially not if you think there might be a connection between what's going on at the Barinov home and the BH.

Please, keep safe. I don't know what I would do if anything happened to you. Well, I've got to go. I'll write more in my next letter. And please let me know what is happening with you too.

Yours, Alex.

Another hurried letter. Annaveta sighed in disappointment. She wished Alex would have written more, but she knew she should be grateful he wrote anything at all. Her heart hurt for him and all the suffering he'd gone through already. She could tell by the tone of his letter that he carried around so much unresolved anger from his friends' and parents' deaths. She prayed all the hurt and anger would be replaced by love. She would need to write him back later that night.

Right now, she needed to hurry. It was the day for her and her maid Tatyana to go to the small community building in the northwest part of Odessa. They had found that place weeks before, and it was the closest building to where many of the poor people were. It's where they distributed clothes and what food they could.

Stepping out of the carriage in one of the poorest neighbourhoods of the city, she put her sleeve up to her nose so the smell of garbage and sewer wasn't so overpowering. Walking up to the door, she saw many people already waiting to get food and clothing for their families. Little children along with many mamas stood shivering, some of them even with bare feet.

Annaveta used her key to open the lock on the door. Her maid was barely in the door before the cold air came bursting through it, along with the fifty or so people she had seen lined up outside.

She saw a couple of older men with worn out coats. Their shoes were riddled with holes. Women stood there holding their babies, surrounded by toddlers and a few older children.

"Go ahead and sit down while we start cooking the food." She pointed to the only two wood tables in the room. She then turned around and worked with Tatyana to cook some simple stew for fifty or so people. Good thing Aunt Esther's cook had given her plenty of bread along with butter and jam. It wasn't going to be a fancy meal, but it looked like they would all get more than enough to eat.

While the stew simmered, she opened up the bags, wondering where they would find room to lay the clothes out. There was also a bag of shoes. From the looks of the shivering children, she hoped some were in children's sizes.

There were about fifteen bags this time. Many people had generously given to the Junior Red Cross, and she was grateful. The one thing that was missing was more people to help serve all these families. It was Dinah's turn to help today, but Annaveta doubted she'd show.

They had just started laying the clothes on top of a blanket along the far wall of the old building when the door opened. In walked Dinah and Svetlana, along with their maids.

"Well, we're here." Dinah breezed into the room, looking out of place with her fur coat and long skirts. Svetlana's velvet dress and long coat with fur trim were also inappropriate. "Of course, neither Svetlana nor I will be staying, but we've decided to give you our maids, Nonna and Oksana, to help you for the day." Dinah moved her hand to encourage her maid to move along toward Tatyana.

"Thanks, it will really help." Annaveta stood up and took the extra bags that the maids carried.

"It's terrible in here. How can you stand the smell?" Svetlana looked around at the many disheveled and unwashed bodies.

"We have to look past that, to what these people need, Svetlana. Maybe that could be one thing we could show them how to do is to wash themselves and their clothes and give them bars of soap." Annaveta started thinking out loud.

"I could do that, miss. Me mum and I often helped with others' laundry. I'm good at it." Oksana's plump cheeks jutted out when she smiled, and she seemed happy to help.

"There you go," Dinah said. "Now you have lots of help. We'll be on our way, then. I'll have my driver pick up the maids at the end of the day." Dinah and Svetlana hurried out the door as if they were about to be attacked by the poverty-stricken people in the room.

Annaveta didn't understand Dinah and Svetlana. Where was their compassion? One thing she knew—they really did come from different worlds.

Annaveta organized a small table by the door. There she placed a large wash basin and a bar of soap where people could clean up before they ate.

The maids had just finished organizing the clothes on the blanket in the corner when the stew finished cooking. They quickly put the soup bowls out on the counter along with the bread.

"The food is ready. Come and get it." Annaveta called out to all those who were just waiting and whispering between themselves.

"Mama, this is hot food," one little boy called out. "We should have food like this, with the people who live with us."

Annaveta's heart sank to her toes. How could it be that these children weren't getting hot meals? She wanted to help, so she was committed to doing what she could along with the other members of the Junior Red Cross.

"We're grateful to you for this good food. As you heard, my boy Dmitry hasn't tasted hot food for a really long time. We usually just eat what food we can find," said his mother. She wore an oversized coat and shoes filled with holes. It looked like she had endured many years living homeless.

"I'm happy you like it." Annaveta smiled and looked at the mother, who eyes shimmered with unshed tears. "What's your name?"

"I'm Natalya Chernoff. And these four are my children, Dassa, Dmitry, Emilia, and Polina." She proudly pushed back their unwashed hair so Annaveta could see their faces. "My man went off to war, and we haven't heard anything since. Not sure if he's coming back. So we've had to make do the best we can."

"I'm sorry, Mrs. Chernoff. But we're here to try to help. I'm Annaveta, and that's Tatyana over there." Annaveta found pairs of shoes for the kids, a little bigger than their feet, but they would do. She also found a clean set of clothes for everyone, but there was only one large coat left in the pile. Annaveta found extra blankets instead.

"Do you have a place to sleep at night?" Annaveta held her breath, scared of the answer.

"We make do. When it gets too cold, we have a friend who shares her place with us. We're grateful for the warm clothes and blankets. Now the children won't shiver all night long."

Tatyana and Nonna did the dishes and cleaned up the kitchen while Annaveta found soap bars that could be used to do laundry. They would have to bring a scrub board next time.

"I'll help whoever wants to wash their clothes," Oksana called out to people sitting at the tables, enjoying the warmth of the building. Many children had fallen asleep. "First find some new clothes that fit you, one set per person to start with, and then we'll wash your old clothes."

"I'll help you, as will my oldest girl." Mrs. Chernoff and her daughter Dassa, got busy and filled a couple of old round galvanized steel tubs with water.

"Thanks for your help, Dassa, is it?" Oksana stared at her for a minute longer. "You look enough like Annaveta to be her twin."

"I thought the same. The likeness is uncanny." Mrs. Chernoff squeezed her daughter's chin lightly.

Annaveta looked at the girl. She had long auburn hair, was roughly the same height and build as her, and even her facial features were similar. Dassa met her gaze, and Annaveta offered her a bright smile, which she timidly returned. The girl really did resemble her, but she seemed much more reserved. Given her circumstances, it was no wonder. Annaveta understood that and decided to use humor to draw her out. "We might have to start wearing nametags around here, Dassa."

That made the girl giggle. Annaveta knew from then on she and Dassa would get along just fine.

Annaveta brought the soap for the laundry and then busied herself helping the poor choose clothing that would fit them. Some of the children got shoes that fit. She watched all the activity going on around her and was happy that somehow this small group that had formed.

By the time the day was done and they had fed them all one more time, the sun was setting. Oksana and Nonna had just left, and Aunt Esther's driver had just arrived to take them home.

After the last person had finally left, Annaveta locked up and walked to the waiting carriage, worn out. They had been able to help many people today and it felt so good.

Annaveta sat up suddenly in bed. Her muscles were tense all over and fear had formed knots in her stomach. Wide eyed, she glanced from one thing to the other and breathed a sigh of relief. She was here, safe in her room. Her heart pounded so hard she thought it would burst out of her chest.

What a horrible nightmare. I can't believe that happened. I hope this doesn't come true. But I've got to write to Alex and tell him.

She was almost done with her letter when Tatyana came in.

"Your aunt asked if you were almost ready to go, miss." Tatyana went to her closet and pulled out her dark blue day dress. "Do you want to wear this one? It's very pretty on you."

 Suddenly she remembered that today was Saturday. She needed to hurry. Aunt Esther was more than likely waiting for her. It was the Sabbath. She hurried to dress in her simplest dress. Sure enough, her aunt and uncle waited for her by the door. They got into the carriage and went down the hill to the Synagogue.

They were greeted as usual by many members, including Sacha's parents.

"Sacha has now been promoted to the rank of captain. But he says he misses his mama's cooking. We miss our boy." Mrs. Yudin had tears in her eyes as she spoke of her son. "Everyone is affected by this horrible war. God help it to end soon."

"From your mouth to God's ears." Aunt Esther smiled at her friend as they started walking toward the inner sanctuary. Annaveta fell behind and walked with Mrs. Yudin's daughter, Dinah.

"So how are you?" Dinah flicked her golden brown hair over her shoulder, her gaze looking beyond Annaveta to some of the men who stood at the doors. They had stopped to watch the young ladies enter the sanctuary before they put the black *kippah* on their heads and entered the worship service.

Annaveta wished Dinah would stop flirting with the men. It always made her uncomfortable. Her friend needed to show more decorum especially at Synagogue.

She was happy when they reached the women's section in the upstairs balcony. Sitting down between her aunt and Dinah, Annaveta anxiously waited for the Cantor to begin. She followed the worship and meditation, but found it difficult to relax beside Dinah. She seemed to be always asking her to look at this person's clothes or how the other person did their hair. Annaveta wondered if she ever looked beyond those frivolous things to what really mattered.

The Cantor stood in the middle of the synagogue and began to recite prayers. Annaveta remembered to answer with a loud *amain* when he paused at the end of a prayer. It wasn't long until they began singing some Jewish songs. These were Annaveta's favourites. Memories flooded her of being a little girl, sitting on Zaydeh's lap while he sang to her. Her belly fluttered at the warm memories.

Suddenly, her thoughts jerked back to the present. The balcony shook. Annaveta grabbed Aunt Esther's hand so she wouldn't fall. Some ladies behind them fell out of their chairs. Some gasped and a few others screamed. The Cantor stopped speaking, and his eyes grew wide. Many men rushed toward the balcony.

Annaveta's eyes opened wide as she saw something beyond what anyone else could see. It was like time stood still, and she saw through the veil of her world to the next. An angel held the bottom part of the balcony with his large hands. He wore a white tunic. His blond hair was curly and his eyes shone red, glowing in the darkness of the room. For an instant, fear filled Annaveta, but then he turned to look at her, gave her a big smile and winked.

"Don't worry. You'll all be safe. I've got you." His eyes seemed to sparkle when he looked at her. Something inside her flipped and a bubble of happiness floated up her throat. The fear was gone.

"Annaveta, we've got to go." Someone shook her shoulder, and the fog in her mind cleared. But she knew that everything was going to be fine.

"We're going to be safe, Aunt Esther. No need to panic. I saw an angel holding us up." Annaveta stood up and grabbed her aunt's hand. Aunt Esther looked at her like she had lost her mind. Annaveta just grinned at her as they followed the other ladies.

"Get off the balcony. The beam is about to break!" a short, gray-haired man called up to them. His black prayer cap fell off his head as he waved his arms, the gesture matching the desperate sound of his voice.

The women quickly filed to the stairway. Annaveta followed Aunt Esther and the rest of the crowd down the stairs. Soon everyone was off the balcony. The ladies waited by the doors for the men. Annaveta couldn't resist peaking at the beams underneath the balcony. She was shocked when she saw how the main supporting beam to the balcony had broken in the middle. The whole upper level could have crashed down to the floor, hurting the women and anyone else who got in the way.

Thank God for the angel who protected them.

"How could this have happened?" she overheard a man's bewildered question. "We get this building inspected every year. There have never been any problems."

The men's voices rumbled as they talked between themselves. They were all surprised by the sudden break in the beams.

"Could someone have come in here and tampered with it?" One man asked the question everyone else was afraid to. "And if there's a problem here, maybe there are other places in the building that need to be looked over. We should check the whole building."

The men continued to discuss the possible causes of the near disaster.

Annaveta put her hand to her mouth and gasped. She remembered her conversation with Jarena.

They have a few large buildings, where many of them gather once a week. Some of the buildings are so old, they'd never realize it wasn't an accident.

So this was the horrible evil plot that they had planned. How could they do something so vile?

"Annaveta." Aunt Esther gestured her hand for her to come. "Come. That's a problem for the men to solve."

She went to the front entrance with Aunt Esther and stood there with all the other women.

"Just think, we could have all been killed. I hope they find out who did this."

Dinah Yudin came to stand beside her, flicking imaginary lint off her expensive dress. "This isn't any fun, you know. There are already so few men our age who haven't gone to fight in the war, and now they're busy talking in the sanctuary—which means they aren't giving me any attention. I wore one of my nicest dresses for nothing. It's just ruined my day."

"Honestly, Dinah. Is that all you can think about at a time like this?" Annaveta couldn't keep quiet any longer. She had to speak up.

"Well, it's not that I don't care about anyone else." Dinah shrugged and looked away. "Besides, you can't talk to me like that. I'm the daughter of one of the most respected and wealthiest men in the city. You're just a sad little peasant girl that Roman and Esther Levinson decided to take pity on." The scorn in her tone and words were like acid rain falling on Annaveta's spirit.

Annaveta thought about what she should say and decided it wasn't worth getting into.

"Sorry if I hurt your feelings. I was only trying to tell the truth. But thank you for letting me know where I stand with you." Annaveta mustered up all the quiet dignity she could from inside herself despite the hurt Dinah's words caused her.

"This probably won't be the last time you hear it." Dinah looked at her, disdain dripping from her words, her eyes flashing with anger.

At the sound of doors opening, Dinah turned. "Oh, good, here come the men." Annaveta watched her move to stand by the front doors. She touched her hair and smiled her co-quettish smile to the few single men in the building.

Annaveta couldn't stand to watch.

She suddenly had the need to get as far away from Dinah as possible.

Chapter Fourteen

Nervously Alex awaited his orders. His thumbs twitched as he stood at attention in front of Admiral Alexander Kolchak. Just a few months ago, Admiral Kolchak had been ordered to replace Admiral Eberhardt as commander of the Black Sea Fleet. This new Admiral was a younger man, probably in his thirties. He was tall and dark-haired with a reputation for being fair. Alex hoped he would get the transfer, then he would be out from under the cruel command of Lieutenant Commander Kornilov.

Two other sailors had talked with him yesterday in the mess hall. They had been transferred to the new dreadnought ship *Imperatritsa Mariya,* named after Tsar Nicholas II's mother Tsarina Maria Feodorovna. It was a better ship than the *Ekaterina II*, with more guns and a crew was almost double in size.

"Ensign Wagner."

"Yes, sir."

"I see you have acted honourably toward your fellow comrades, even going out of your way to try to save them. Because of that, I hereby promote you to Sub Lieutenant."

Admiral stood up and walked over to him and pinned the new insignia—one star and one stripe—onto the shoulder of his Navy uniform.

"Thank you, sir." Alex saluted his new Admiral, who saluted back.

"One other thing. You have been officially transferred to the fleet command ship, the *Imperatritsa Mariya*. Report there today for duty."

"Yes, sir." Alex saluted one last time, turned on his heel, and exited his office.

He hurried to the Sevastopol dock where the two Navy ships were anchored side by side. He went onto the *Ekaterina II* and hurried to his cabin. As he gathered his gear, he ran into Moeshe and Boris.

"You've been transferred, then." Boris said the words like he'd lost his best friend.

"To the new dreadnought, the *Imperatritsa Mariya*. How about you?" Alex finished putting his clothes and journal into his bag and looked up at his friends.

"I'm staying." Boris said his voice full of regret. "I'm still under Lieutenant Kornilov's command, I'm afraid. The good news is that we're still in the same fleet."

"And whenever we get leave, we'll make the most of it, my friend." Alex tried to cheer him, but didn't know quite what to say. "What about you, Moeshe?"

"I'm transferring with you to the new dreadnought. Did you know that she is the lead ship of her class?" Moeshe went on to describe the four steam turbines, the four anti-aircraft guns, and gun turrets that were positioned the length of the ship.

"Okay. We understand it's a good ship, Moeshe." Alex laughed at his friend's ability to describe the merits of the new dreadnought down to the last detail. "You've done your research, that's good. They'll probably promote you."

"Well, that's the last of it." Alex pulled on Boris's hand and surprised him with a big hug. "Be thinking of you here, comrade. We'll see each other at some point at Sevastopol."

"I know." Boris grimaced and sighed as a look of resignation came over him. "Well then, get on with you two. I'll see you later."

Moeshe and Alex went topside, waving goodbye to many other friends as they left the *Ekaterina II.*

"It will be good to have Admiral Kolchak in command of the fleet," Alex said. "He seems a decent and fair man." They walked the gangplank up into the *Imperatritsa Mariya.* Many of the ensigns saluted Alex as they walked by.

Moeshe looked at his uniform. "Sorry, I didn't see your new insignia. Congratulations, Sub Lieutenant Wagner."

"Thanks. I hope it happens for you soon, too." They reached the bottom berths of the new ship and searched for their assigned bunks.

"Yeah, well, meanwhile, I'm going to enjoy getting to know the details of this new ship." Moeshe grinned and took out his book. It was full of data about the new ship.

"See you topside in an hour. All new transfers and recruits are to report." Alex found his bunk and got all his stuff arranged neatly. He hoped there wouldn't be too many surprises here.

After six weeks of prowling the Black Sea, they finally got a glimpse of the Ottoman Navy's flagship, *SMS Groeben*. It was just the break that Admiral Kolchak was hoping for. The *Imperatritsa Mariya* prepared for battle.

"It's time to for us to control the Black Sea. We're going to use the tactical advantage we have with this new flagship to get rid of the their fleet here. We've just intercepted radio transmissions from the Ottoman battlecruiser *Yavuz*. We're on our way, along with the *Ekaterina Velikaya,* to catch her in her return from bombarding the Tuapse port. Ready the battle stations." Admiral Kolchak's determination and fearless actions contrasted that of the former Admiral Eberhardt. It was clear why the upper brass replaced the former Admiral.

Admiral Kolchak spoke to the sailors and said they had just received the mines they wanted from Petrograd—formerly St. Petersburg—and his goal was to mine the entrance to the Bosporus to stop any more Ottoman ships from entering the Black Sea. They needed to be on the lookout for Ottoman ships, although he was confident that with their new flagship they would be able to outgun even the German Admiral Souchon's flagship.

Alex was on the top deck overseeing the ten ensigns who had been placed under his command. Ever since his promotion to Sub Lieutenant, he had more responsibility and reported more details to his new Quartermaster.

"We need to check the new 130mm B7 semi-automatic guns. I want you sailors to form two groups." Alex strategized how to get the ammunition organized before the real battle began. "Half of you need to check the six guns from the forward turret to the rear funnel, and you other five need to check the cluster of guns around the rear turret."

He led the men to to the different sections of the ship and helped the sailors get familiar with the working of these new guns that had just been delivered from a manufacturing company in Great Britain.

The men took turns checking the details of the guns to make sure all was in order. Alex hurried them. He fully expected a battle at any time.

The Ottoman ship *Yavuz* dodged north toward the Bulgarian coastline. Alex looked out along the coast and could barely make out the outline of the ex-German battlecruiser.

"Ready the guns. It won't be long until we're in firing range." Lieutenant Levinson commanded all the men who worked with the many gun turrets and other guns mounted on casemates. Alex stood behind his men as they readied their guns.

"Stand down, sailors. We've lost them." Admiral Kolchak's stoic tones funneled loud and clear through the voice pipe.

"Relieve the big guns of their shells." Lieutenant Levinson's calm voice didn't seem to change whether they braced for a fight or not. Alex hadn't had much chance to talk to him since they had both been transferred to the new ship. They were acquaintances, but not friends, at least not yet. Most of the time the Lieutenant was so busy that he only nodded to him. Alex wasn't really sure where he stood with Jude. Alex remembered how it had taken Jude's father a bit of time before he accepted him. Maybe it would be similar with Jude. Then there was Annaveta, stuck in the middle between himself and her uncle. She desperately wanted to please the man who was the only positive father-figure in her life, yet she also said she loved Alex. Some days it made him angry that she continued to put her uncle and aunt before him.

He took most of his frustration out on the Germans. They had hurt his heart more than anyone, anyway.

He heard the curses and loud sighs of disappointment from many of the men because they had lost their enemy once again. He couldn't wait to give the Germans the crushing blow that they had coming.

Soon he noticed their ship was turning around. Admiral Kolchak must have decided to head north. It was only a matter of time before they would encounter the Germans or the Ottomans again.

Early the next morning, they saw the Ottoman army marching along the coast, their supply columns in the middle and at the end of the long row of marching troops.

"Our orders are to shoot at the Ottoman supply columns. It looks like they are on their way to Trebizond to take the city. We'll disable them, and at some point they'll give up." Lieutenant Levinson spoke to the sailors, giving them the new strategy.

"Battle stations!" He called out the order and all the sailors went to their assigned posts.

Within about an hour, they had disabled all of the Turkish

supply columns and had slowed the progress of the army to a crawl. It was mid-afternoon when the Turkish army withdrew and began marching back.

Admiral Kolchak's voice echoed over the voice pipe. "Well done, sailors! The Ottoman troops are headed home where they belong. However, we've been alerted by radio intercepts that another Ottoman ship, the *Lidilli* is on it's way back from the Russian harbour of Novorossiysk. Most likely they've set up mines there to blow up our ships and submarines. We'll try to catch her on return. Be prepared to skirmish with the *Lidilli*."

Alex wiped the sweat from his forehead with the handkerchief he kept in his pocket. The weather in this part of the country had a reputation for being one of the most hot and humid areas of Russia. They were only a few miles out of one of the few non-freezing bays when they spotted the *Lidilli*. Alex looked out the window and saw the remains of another sailing vessel off the coast of Tuapse. It looked like the Turkish vessel had been busy.

We'll see who gets the last laugh.

"Battle stations!" The expected call came loud and clear throughout the voice pipe.

"Fire!" Lieutenant Levinson's voice called out the order to all the sailors manning the guns. The first volley of shots rang out and shot too far in front of the *Lidilli*. The second volley of shots missed behind the ship.

The *Lidilli* picked up speed with the *Imperatritsa Mariya* in close pursuit. The light cruiser shot a few volleys in their direction, trying to disable them. They only splinted the side and front of their ship, nothing more.

It wasn't long before a few shots hit their target. The *Lidilli* slowed. It looked like they had damaged her rudder. Now the light cruiser was more like a lame duck facing a hungry animal coming in for the kill.

The *Lidilli* fired her big guns, which toppled the casemates of their dreadnought. A few of the guns broke off from the steel cavity which was supposed to hold them secure. Alex watched in horror as the gun swung at Lieutenant Levinson and the other sailor beside him. The force of the blow threw them overboard. Alex glanced outside to see the Lieutenant and the other sailor floating in the water, unconscious. As shots continued to fire, he didn't see anyone jump into the water to rescue them. *I can't let them drown.*

Alex dove into the water and resurfaced for air still a good ten yards from the men. Their ship continued its assault until explosion rocked the *Lidilli*. A huge fire blazed on the much smaller ship. He heard screams of pain and terror from the *Lidilli* in spite of the quarter mile distance between the two ships. Many of the men went down as the fire spread quickly to the whole and sank.

By the time Alex reached Lieutenant Levinson, the sailor in the water beside him had revived and started to cough up water. Alex reached for him and held him up to let him cough it out. Another sailor swam toward him to help. It was Moeshe.

"Here, you can help this sailor, I'll take the lieutenant." Alex's words came out in between quick breaths. He was beginning to tire of treading water.

"Got him." Moeshe put most of the sailor's weight onto his back and Alex did the same with Lieutenant Levinson, who was still unconscious.

With strong, steady strokes, they made their way back to the *Imperatritsa Mariya.* Two ropes were lowered down the side of the ship, with some strong boards made into a bench in the middle. Alex lowered the lieutenant onto it and strapped him in. The men started pulling him topside. Soon they lowered the ropes again and the other sailor was pulled up. Alex and Moeshe climbed the ladder that the men had put over the side of the ship.

As soon as Alex reached the top deck he saw the medic attending to the lieutenant, trying to pump out excess water from his lungs. He choked and sputtered, and a few seconds later could breathe normally once more.

"There you are," the medic said. "Happy to have you back in the land of the living, Lieutenant Levinson. Some other sailors weren't as lucky. This sailor saved your life. He jumped into the sea as soon as he saw the large gun strike you down."

"Thanks, Wagner. I'm in your debt." Jude Levinson looked more like a scared little boy than like one of the top officers of the ship at that moment. His face was red from the effort to breathe properly, and it sounded like he was still trying to catch his breath. "You're a good man."

"I'm just grateful I saw you and could help you out, sir." Seeing the lieutenant was in good hands, Alex saluted and turned on his heel. He walked away, hoping to change into dry clothes, but was cornered by the Admiral's First Lieutenant, Igor Vasilyev.

"There are some German men in the water now because their ship has sunk. Some of them don't look like they're very good swimmers. I need you to go and talk to them, and I'll send a few other men to go get them. Take two of the life boats."

"Yes, sir." Alex nodded and found the other sailors who were also ordered to get the German men. As soon as the boats were in the water, they paddled toward the debris and the German sailors who were trying to stay afloat.

The rage that Alex normally felt for the Germans bubbled to the surface.

I would rather eat rattlesnake than save one of these German men. They killed my mama and papa. They are vile and loathsome. How can I actually save one of them?

He was about to suggest that he would keep the boat steady while they hauled in the the men, when he saw the Germans in the water, struggling for air. Alex looked from one man to the other, seeing them as struggling men, not as bloody killers. His eyes looked into their eyes and he saw the fear, horror, panic, and distress there. For the first time, he saw them as people, not as the monsters he had originally believed them to be.

They were just following orders, just like he was doing. He was surprised that he felt a little bit of compassion for these men as they pulled them from the water and into the life boats. Alex wasn't sure that he liked what was happening to him. He remembered Otto's words, "You need to forgive them." He wasn't at that point yet, but he didn't feel the rage that he once had. Otto would have been pleased.

They brought back sixteen men from the *Lidilli's* wreckage. It wasn't many, considering the ship had a complement of over three hundred. Alex found he was able to understand what the German men were saying, even though his Volga German dialect was slightly different.

"So now we are prisoners of war. We should have swum for

the other shore when we had a chance," one of the men told his comrade.

"And we would have died trying to swim those eight miles to the other side," he shot back.

"It would have been better to die at the hands of the Russians. We'll probably be sent to Siberia to starve. At least our comrades who died are pain free now."

Alex saw the despair in the man's eyes and wondered how long he would last in a Russian prisoner of war camp. It was true that many sent to Siberia had to do hard labor in order to pay for food and clothing. He wouldn't wish that on anyone.

They reached the boat, and the men climbed the ladder to the top deck. Alex looked up and saw the sailors pointing their guns at the German POWs, trying to lessen their chances of escape.

One man dove into the water and started swimming away. He was shot, and that stopped the other men from trying.

Out of all the sailors, Alex was one of the few who spoke German, so the Admiral used him as a translator. They were put in the ship's hold and given food and water rations.

Alex was grateful when their ship pulled into the Sevastopol port two days later. Then prisoners were transferred to a truck waiting to take them to the nearest Russian prisoner of war camp.

Alex watched them get into the truck, despair written over their faces. He was surprised at the compassion that welled up.

As soon as the prisoners were gone, the mail arrived at the ship. Each sailor retrieved his own. He brought Lieutenant Levinson's one letter to him. He wanted to see how he was doing.

"How are you feeling sir?" Alex stood at the doorway of Lieutenant Levinson's quarters.

"Been better. My head is still throbbing a lot." He lay on his cot, his hand on his forehead. He looked at Alex as if deciding something, then said, "Admiral Kolchak said I could have a week's leave, to try to heal. I need help going home. I'm wondering if you would like to join me?"

"That would be great, sir. When do we leave?" Alex was eager to be off the ship, even for a short time.

"We'll catch the evening's train, then. I'll let the Admiral know. Thanks, again." The lieutenant grinned at him. Alex knew that he realized there was a bigger reason that he wanted to be home. It would be so good to see Annaveta again. It had been too long.

"Thank you, sir." Then Alex remembered why he'd stopped by. "I almost forgot. This letter came for you."

"Thanks for bringing it by. Come back here right after you've had your meal."

"Yes, sir." Alex couldn't believe he had the chance to go back and see Annaveta.

He opened up the letter he read from her as he was waiting for the lieutenant at the train station. It was good to hear that she missed him. But a feeling of dread overcame him when he read about the dream she had. She was trying to warn him, but little did she know she had described the battle they just had with the German ship. He was surprised again by how she foresaw things to come.

Alex was looking forward to seeing Annaveta. He hoped by the end of this visit, she would no longer keep him at arms' length. He hoped by the end of this visit, she would no longer be angry and offended at him. He hoped by the end of this visit, she would choose to forgive him.

Chapter Fifteen

"What if our son is one of the sailors that died?" Aunt Esther's shaky hand pointed to the morning newspaper as she questioned her husband. Annaveta felt like she couldn't breathe.

"It didn't sound like it was his ship that went down, my dear." Uncle Roman grabbed the Odessa news written for July 30,1916. "Here, this is what it says. *On the twenty-second day of July, one of our newest dreadnoughts suffered significant damage to her hull from a skirmish with a German light cruiser, the* Lidilli. *Our own* Imperatritsa Mariya *attacked the smaller ship as it returned from mining the harbor at Novorossiysk on July 21. The* Lidilli *got in a few well aimed shots which damaged some artillery as well as left three men killed and nine more wounded. Soon after the* Imperatritsa Mariya *blasted some of her big guns. One of those shots hit the casement that held the artillery, and the forward shell magazine exploded. Out of the approximately three hundred sailors on board, only sixteen were rescued and later sent on to Prisoner of war camps."* Uncle Roman took off his reading spectacles, put the paper down, and hung onto his wife's hand. "See, there were only a few wounded. But if it makes you feel better, I'll send off a telegram to the war office for more information."

"Please do, Roman. I won't be able to sleep properly until we get word of what has happened to our son." Aunt Esther wiped the tears that streamed down her cheeks.

"I hope everything will be all right, Aunt Esther." Annaveta got up from her place at the table and went to sit beside her aunt. She reached for her hand, not sure what to say, only wanting her aunt to know she wasn't alone.

"You, my dear girl, are a source of strength and happiness to your uncle and me. Thank you." Aunt Esther squeezed her hand, and they sat there in silence.

"There are still duties that need to be attended to today, despite the news." Aunt Esther's usual stoic disposition was back. "We go to the hospital this morning, and this afternoon we'll get after some business at home."

"You've always been good at getting things done, Esther. I'm not concerned." Uncle Roman winked at Annaveta as he teased his wife. "Oh, by the way, Annaveta, I thought I should let you know the building in the poorer neighbourhood, the one we own, we've had an offer on it. It's actually your friend Jarena's father, who is in real estate. He says he's been buying up old property for years. He started in 1905. Seems he likes replacing the old and building new. He's offering almost double what it's worth. It's tempting to sell. What do you think?"

"Oh, Uncle Roman, don't sell. Couldn't you hold onto it for a little longer? It's been so good to use that old building for our Junior Red Cross Society members." Fear formed a lump in Annaveta's throat at the thought of a member of the Black Hand owning that building. If Mr. Barinov owned it, they would have to find another building to use that was close to the same neighbourhood. She was sure the Black Hand wouldn't be willing to let them use the building that served the same people they were trying to get rid of.

"Then we won't sell, not if you're putting it to such good use."

"Thank you, Uncle. I'm glad there are good people like you and Aunt who help out the poor in their community. You're an inspiration." Annaveta stood up and kissed his cheek.

"Well, I'll do more of it if I get more kisses like that from my favorite niece." He winked at her.

"Oh, you two." Aunt Esther sighed, but a smile tugged at the corner of her lips. "Come on then, my dear. We need to get going." Aunt Esther kissed her husband on the forehead and squeezed his shoulder before they left.

As soon as the driver dropped them off at the front entrance of the hospital, they were busy. Annaveta walked around to each able to encourage and write letters for more wounded soldiers. By the time they left three hours later, Annaveta felt weary.

"I wish we could take away their pain," Aunt Esther said. "But maybe our being there has helped a little."

"The soldier I talked to today said he wished he could see his wife and son one last time. He dictated a last letter to his family. It was so sad. When I talked to the nurse before we left, she said at most he only has a week to live." Annaveta wiped a stray tear from her eye as she looked out the carriage window.

"Where does his family live?"

"St. Petersburg is the address he gave me."

"Let's telegram his wife and see if she can come."

"What if she doesn't have any money?"

"Oh, I'll take care of that. Some of our investments are in a bank in St. Petersburg, so we can get what she needs for the train fare." Aunt Esther's s face lit up. "It feels so good to help someone else in some small way, doesn't it?"

"It does, Aunt Esther. It really does." Annaveta's heart was happy. She prayed that the soldier would live long enough to see his wife and child one last time. She wished they could help more people in ways like that.

The driver pulled the carriage up the hill to the estate. When they drove down the lane she saw two dappled mares hitched to a wagon. It was the old man who made deliveries in Odessa.

"Boris Rusnak, did you come here for Cook's fresh baked bread rolls?" Aunt Esther teased the weathered old man who stood at the back of his wagon, putting a cloth covered loaf of bread into one of his wooden boxes.

"Esther Levinson, you always did know my weakness for Edda's fresh baked bread." The old farmer snapped the suspenders holding up a worn and loose pair of faded brown trousers. "I also brought a surprise home for you. You'll have to go inside to see it."

"Oh, Boris, how thoughtful of you. I love surprises." They waved to him as he pulled himself up onto the wagon bench. "Enjoy the bread."

Aunt Esther laughed a little as they walked up the stairs to the house. ""He's a good man. I like him. Well, what do you think about eating outside today? The weather is so nice."

"That would be lovely." Sometimes Annaveta felt a little guilty of the food and clothes and shelter they had, when just down the hill there were many people, so poor that were thankful if they even had one of the three. She wanted to help them because she remembered what it felt like to be so poor that she had to search for food, to walk during the cold winter months with only her bark shoes on her feet, or to help mama make soup so thin it was hardly more than boiled water. So she was grateful for how her life had changed for the better, and she wanted to do what she could to help others live better lives, too.

Larson held the door open, and Aunt Esther preceded her into the house. Annaveta was surprised when she heard her aunt's startled cry.

"You're alive!"

Annaveta walked through the door just in time to see Aunt Esther pull Jude close to her in a tight hug. Standing behind them, Alex looked on, a happy grin on his face.

"Boris Rusnak told me he brought a surprise, but I never thought it would be you. I'm so happy." Aunt Esther pulled back from her son, and putting her hands to the sides of his cheeks, she looked him square in the eyes. "But you're not well, are you?"

"Ah, Mama, you know me too well." Jude leaned heavily on Alex, who moved forward to help him. "I got a bump on the head during our last skirmish with German ships. I'll be good again after I've had some time to rest. The Admiral thought I would heal faster at home." Jude spoke to his Mama, who led him to a chair to sit down.

Annaveta looked at Alex, who stood close to her cousin. He looked dashing in his dark blue Navy Uniform. Shiny silver buttons ran down the front of the long coat. Matching silver shoulder insignia and bars that went with his new rank decorated his coat. She looked up at his face and still felt unsure about him. She wondered if he was still angry like when he left to join the Navy.

Can I trust him now? Has his heart changed from the anger and meanness I saw that reminded me of papa's drunken rages? I can't be with a man who is like my papa. There's no way I can go through the rest of my life fearful and scared of what might happen. Maybe he has changed. I need to see it for myself.

Annaveta gave Alex a small smile as he walked up to her. "Surprised?"

"Very surprised. It's too bad my cousin was hurt, but I'm happy you've been able to help him.

"Come. We'll go sit in the small breakfast room and talk. You need to sit down, Jude." Esther nodded at Larson to take care of things.

"Esther, I thought I heard voices out here, what—" Roman came to a sudden stop, and his jaw dropped. "Jude. We weren't sure if what the newspapers said was true. We worried for you."

"I'm a little wounded, but otherwise I'm doing well, Papa." Jude looked over at Alex. "If it wasn't for Alex's quick actions, I wouldn't be here today."

"What happened?" Roman looked from Jude to Alex and back to his son.

"Roman, let's go sit for luncheon and Jude can tell us all."
Esther led the way to the breakfast room. She turned and
whispered to Annaveta as they sat down at the table. "With
Jude not feeling well, we'll sit inside today. Maybe later this
week, if he feels up to it, we'll eat outside."

Annaveta nodded and soon the maids served luncheon.

"So tell us the story, Jude." Aunt Esther spoke after everyone
had eaten.

"Not much to tell, Mama. The German ship hit one of our
big guns, which in turn hit me and knocked me into the sea.
I was unconscious. Alex saw what happened and jumped into
the water after me. He saved me and another sailor."

"Well done, Alex. That was a brave thing to do." Roman
Levinson's eyes were misty. "Thank you for saving the life of
our son."

"I just did what needed to be done, sir." Alex looked uncomfortable with the praise.

"Well, it took courage. Esther and I are grateful."

Annaveta looked at the play of emotions across her uncle's
face and realized his heart was softening toward Alex. It
made her happy to see the change in him.

"At the Admiral's request, Alex took a few sailors to save the
sixteen men who survived the destruction of the *Lidilli*. Alex
translated between them and the Admiral and other sailors
until we got to port and sent them to the prisoner of war
camps. He has also helped me get around since I was hurt.
He's a good man to have around." Jude gave Alex a grin.

"You make me sound like some kind of guardian angel." Alex grinned, and Annaveta's heart was glad they were finally getting along. The more she thought of Alex saving those Germans, the more she realized how difficult that must have been for him. She was surprised he had done it at all.

"Well, we're all happy you're home. Maria, would you pour tea?" Aunt Esther waited until she had finished pouring and then looked at her son. "How long can you both stay?"

"Admiral Kolchak told Alex to be back in two weeks, but as for me, he said to make sure I got lots of rest before I returned to duty." Jude brought a shaky hand to his head. "Which is maybe what I should do right now."

"Yes, that's what you need. Lots of rest. Alex, if you could help Jude to his room, I'll double check that he has everything he needs." Annaveta watched as the three of them left the room. She hoped she would have a chance to talk with Alex soon.

"Watch and see, it won't be long before your Aunt Esther plans a dinner party, now that her boy is home." Uncle Roman's eyes seemed to flicker with pleasure.

Annaveta agreed that her aunt probably had something like that in mind.

Annaveta stood in front of the mirror and ran her hand down the long cream-coloured floor-length dress. She turned to the side and admired how the pleats pulled in at her waist. The sleeves were just over her shoulders, and the neckline was cut in a large circular boat neck style, daringly low. Aunt Esther said that style was all the rage in Paris. Annaveta tried to pull up the low cut bodice, so her bosom wouldn't show quite so much.

She had to admit the dress looked good. Even though she could barely breathe because of the tight corset, she figured she could handle it for one night. She hoped Aunt Esther would be pleased.

Tatyana had just finished putting her hair up into a French twist and a few tendrils lay on her cheeks. "You look beautiful, miss."

"Thank you for your hard work. I like my hair like this." Annaveta took one last look, and turned around. She squeezed Tatyana's shoulder and walked toward the door. "It's time to meet all of Aunt Esther's many guests."

By the time she reached the end of the long hallway leading toward the large dining room, she heard Larson and Maria offering to take the women's wraps. As she walked into the dining room, she saw her aunt and uncle receiving people along with Jude.

"Ah, there she is. Annaveta, you remember Mr. And Mrs. Yudin?" Aunt Esther held out her hand and Annaveta grasped it like a lifeline. For some reason she always felt she was being looked over like a horse at an auction when she went to these dinner parties. Next she expected they would want to see her teeth.

"Of course. How do you do?" Annaveta pushed aside those nasty thoughts and nodded and curtsied like her aunt taught her.

"As Providence would have it, our Sacha is also home for a week." Mrs. Yudin's adoring eyes looked up at her tall son. Annaveta looked at Sacha with a small grin on her face. He winked at her and she blushed.

Annaveta turned to Dinah, who smiled nicely at Aunt Esther but only nodded to her. Dinah flirted easily with Jude, who seemed to enjoy it, much to Annaveta's annoyance.

It seemed like suddenly there were waves of people coming through the dining room doors. Uncle Roman was right. It was like Aunt Esther had prepared the fatted calf for the lost son who had come home. Annaveta welcomed Anastasia Borovitz, her parents, and a tall blond brother who she hadn't met before. Her other friends, Moriah Lapin and Svetlana Borodin arrived with their parents. Moriah's brother had been killed in the war a little over a year ago. Svetlana had two other sisters who were much younger, so they stayed home with their nanny.

Judge Saratov arrived with his timid wife and their two sons. David, the serious one, was limping. No doubt he was on leave from his wounds. Annaveta noticed that Yuri was missing from their group of friends.

"Will you go and double check that Cook is ready with the food? I think almost everyone has arrived," Aunt Esther whispered in her ear.

"Of course, Aunt." Annaveta was only too happy to take a break from the line up. Especially when she saw Jarena enter with her papa, step-mama and step-brother. That man—her father—filled her with fear, and she would rather avoid him than meet him. She hurried to the kitchen to ask Cook how much longer until the food was ready.

"It's ready now, miss. Tell your aunt once everyone is seated, we'll serve."

"I'll let her know."

There were two long tables set up to seat everyone in the dining room. Soon Aunt Esther directed everyone to their seats. Annaveta found herself seated with David Saratov on her right and Sacha on her left. She could tell Aunt Esther was trying to do her best to make sure everyone had a chance to talk to people they hadn't seen for awhile.

"I hope your leg is healing well." She looked over at David, who seemed lost in thought as he sipped Uncle Roman's favourite red wine.

"It's doing well enough." David eyes filled with a seriousness as he looked around at the people at this table. His eyebrows pulled together as his eyes finally rested on her. "How do you stand it—being here, I mean? Here we are eating, drinking, and being merry when all the while right now people are starving and dying for our country. And now that the Tsar has taken command of whole of Russia's army, the situation is even worse. The soldiers don't have enough guns or food. They're sent out to be murdered, and no one is doing anything about it." He shot back the rest of his wine and stared at her with dark, soulful eyes.

"I didn't realize the situation was that bad. I guess they don't tell us everything in the newspapers, do they?" Annaveta shivered at the thought.

Beside her, David let out a bitter laugh. "Not half of what's really going on. And someone really needs to let everyone know what's going on out there. Those men need help, and now they won't let me go back and help them because of my beat-up leg. I feel so helpless." David held up his wine glass for the maid to refill it. Annaveta could tell he had decided to drown his sorrows, to forget all the misery around him.

"David, have you thought that there might be another way you might help the soldiers?" Annaveta hoped he'd consider her idea. "I do know what you mean about feeling helpless and wondering what I could do to help. That's part of the reason I started the Junior Red Cross. I want to help those widows and families affected by the war. Now that we have more women helping out, we've been able to help even more people. It's really been a big help to many of the poor families here in Odessa." Annaveta played with the corners of her napkin as she spoke, thinking of the law degree David had just finished before the war started. "I think you could do more. You could write a weekly column in a newspaper or start your own brochure that tells what's really going on in the war. Since you can't go back to serve on the front lines, you could think of other ways you could use your great legal mind."

"Hmm, hadn't thought of doing something like that. You might be on to something there. I'll have to think about that a little more. There are some things I could do to help, and I could always get advice from Papa." He grinned. "You have a good heart, Annaveta, and have given me a spark of hope." He raised his glass as a toast to her and took a drink.

"Thank you, David. We can all do a little something to help."

Soon the maids came with their food. There were many appetizers and other side dishes to enjoy before the main meal. Soon David's attention was taken by the blonde-haired young lady seated on his other side. Annaveta looked around and realized Aunt Esther had made good on her promise to invite a few more people Jude and Annaveta's age, and she admitted she also needed more people to even out the numbers. Annaveta smiled at her aunt's obvious attempt to bring suitable friends into her and her cousin's life. She noticed Jarena seated beside Moriah, talking and laughing together. She was happy they enjoyed each other's company. She was grateful Mr. and Mrs. Barinov and their son were seated at the other, larger table. She shivered at the thought of actually talking to him one day, which was bound to happen since she was good friends with his daughter.

"Is sitting beside me so distasteful? Your shudder of disgust makes me nervous." Sacha grinned at her.

"What do you mean?" Annaveta scrambled to figure out where this question was coming from.

"I did take liberties last time we spoke." He leaned over and whispered in her ear. "I only have beautiful memories of those stolen moments in Mama's moonlit garden."

Annaveta's shaky hands adjusted the napkin on her lap, and she shivered as he whispered in her ear. She hoped he had forgotten about that. She looked across the table to where Alex sat. She still felt guilty about that kiss, but was glad he knew about it. It seemed like she had a knack for getting him upset with her. When she looked at him again, she saw he was in a deep conversation with that flirt, Nadia Borowitz. Well, maybe she didn't feel quite so bad then, not when he had that siren so close to him, breathing down his neck. Alex looked up at Nadia and leaned his head in closer to listen to what she was saying. Annaveta loved him, but at this moment, she didn't like him very much.

"I remember." She pushed her feelings of guilt aside and looked up at Sacha. "And no, sitting by your side isn't distasteful. You're quite fun to be with, even though you are a terrible flirt." She grinned up at him as he leaned back, a fake look of surprise on his face.

"You wound me, my dear." Sacha put his hand over his heart. "I've meant every compliment I've ever given you, in words or actions."

"See, that's exactly what I mean." She shook her head, and her half-smile betrayed her so her words were more like teasing and less like scolding.

Orchestra music filtered in from the great room, signaling the time for the dancing. Annaveta sighed in relief.

"Dancing is beginning in the great room," Larson announced to everyone as he stood at the doorway.

"Looks like that's our cue." Sacha pulled out her chair and Annaveta stood and brushed off any crumbs from her dress.

Sacha offered his elbow, she put her hand lightly on top of his arm and he led her into the great room. Her aunt and uncle started off the dancing with a waltz, and Annaveta loved how they moved in sync with the rhythm of each other. It seemed like a testimony to their love and marriage.

Next Uncle Roman came to ask her to dance with him. Aunt Esther danced with Jude. Annaveta felt special.

"I hope I don't accidentally step on your toes, my dear. I'm not as light on my feet as I once was." Uncle Roman laughed at his awkward dance steps.

"I'm just happy to dance with my favourite uncle." She looked up at him and realized how grateful she was to have him and her aunt in her life.

"Looks like someone else wants to take you away from me. Enjoy yourself, my dear." The song ended and Sacha was right there, ready to claim her for the next dance.

"I see Alex has been stolen off by Miss Borowitz, so I can enjoy this dance with you." Sacha pulled her close to him, and she pulled away a little.

"So tell me about the people you know here." Annaveta breathed a sigh of relief when he started talking about how long he'd known David and his anger that a few of his friends had been killed in action. He talked at length about his dreams of travel and adventure and how the war had stolen that from him.

"You'll make it through this and have your chance to travel." Annaveta's words seemed to give him courage. He held her close until the dance was over.

"My turn with the beautiful lady, Sacha." Alex's voice came from behind her and held a challenge. Sacha narrowed his eyes.

"Thanks for the wonderful dance, Sacha. I promised Alex a dance, too." Annaveta hoped her words would stop any fight brewing. Sacha walked off the dance floor, and Alex took her in his arms.

"Sacha always seems to be wherever you are, doesn't he?" Alex's jealous tones brought a tightness to her chest.

"You mean kind of like how Nadia is slithering close to you tonight?" Annaveta's eyes narrowed in challenge.

He winced at her words.

"You're right. That was a little hypocritical of me, wasn't it? Sorry. Let's just enjoy this dance together." Alex pulled her closer and they danced another slow song. It took Annaveta until the song started to fade before her anger left her.

"I need a little rest." She walked toward where the cool drinks were being served. Seeing Jarena standing there, she went up to her.

"I haven't talked to you yet, Jarena. Are you enjoying the music and dancing?" Annaveta waited while the maid poured her drink.

"It's so nice, Annaveta. Thanks for inviting me." Jarena leaned closer and whispered. "I even met a cute guy that I really like. That's a first for me."

Annaveta giggled with her as Jarena explained how they had literally bumped into each other.

"Jarena, it's time for us to head home." A deep male voice spoke firmly behind her. Jarena turned around, as did Annaveta.

"Introduce me to your friend before we go." Annaveta looked at Jarena's father, fear pulsating in her throat, cutting off her breath. He stood beside his pretty wife and his son, his dark brown eyes piercing hers. A slight smile—that didn't seem real—on his face. His white sleeves came up to his wrist, so she couldn't see if he had the tattooed symbol of the Black Hand.

"Papa, this is my friend, Annaveta Travotsky. She's Mrs. Levinson's niece." Jarena introduced them and her papa reached over and kissed the top of her hand. She pasted a firm smile on her face, despite the fear that pounded in her heart.

"Ah, you're the niece Esther keeps talking about. Well, I'm glad you're here, adding even more beauty to our fair city and making my Jarena happy at the same time." His polished words made Annaveta even more wary because she couldn't figure out his true thoughts about her. "This is my wife, and my son Anton."

"Thanks for your welcome. It's nice to meet you and your wife, Mr. Barinov, and your son I've already been introduced to." She nodded to all three. "Maybe we'll see you again soon." The polite words came out of her mouth even though deep inside she hoped she never saw him again.

"Oh, you can be sure we will meet again soon." Mr. Barinov's eyes narrowed at her, and he nodded his head as a final good-bye before all three of them walked toward the entryway.

Annaveta stood there shaking. She was scared she'd have to come face to face with him again.

Chapter Sixteen

Alex ran the sandpaper over the newly completed bench. Mrs. Levinson said she wanted it for the entrance to Roman's office. Too many men came in with boots and shoes and needed to sit down to take them off and put them back on. She liked all the other work Alex had done for them, so she put him to work again now that he was home for a few weeks.

Alex didn't mind. He loved crafting new things with his hands and creating something that people enjoyed. It also helped that he was saving up quite a big of money, which he was sure he would need after the war. He hoped he would be able to start his new life with Annaveta then. He didn't like that argued so much lately. They needed to spend some time together, just the two of them, so they could really talk. Most likely that wasn't going to happen today, though.

A loud knock at the door interrupted his thoughts. "You ready to go?" Annaveta stood there in a simple brown dress and her most practical shoes. She had asked if he would come with her and her maid to help fix things up at the homeless shelter. Her uncle had told her she could do what she liked in that building to rebuild or reconstruct things in whatever way would help her serve more of the poor people.

So Alex agreed to help her.

"Just let me gather my tools." He put his tools in the wooden toolbox he made for himself.

They walked out into the cool morning air to the waiting carriage.

"I'm so glad you're coming." Annaveta smiled at him as they entered the carriage. "The building needs some fixing."

"I'll do what I can to help." Alex nodded at Tatyana. He listened to Annaveta describe the many different people that walked through their homeless shelter since they started it almost two years ago. By the time the carriage parked outside the old building, Alex felt like he knew most of them.

Alex followed Tatyana and Annaveta into the large, run down building. He saw the kitchen and the two tables they had set up. It seemed like the kitchen had been fixed up, but not the rest of the rooms in the place. The building was actually an old, dilapidated, eight-room house that Annaveta had talked her uncle into making into a place for homeless women and children who had no place to go.

He started on the main floor and worked his way to the bed-rooms. Alex saw Annaveta go up the stairs with one of the mothers, so he took his tools and began repairing the holes in the wall. He had to step around children and mothers, but soon he was done on the main floor.

Out of the corner of his eye, he saw a slim form turn the corner, long auburn hair hanging down her back. Annaveta. Unable to resist, he crept up behind her and grabbed her waist to spin her around. "Hi!"

She squeaked.

He was taken aback when he he looked into her face and realized his error. "I'm sorry, miss. I made a mistake. From behind, you look just like someone else. My apologies."

The girl's face turned a shade of red, similar to his own. Alex made a hasty retreat and soon bounded up the stairs looking for the real Annaveta.

He found her in one of the bedrooms that had more than its share of holes in the walls and on the floors.

"I met your look-alike."

"Oh, you mean Dassa. Everyone says we could have been twins. I guess everyone has a double somewhere." Annaveta shrugged and turned away when someone called her name. Then she hurried off, needed again by someone else.

Alex decided he would have to be careful from then on. He didn't want to make that mistake again.

He set down his toolbox and got to work. Mr. Levinson had reminded him that there was extra wood for repairs in the basement. He realized this room needed a lot of work, so he went to the basement to haul up more wood strips to fix the weak and damaged walls.

His mind was on the dinner and dance a few nights ago. He didn't like that whenever Sacha came to these events he stole Annaveta's attention. And yet he realized Annaveta's words the other night were true. He was a hypocrite if he got upset at her when he was doing the same thing. The fact was, it was nice to have Nadia's attention, but she was not the sort of girl he could ever have a meaningful or long term relationship with. She was a flirt, and not at all the sort of woman he could ever bring home to his mama.

A deep sadness filled him as he thought of the death of his parents and his other friends who had died. He couldn't wait until the war was over. He walked up the stairs, each step feeling like a heavy weight, until the light laughter of Annaveta and her maids wound its way up the curvy staircase to his ears. In some small way, that sound made his day. It was like a glimmer of hope that the world could be made right again.

He fixed the walls in three of the rooms. As he was finishing the fourth room, Annaveta came through the door.

"You've done so much already, Alex. Thank you." She came over and kissed him on the cheek and danced around the room. "I'm so excited. This is going to help so many of the poor women and children." She stopped, her cheeks turning red. "Sorry, I get really ridiculous when I'm excited. I really came upstairs to tell you that lunch is ready. Come and take a break from all your hard work." She pulled his hand.

He couldn't resist. He pulled her close and put his arms around her. She put her head back and laughed up at him. Her full lips were so close to his own, he couldn't resist kissing them. At first his lips met hers softly, and he savored the sweetness. And the more his lips lingered on hers, the more his passion grew.

Annaveta pulled herself gently out of his arms. "Alex, they're waiting for us downstairs. Let's go, before they come looking for us." She smiled that shy smile of hers that he loved so much.

"So soon?" Alex sighed in response to her nod. He loved

the time they had together and wished it would last longer. Forever might be just be long enough.

They went downstairs, and Alex helped dish out food to the many poor people who came through the doors. Soon everyone had eaten, and Annaveta put a plate of food in front of him.

"It's your turn. I ate a little already, or I'd sit down with you." She squeezed his shoulder and went to talk to a young mother with three children by her side. Two of the children knew her well enough that they hugged her, excited to see her. He watched as she went around the room talking to some young boys who were sitting on the floor, and then to a couple of older men who seemed like they had given up on life. Annaveta had them each smiling by the time she had finished talking with them. She amazed him with all she had to give to people. The cynical side of him wondered if any of them would take advantage of her good nature, but he knew Annaveta would only tell him that this was what she needed to do right now.

He stood up and took his dirty plate to the girls washing dishes. Seeing some garbage, he decided he would take it out to the barrel and burn what was there.

Alex opened the back door and walked to where the burning barrel was nestled between the small carriage house and the back of the house. He dumped the garbage into the bin and fumbled for the matches he had put in his pocket.

Without warning, he saw movement on the other side of the carriage house. Picking up a long thick stick he saw on the ground, he walked cautiously toward the intruder. Reaching the corner of the building just beyond the large door, he stopped. The sound of heavy breathing and digging reached his ears. He wondered what was going on. Peering around the corner, he saw a tall skinny man with black hair shoveling a large hole of dirt at the far end of the carriage house.

"Hey! What are you doing?" Alex stood there with his hands on his hips.

"None of your business." The man turned and looked at him, his eyes wide in surprise at the interruption. Picking up his jacket on the ground, he grabbed the shovel and began walking away.

"Wait. I know who owns this land and the buildings on it, and I know you shouldn't be digging here. What are you looking for?" Alex followed him behind the carriage house toward the street, needing answers.

Instead of answering, the man ran across the street to a waiting motor car. Soon he disappeared in the fog-covered street.

He walked back to the side of the carriage house and looked at the freshly dug hole. He couldn't see anything in there besides dirt and some clay. What was that man looking for?

Alex went to the burning barrel, lit a match, and threw it in. As the flames licked up the garbage, a thought came to him. Why would a man dressed in nice clothes be on Roman Levinson's property digging in the dirt? What was going on? He walked around the yard to see if there were any other places that had been dug up. He saw a few places where there were dirt covered mounds, revealing that someone had been digging here, but had covered up his tracks. As he reached the back of the property, against the edge of the trees he saw another open hole. When he looked inside that one, it was the same thing. Only dirt inside. What was the man looking for?

He heard a motorcar drive up. It stopped just before it reached the front of the house. Three men walked toward the back of the land. The hair on the back of Alex's neck stood on end, and he headed toward the trees that lined the back of the property. He found a thick clump of brush and crouched behind it. Soon he heard them talking.

"Did you offer him more money?" one of the men asked. That voice sounded familiar. He wanted to move so that he could see the men's faces, but he didn't want to risk them hearing him.

"I offered him double the value of the property, but he still wouldn't sell. I'm not sure what the holdup is." The man sounded frustrated that he wasn't getting his own way. Alex thought about what they could be talking about. Did they mean this property? Is that why they were here looking it over, because they wanted to buy it?

"It's been my experience that sometimes people need a little encouragement to see things my way." Alex moved a little so he could catch a glimpse of the men. Nothing. They kept moving. "Sometimes you have to disrupt those things or people that are most important to them, to get them to see why they need to sell this land to you."

"Any ideas on how I could convince him to sell would be very helpful."

"Find out about his life. Those people he loves and things that are most important to him. Then we begin to bring pain to it. It's simple."

Alex heard more scuffling noises as they walked on the rough dirt at the back of the property.

"I'll do that. This week I'll get the information I need about Mr. Levinson. I'll do whatever it takes to get this land. There's too much to lose for it not to go my way." Something clunked against the hard earth. Alex could see the shapes of the men. One bent over to pick up a shovel and began dumping ground back into another large hole.

"Looks like our man has been busy trying to find the secret. Why didn't he cover up these holes? I told him to be discreet. I'll need to talk to him next time he comes in to report."

"Have you heard anything more about our red-haired fire-ball?" the third man asked.

Alex knew that voice. It was all too familiar. Monsieur Arnaud. Which meant the other man was Misha. They were supposed to be in prison for their part in the assassination of Archduke Franz Ferdinand. Someone must have helped them escape. The Black Hand had its fingerprint all over this.

Alex's stomach clenched with dread.

"Actually, that was my interesting discovery the other day when I went to the Levinson's dinner and ball." The first man was talking. He was Jarena's papa. What was his name again? "Turns out that my daughter's best friend is the same red-haired girl you know from Noltava. She is Levinson's niece."

"Well, well, well. I'll have to think about how I can make the most of this little piece of news." Misha's arrogant laugh brought Alex back in time to when he held Annaveta in the baron's basement and separated the two of them. A sense of foreboding filled him as he heard their footsteps fade. The sound of their motorcar starting up and driving away returned Alex to his senses. He stood up from behind the trees and hurried across the ground to the house.

He found Annaveta upstairs, busy with the other maids cleaning up the rooms he already fixed.

"Oh, good. You're back. You still need to see what you can do to fix the other three rooms." Annaveta turned around to face him, her wet cloth dripping on the floor. "What is it? You look like you've seen a ghost!" She put her cloth down in the pail and pulled his arm to walk into one of the empty rooms on the floor. "Tell me."

He told her all that had heard and seen outside, and about the threat against her and her uncle.

"Thanks for telling me and not hiding the truth" Annaveta grimaced and paced the length of the room. "I can't say I'm surprised that the man from the train was in someway working with other members of the Black Hand. But I'm shocked that Misha and Monsieur Arnaud escaped from the Sarajevo prison." Her eyes closed and her body shuddered at the thought of it.

Alex stared out the window and rubbed his chin. "The hard part is going to be trying to keep you safe. I don't know if they've seen you at this house yet, Annaveta. But it won't be long until they know you come here regularly." Alex frowned at her. "At the very least you have to change up the days you come here, or it will be too easy for them to try to harm you."

"I agree. I'll talk to the women and children who are moving into this house and tell them I'll come on different days." Annaveta paced in the small room. "We'll just have to do that for now until the police catch them and send them back to prison."

"That's the other detail we need to think about. Maybe we should ask your uncle to put a few men in the house as

guards. I just don't trust that they won't try anything stupid."
Alex ran a hand through his blond curls, worry making his
body tense like a man facing a firing squad.

"The next thing we need to do is to find out why they seem
so desperate to have this land. Why are they digging in the
back yard? What are they hoping to find, and why is it so
important to them?" Annaveta walked over to Alex and
grabbed his hand. "Come. It's time to start our search."

Chapter Seventeen

Annaveta's heart raced as fast as the clipping heels of the horses that pulled the carriage. She couldn't believe those men—monsters really—had escaped from prison.

Her worst nightmare was coming true. They were in Odessa and for some reason wanted not only her, but the land Uncle Roman owned. She had to find out why this was so important to them. Misha wouldn't give up harassing her. She couldn't imagine he would until either one of them was dead or out of the country.

"David's the dark-haired man with the limp, right? I think I remember meeting him at Mrs. Levinson's dinner last week." Alex sat across from her in the carriage.

"Yes, that's him. He graduated with his law degree at the University before he joined the army. Now, because of his injury, he can't go back to war, so he's healing at home, and he's looking for a new purpose." Annaveta pushed back a few stray strands of hair with shaky hands. "I know he'll help guide us to the right information about that land, and maybe he'll answer some other questions."

"I'm sure he will." Alex's blue eyes seemed to bore a hole into her own as he searched hers. He gently pulled her hand from her hair and held both cold hands in his own. "I know you're scared. I am, too. But you must know I will do everything in my power to keep you safe."

"I do. And it makes me feel so much better, Alex. Truly. But I still feel like I need answers." The carriage stopped outside Judge Saratov's large house, only a few blocks from the centre of the city. They asked the driver to wait and approached the imposing structure. Annaveta knocked, and soon a maid answered.

"What can I do for you, miss?" A pleasant-faced woman answered the door dressed in a gray ankle-length uniform with a white apron and collar.

"Would you tell Mr. David Saratov that Annaveta Travotsky and Alex Wagner are here to see him?" Annaveta stood shivering in the cold afternoon air.

"Just wait here, miss. I'll see if he's receiving visitors."

Annaveta looked up at the storm clouds gathering in the sky above them. A sense of foreboding came over her as she waited.

The large wooden door opened once more. "Mr. Saratov says you are to come inside. He'll see you in the library."

Annaveta and Alex entered the large house and stared in awe at the grand staircase that spiraled up to the second floor of the house. The maid took their coats, and they followed her down the long hallway. Soon they entered a room covered floor to ceiling in books.

"I'll be back with tea." The maid left the room and closed the massive door behind her.

"Have you ever seen so many books in one room?" Annaveta saw a large desk in one corner of the room with papers all over it. Alex sat on one of two couches in front of a large fireplace. Annaveta walked over to the fireplace to warm her hands.

"Ah, Miss Travotsky and Mr. Wagner, what a nice surprise." David entered the room and closed the door behind him. He walked over to them and clasped their hands, then waved for them to sit.

"So what's on your mind? Or is there another dinner party that your aunt has planned for us poor blokes?" David grimaced as he waited for Annaveta's answer.

"Now, David. I know how much you hate being subjected to the crush of people and all that dancing. Would I come here just to see if I could add to your misery?" Annaveta teased him and was happy to see his cheeks turn slightly red. "No, I have something much more pressing to discuss with you. This will be a task that challenges your skills as a lawyer, and will even give you practice at being a spy."

David laughed out loud. Annaveta glanced at Alex and saw him raise one eyebrow in question.

"All right, now you have me really curious." The maid entered with a tea tray. As soon as she set it down, Annaveta poured tea for everyone. "So tell it to me straight, Annaveta. What is this undercover task you have in mind that would force me into my new role as a spy?"

"Let me start from the beginning. This is all confidential, of course." Annaveta took a big breath knowing she needed to tell all, and for some reason felt quite nervous doing it.

"Of course." David sipped his tea and Alex nodded for her to continue.

She told David everything from back when her parents died in the house fire to the men Alex saw in the back of the Junior Red Cross facility.

"Sounds like you've been through quite a lot already." David shook his head and looked at both of them in amazement. "So you want me to help you catch these men?"

"In a round about way, yes." Annaveta sighed. "You see, Jarena's father offered Uncle Roman double the price for that property, and we couldn't figure out why he would do that. But when Alex saw the deep holes someone dug around the property, we realized we really need answers. So that's why we came to you. Who better to ask how to find information on a house that was built in 1899? We want to find out about not only that land, but also about Mr. Barinov's land and the parcels he has bought in Odessa."

"Ah, so we are doing some research mixed with a little spying. Sounds like this might be fun," David said. "What we need to do is look back at the historical records, which include surveys of the land in question and the transfer of ownership since 1899." David pulled a paper out of his pocket and began to write down the information. He stopped and looked up at them. "One more thing. We should do a search for any other information linked with the land, like oil and gas and mineral rights." ·

"Sounds good. So what is our first step?" Annaveta was ready to get it all done at that moment.

"We need to go to the land office. The building will be closed for the rest of today. Why don't we plan to meet there first thing tomorrow morning?" David put down his tea cup on the side table.

"That sounds really good. Thank you for your help." Alex stood up and shook David's hand. "It sets my mind at ease knowing you'll be helping Annaveta after I head back to my assignment."

"Of course. If it wasn't for this twisted leg, I'd be joining you." David grimaced as he stood up. He rubbed his leg and limped behind them out of the library to the front door.

"Right now, I'm glad you are here to help us find some answers."

"David, we'll see you at the land office tomorrow morning." Annaveta smiled up at him.

"Here's to my new duties as spy." David's laugh echoed through the door as she and Alex walked toward their waiting carriage.

David was already waiting inside the land office when they arrived. He was talking to the clerk, asking to see records dating back to the early 1890s, specifically those focused on the northwest side of Odessa. The clerk, an older man with a straight face, gray hair, and mustache, frowned at Annaveta as she followed Alex and David to a separate room to look at the records. She guessed they didn't see many women in this office.

"We want to look at the records for each year to find who owned the land. We're also looking for information from surveys of the land, and mineral exploration and rights." David handed Annaveta a file labeled 1900. Looked like they would most likely be there awhile.

"I found the land title of the man who bought the land and built the house in April 1899. It says here it was Vassily Krupin. Looks like he requested a simple survey done, and that was all before he bought the house." Annaveta flipped through more pages in the document. "For some reason the documents proving Mordecai Goldstein bought the property from Mr. Krupin are missing." Soon they had gone through the other years with no new information to be found. Then Annaveta began to read about the Jewish Pogrom of 1905.

"There were over eight hundred people killed and several thousand wounded. Also, a little more than sixteen hundred Jewish houses, apartments, and stores were damaged in the pogrom." Annaveta read down to learn more specifics about the attacks. "It looks like northwest Odessa was one of the areas where Jews were attacked and pulled out of their houses, killed, and their houses burned. That's where Zaydeh and Bubbeh lived."

Annaveta's voice choked as she read about the awful truth of what happened on that horrible day. She remembered when she had asked her aunt about that pogrom. Her aunt couldn't speak of it. Instead she told Annaveta of a different pogrom when she was a little girl. Her brothers had been killed in that one. Aunt Esther said because she had blonde hair and blue eyes, she was often the one sent to buy things for her family. Bubbeh said because she didn't didn't look Jewish, she would be treated with more kindness, and it would be easier to get the groceries they needed.

Annaveta couldn't believe all the suffering her family went through. She looked at the documents that gave more details on what happened after the Pogrom of 1905. "It looks like three months after the fire, a tract of land that included Mr. Mordecai Goldstein's home and two other homes was sold to Mr. Barinov."

She looked over at Alex and David. "I guess that's that. Mr. Barinov bought the land. It's his to use however he sees fit."

"Wait a minute." David was looking at another document. "Here's a map made just last year of the city of Odessa. But when I compare it with the map from 1905, I see the houses that were burned in the pogrom are now a part of Mr. Barinov's large estate. What I don't understand is how he could combine all those small portions of land into his estate, when only two of these houses were sold to him. It's very confusing. I need to research this further. One thing is certain, though. He has continued to expand his land only in this specific area. I wonder if there's a reason for that?" David shook his head and continued to look through the documents. "I'll need to ask my father about these documents."

Annaveta was grateful to not only have David's help, but also that of Judge Saratov. With all his years of practicing law, she was confident he would be able to shed some light on any information that they were missing.

"I'm looking here at the search for mineral rights on the land around the northwest part of Odessa." Alex was searching through documents that dated back quite a few years. "Mordecai Goldstein didn't ask for a search done on his land, but as soon as Mr. Ulinov acquired the land in early 1906, a search for minerals was done. However, there's a note here that says, '*At the request of the buyer, findings from this search have been withheld from the public.*' David, what are your thoughts on this new information?" Alex looked up at David, a crease marring his smooth forehead.

"I, too, thought that was public information. That's another thing I'll need to research." David grimaced as he wrote more information in his notebook. "There seem to be too many unknowns and withheld information in these documents. It makes me wonder what we're really dealing with here." He looked over at Alex then Annaveta, and his expression softened. "I'll keep researching, and I'll ask my father for advice. Right now, you'll just need to be patient as we sort this out."

"I'm not very patient, but I'll try." Each of them put the documents back in their right places, and David carried what they had to the clerk to file. Then she turned toward David. "I really appreciate your help with this."

They walked outside into a slight drizzle.

"Come on," David said. "I'll give you a ride back." They followed him to what looked like a newer motorcar. It was quite late in the afternoon, and Annaveta was sure her Aunt would be worried. The fastest way home would be best. They got inside, and soon David had them on the road. She was pleasantly surprised at how fast and smooth the ride was to Uncle Roman and Aunt Esther's estate.

They waved goodbye to David as he raced off in his roadster.

Alex and Annaveta went inside the house and had just taken off their coats when Aunt Esther walked toward them. She wrung her hands. Something must have upset her.

"Aunt Esther, you're as white as a ghost. What happened? Is Jude feeling worse?" Annaveta looked into her eyes and waited for an answer.

"We just got word that one of the girls from the shelter was kidnapped late last night." Aunt Esther paced in front of them. "To make matters worse, it was a girl with the long auburn hair like you."

"Dassa. They took Dassa." Annaveta felt tears escape from the corner of her eyes. She knew the girl was sixteen and was the only helper her mama had with her three younger siblings. Her mama had commented that Dassa and Annaveta could be mistaken for twins. "Did the kidnappers send a note to say what they want? How do we get her back? Her mama will be worried sick. I should go over there and—"

"No, you should not go over there." Alex interrupted her thoughts that were like a runaway train. "Don't you see? They were trying to take you. The kidnappers got the wrong girl. So I'm sure they won't give up just because they made one mistake."

"You're quite right, Alex." Aunt Esther lifted up Annaveta's chin so she could look her in the eye. "Who they really want is you. They made that quite clear." Her aunt put her hand into the side pocket of her skirt and handed her a note. "This was brought by messenger a little while ago. Read it."

Annaveta's hands shook as she opened the note. Alex came to stand beside her and they read it together.

We got the wrong girl this time. We won't make that mistake again. Mr. Levinson, don't you think it is time for you to sell this property?

Annaveta choked back a sob, and Aunt Esther pulled her into her arms. "There, there. We'll get this sorted out. We'll do everything we can to keep you safe." Annaveta pulled back from her aunt's hold.

"But Aunt Esther. I'm not so worried about me. I'm wondering who is going to protect all those innocent women and children living there." Annaveta rubbed her neck and took deep breaths to try to relieve the tension. "The Black Hand is behind this. And Alex and I both know they will do whatever it takes to get what they want. Even killing the innocent."

Chapter Eighteen

His hands moved the brush gently across the back of the bench. Almost done. Alex hoped Esther Levinson would be pleased with it.

His thoughts flittered from one thing to the next, all having to do with his worry about how to keep Annaveta safe and protected. He left tomorrow and couldn't stand thinking about all the things that the Black Hand could and would do to her if given the chance.

"Here you are." Roman entered the carriage house with a flourish, sort of the same way he did most things. "I thought you might be here finishing all the projects we gave you. Looks really good, Alex. You definitely have a gift for crafting beautiful furniture." He ran his hands down a few smaller pieces.

Roman clenched his jaw. "I wanted to talk to you about this whole business with the Black Hand and the threats I've been getting. The address on the back of these notes is an abandoned warehouse, at number seven Mykolaivs Road, down by the docks. I've already told the police about the warehouse and they said it was empty. The police also know about the girl, so they are trying to find her. But I need to know more of what's going on. I know you explained the whole story of what happened before you and Annaveta arrived here, but I guess it's what has happened since that is a little muddled for me."

Alex tensed as he remembered. "We were followed here by a man from the Black Hand. He was on the train with us. Then we didn't see him again until that dinner at the Yudin estate. By that time, Annaveta was friends with Jarena. Annaveta was getting to know her, hoping to get more information."

"Sounds risky." Mr. Levinson sucked in a quick breath.

"It was, but you know how determined your niece can be."

Roman grimaced and nodded.

Alex went on. "Annaveta found some clues at Jarena's house as to the Black Hand's bigger plan to hurt more Jews and Germans. Then we found out that the Black Hand members that hurt Annaveta when we were in St. Petersburg had escaped from the Sarajevo prison. Then recently, when I was at the shelter fixing the walls, I went outside and saw a man digging in the back yard, looking for something. When I heard a motorcar stop, I hid behind some bushes and overheard them talking. I recognized two of the voices as Misha's and Monsieur Arnaud's, and I think the other voice was Mr. Barinov."

"What did they say?"

"They were talking about how they would need to convince you that you needed to sell the property to them. And how they had hired the man I saw to dig in the backyard and look for something. They didn't say what." Alex wiped his hands on a clean cloth and looked up at the tense man standing in front of him.

"Well, that does help me understand more of what's going on." Alex had never seen the strong Roman Levinson look more ashen-faced. Alex understood. He felt the same way when the people who were important to him were in danger.

"If you're done here, I thought I would take you to the shelter. Annaveta doesn't know yet, but I hired some bodyguards. She needs to have more protection, and so do the people there." They walked out together into the cool morning air. Getting into the carriage, Roman handed him a note. "Here, read this. I wrote a response to the Black Hand. I'll have one of my bodyguards hand deliver it to the same address—the warehouse at number seven Mykolaivs Road— this morning. I told them there was another investor and there is. It's my son Jude. And since he happens to be in the Navy, I'm hoping it will delay things a bit."

Alex opened the note.

I received your note and I am presently contacting my lawyer to see the steps I need to take to sell that property. There is another investor involved who I will need to contact. I need his approval before the sale can go through. I will contact you when I know more.

"Think that will hold them off a little longer?"

"Maybe for a few days at most, and then they'll be back. The Black Hand doesn't give up so easily." Alex handed the note back.

"There must be something more I can do. I've been thinking, but I can't seem to come up with anything." Roman ran his fingers through his graying hair. The carriage pulled up to the shelter. They got out, and Roman introduced Alex to the four bodyguards he hired. Two were for the day shift and two were for the nightshift.

Dassa's mama wept as she talked with Roman. Her children clung to her skirts. One little guy cried. Alex picked him up and tickled him. It worked. He stopped crying and started giggling instead.

"I just don't know where to look to find her," the sobbing woman told Mr. Levinson.

"I have contacted the police, Mrs. Torres." He put his hand on her shoulder. They are doing all they can to look for your daughter."

"What about my babies and the rest of the people who live here now? What will we do if they come back and try to hurt us or take someone else?" She wrung her hands and cried. By this time, almost all of the people living there had surrounded Annaveta's uncle.

"We've hired bodyguards to protect you. I believe you'll be safe. Now don't worry. Instead, try to cheer your children and each other." Roman waved at Alex with his hand. Alex handed the boy back to his mama, and they stepped outside.

Alex looked around the building and the yard but couldn't see anyone or anything unusual. So they got into the waiting carriage.

"I need to inquire at the police station to see if they have found any more information on Mrs. Torres' daughter," Roman said. "But I can get the driver to take you home."

"Actually, I have another stop I need to make today, too. Maybe I'll have your driver take me there, and then I'll find my own way back to your place."

"Good, then." Roman got out at the police station and Alex gave the address to the driver.

As he walked up the stairs to David Saratov's home, his mind raced.

It wasn't long before the maid invited him inside, and he was escorted to the library where David waited for him.

"Good to see you, Alex." David shook his hand and invited him to sit down. "You're probably wanting to learn what I've uncovered in my research."

"That's one of the reasons I came to see you, yes." Alex sat forward on the couch, his elbows on his knees, looking at David and waiting for him to speak.

"I'll start with what I've learned." David reached for a notepad full of research he'd done. "I've discovered a few things. In 1905, none of the Jews sold to outsiders. If they were to sell their property, they sold it to other Jewish people or passed it down to their children. In all the research I did, I didn't find a single occurrence of Jewish shops or houses being sold to outsiders. So there is no way Mr. Barinov could have bought it. My father and I are digging deeper into what we found, because it means that Mr. Barinov doesn't own as much property as he thinks. We also discovered a neighbour who knew Mordecai and Zahava Goldstein. That should help us find out more." David paused and rubbed his chin. "I told the Judge about the mineral rights being withheld from the public, and he told me a private citizen wasn't legally able to do that. That could only come from Tsar Nicholas himself. So I'm going through some political red tape to get that codicil removed from the legal documents. That's where things are. And who knows what I'll uncover next."

"Sounds like you've found a great deal. Thank you for that." Alex appreciated all the effort David put into the search.

"What else can I do while I'm here at home, healing? It's rather fun digging up new information that will, at the very least, slow the Black Hand from achieving their goals." David chuckled. "Besides, Annaveta made it sound like doing this was my duty to my country. How could I say no?"

"Yes, she does have a way of talking a person into doing things. Which brings me to the favour I wanted to ask." Alex looked at David and then down at his hands, not sure how to say this.

"Speak man. You know I'll do what I can to help out." David sat back in his chair.

"That's good to know, because this might be a request that seems a bit unusual." Alex took a deep breath. "I head back late tomorrow to my new assignment, and I wanted to ask you to do what you could to watch over Annaveta. To protect her. She has a way of leaping into new adventures without thinking first, and sometimes following her heart gets her into situations where she gets hurt. Will you just check in on her once in a while? Her uncle has hired security guards, but I'd feel better knowing someone we know and trust is looking out for her." Alex appealed to David, hoping he would agree to help him.

"I promise I will do what I can to look out for her. I can't be with her all the time, but I'll check up on her and do what I can." David nodded and put out the cigarette he'd been smoking.

"Thank you. I feel so much better. Now I can be a little more at peace going off to war." Alex stood up and held out his hand.

David rose awkwardly, favouring his left leg, and shook his hand. "I appreciate your faith in me. And will do all I can to live up to that level of trust." He walked Alex to the front door.

"Oh, one other thing." Alex put his coat on and reached for the door handle. "Let's just keep this between us men. Annaveta doesn't need to know that I asked you to look out for her. It might not make her too happy knowing that." Alex grinned at David and walked out into the foggy Saturday afternoon.

He felt good knowing there was someone else who would help keep Annaveta safe. Now he could go back to the Navy with one more weight lifted off his shoulders.

He woke quite early the next morning, as he had asked Annaveta to meet him at the place he'd started to think of as *their hill*. They were starting early because he still wanted to go to the German Lutheran church service before he had to leave on the late afternoon train. Alex was glad they still had this time together. They were going to take the horses this time. He went to the barn and found Pavel already there saddling Beauty for Annaveta.

"It's a good day for a run in the meadow." Annaveta's cheeks flushed with the glow of doing what she loved—spending time with the horse Aunt Esther had given her.

Pavel brought both horses—Star, a gelding, and Beauty, a bay mare.

Alex watched as Annaveta swung her leg up into the saddle, looking beautiful in a new green riding habit. She grabbed the reins and gave the horse her head before Alex could get onto Star.

Alex sat in the saddle like he was born to it and coaxed Star into a gallop. He appreciated the fact that he was chasing Beauty – both the horse and her rider - across the wide expanse of meadow and it exhilarated him. When they reached the downward slope that led to the creek, Annaveta slowed down and looked behind her.

He caught up to her and smiled.

"I'm jealous," she said. "You're so much better at riding than I am."

"I've been riding since I was small, so I have gotten used to it." Alex patted the horse's glossy black coat. "Star here is a smooth ride, much like Blackie, our gelding at home. I hadn't realized how much I missed riding until now." They started walking their horses side by side, heading down toward the creek.

"It's good that you have had some time here for a little while, even though I'm sorry my cousin was hurt." Annaveta looked over at him. Alex tried to shake off the memories of that day.

"I'm grateful I could be here too. I'm grateful for the chance to get away from all the dying, even if it's only for a couple of weeks." A dark foreboding filled him.

"That must have been difficult to save not only Jude's life, but to save those German sailors." Annaveta said with compassion—like he'd heard before—in her voice.

"It was one of the hardest things I've ever done." Alex looked down at his hands and gripped the reins as the memory came back. "When Admiral Kolchak said I needed to go rescue those German sailors, my first thought was that I would just as soon like to take a gun and shoot them all. But as our lifeboats got closer, and I saw the whites of their eyes, the enemy suddenly became men following orders, just like I was. It was like the hatred and the evil I had in my heart for the men who killed my parents suddenly left. I can't really explain it. I expected to hate them, and yet when I heard them speak of their fear of going to the Russian prisoner of war camps, I was surprised by the compassion that I felt for them. I'm still not at the point where I've forgiven them, but at least the hatred is gone now."

"I'm speechless. That's so good." Annaveta looked like she didn't know what to say.

'One other thing." Alex put his hand on her mare's reins and tugged Beauty to a stop. He looked over at her and held her hands. "I want to tell you how sorry I am for how I acted the day that I left. I don't know what I was thinking, all but demanding we get married and just run away from everything. Maybe I was in shock from my parents' deaths, I don't know. And I'm very sorry for getting so angry that day." Alex saw tears glistening in her eyes. "What is it?"

"Thank you for explaining." Tears fell down her cheeks. "You really scared me that day. Your anger reminded me of how my papa used to be. I wasn't sure if I could trust you anymore."

He wiped her tears with this thumb and kissed her forehead. "I'm so sorry. I never want to do that again. I value your trust in me. Forgive me?"

Annaveta nodded. "I do forgive you. We'll begin again."

"Sounds good." Alex moved his hand from hers as his horse spooked from a squirrel that ran up a nearby tree.

"Race you to the bottom." Annaveta spurred her mare to a gallop, flying toward the creek.

"Hey, Red. No fair." Alex yelled out and soon Star's long legs had them close behind her. They caught up when Annaveta reached the creek bottom.

She hopped off Beauty and walked her toward the water. Alex got off his horse and in one swift motion grabbed her around the waist and pulled her to him. She laughed as he twirled her around and set her down on her feet. He tightened his hold around her waist. The morning sun was just peeking through the clouds. He was surprised when Annaveta reached up and moved his blond curls away from his forehead. His hands played with her long auburn hair, and he brought a fistful of her tresses to his chcck.

"You never cease to surprise me, Red. I like it." He put both hands on the side of her face and kissed her until she was breathless. His heart raced from having her near.

"I kind of like you too, blondie."

He pulled her close and kissed her again. "I'm convinced. I really do love you."

Annaveta frowned.

"Why are you sad?"

"I'm just worried that something will happen to tear us apart again."

Alex rubbed his thumb gently across her forehead where a crease had formed. He'd been with her during some of the hardest days of her life, so he could tell when she worried. He recognized the tell-tale signs—the sparkle was gone from her eyes and with it, a familiar wrinkle on her forehead had appeared. "We're strong together. We'll make it through." Alex kissed her forehead and held her close, his cheek pressing softly against her the top of her head.

Annaveta sighed. He loved having her in his arms but wasn't convinced there wouldn't be something else in their lives that would try to pull them apart.

He frowned when he saw her twist the three corded bracelet that he given her. Doubt, it seemed, was a constant companion to them both.

Chapter Nineteen

Annaveta walked beside Alex up the stairs of the old Lutheran Church. Being there brought back so many memories of living with the Wagner family in Pleve colony. It also reminded her of the last time they were in this church—for the memorial service to honour Alex's parents.

They made their way into the church and split to go to the separate men and women's sections. The pastor spoke about the importance of forgiving and loving those who have hurt you.

Annaveta could think of several people who had hurt her. She looked around. Aunt Esther's Cook Edda sat two benches ahead of her and some other women. Everyone had sad and weary faces. Annaveta could relate. She was so tired. Tired of trying to fit in, tired of fighting old and new enemies, and tired of the war.

It was August 1916 and everyone was worn out. A feeling of hopelessness saturated the air around her. With news from St. Petersburg of people standing in line for hours just to get bread for their families, it was starting to feel more hopeless everyday. The situation wasn't quite so bad yet in Odessa, but there was a food shortage. People everywhere spoke of how disillusioned they were with the war and the leadership of Tsar Nicholas and his cabinet ministers.

Jarena's brother told her many of the soldiers didn't even know what the war was about. One peasant conscript under his leadership told him he didn't know why he was going to kill the Germans. He didn't know who was more the enemy, the Germans or the company commander. With lice biting at him in the trenches, hunger gnawing constantly at his stomach, he felt more hopeless everyday that the war went on.

From snippets of conversation at the breakfast table with Jude, Aunt Esther, and Uncle Roman, Annaveta had started to see the bigger picture of the devastating effect war had on her country. She hoped it would all come to an end soon. She looked at the men's side of the church and saw mostly older men, all with defeated looks covering their faces.

Without warning, Alex stood up and went to the back of the church. Wondering what he was doing, Annaveta stood up to follow him. The pastor kept speaking despite the distractions around him.

"What happened?" Annaveta finally found Alex outside, walking toward the back of the large Lutheran church.

"During the service, I felt an urgent need to get up because I thought I smelled smoke. I asked some of the men beside me, but they couldn't smell it. I need to find out where it's coming from."

Annaveta walked faster to keep up with him. Soon they saw black smoke coming out of a couple windows and a side door on the back of the church.

"I'm going in. You stay out here. I don't want you getting hurt." Alex put his light coat against his nose so he wouldn't breathe in too much smoke and pulled hard on the door. He stepped into the black smoke and disappeared before she could reply.

She worried when she heard groaning and shuffling mixed with a lot of coughing. She spotted a covered well at the back of the church and ran to it. She hurried to bring the bucket up with some water and ran to where Alex was, water sloshing over the side of the pail as she went. When she reached the door, she saw a few men running toward the well.

Good, there's more help. The faster we can put the fire out the better.

She went into the black smoke, and since she couldn't see where anything was, she threw the water into the thick blackness.

"Alex, are you there?" She heard a feeble moan. Unable to see, she reached out but found nothing. Walking up some steps, she groped around again. The heat from the fire was intense, but she found him. She grasped his hands and dragged his body back to the entrance. She managed to pull him through the door, both of them choking and gasping for air. Some men helped carry him away from the church, and lay him on the grass. Annaveta saw the men form a line from the well to the door of the church to put out the fire.

"Oh, Alex, wake up." Annaveta leaned over him and tapped his face lightly. She repeated it over and over until he moaned and opened his eyes.

He tried to sit up and coughed. "I just need to catch my breath."

Annaveta helped hold him upright as he coughed. After a few minutes, he settled down and began breathe regularly. "Looks like the men are getting it out."

"They wouldn't have noticed the fire without you." Annaveta felt a new respect for Alex. "I'm just glad you're doing well after breathing in all that smoke."

"Thanks for getting me out." Alex looked at her and put a shaky hand to her cheek.

She let out a long sigh, grateful he was alive. "You must have a few angels looking out for you." She gave a little laugh as she thought of all the times he could have died and didn't.

"You are definitely one of them."

Alex's whispered words made her blush. He started to kiss her, but a booming voice interrupted him.

"We got the fire out!"

A cheer erupted from the long line of men standing along the side of the church with buckets in their hands.

"I want to see inside the church now." Alex stood unsteadily to his feet.

"But—"

"I have to, Annaveta." Alex began to walk, and she helped steady him. "I must see if this fire was deliberately set."

Annaveta breathed in quickly as she thought of what it might mean.

He walked into the room with Annaveta behind him, their feet sloshing the water that was all around the room. They couldn't see where or how the fire started, so they retreated.

"Look, there's some red paint or something on the wall behind the door." Alex pulled the door so it was more closed.

Annaveta gasped in surprise and covered her mouth at what she saw written there.

All Germans must die.

The words were written in Russian inside the circle of the black skull—the symbol of the Black Hand. There was nothing else, only the sign.

"Well, now we know who started the fire." Alex shook his head and grabbed Annaveta's hand as they walked out the door.

"We need to get the police to come and look at what happened here." Alex talked to the pastor, who by this time was out on the grass talking to the men from his congregation. He told them the details of what they would find inside.

"Danke, Alex Wagner. You have been an angel in disguise to us today." The pastor shook his hand.

"I'm just happy we got the fire out in time."

Someone else walked up to talk to the pastor, so Annaveta and Alex left the church yard.

"I need to get back and change, and then I have to leave. But I won't leave at ease. Too much has happened, and I'm more than a little worried. Especially for your safety, Annaveta."

They hired a carriage driver to bring them to Annaveta's family's home. The driver brought them to the estate, and Alex asked him to wait. Soon Alex came out of the guest house clean again, dashing in his dark blue Navy uniform. He spoke to Roman and Esther and Jude, who Annaveta had brought outside to send him off.

"Will you promise to always let someone know where you're going, and if at all possible have someone with you when you go out?" Alex held her hand and kissed it.

"I promise to be careful. You will too?" She feared for him going back to war. It scared her since she heard of Alex's close calls with death. Although, he had been in danger at the church and had nearly died too.

"I will. You'll write to me and let me know what's happening with the property and what the police find out?" She didn't want to let him go for fear he wouldn't come back.

"You know I will." A small smile filled her face.

Alex leaned down and kissed her cheek. "I wish I could kiss you properly, but I must do the correct thing with all these eyes watching." He kissed her hand one more time, then let go and waved at everyone else. He saluted Lieutenant Levinson and got into the carriage.

Annaveta watched him go, wondering how long it would be until she would see him again.

A few days later, Annaveta went with Aunt Esther to help

out at the hospital again. She smiled as she remembered the nurse describing a woman coming from St. Petersburg to see her dying soldier husband one last time. She said someone had sent her a telegram and had given her money to come on the train. The nurse said his sharing last few hours in the world with his family was beautiful and touching.

Those moments made all the discouraging days worth it. Annaveta was inspired to do what she could for these poor men. Especially since she didn't know when she would see Alex again.

When she was saying goodbye to the last man in ward, she spotted Jarena standing at the door. Annaveta walked over to her friend, who kept making furtive glances out into the hall as if worried someone else would show up.

"Quick, lets go to this alcove, hidden away from everyone." Jarena pulled Annaveta under the archway so they stood in the corner behind some linen shelves. "I can't talk long. My father is coming to pick me up here soon. He said I can't go to the shelter anymore to see you and to help. I'm not happy about that at all."

"What reason did your papa give?" Annaveta wondered what her father knew about her or what she was doing.

"Papa says he doesn't think what you're doing is safe. That's he knows some people who are already upset by you helping the poor people there. He says because he wants to protect me, he can't allow me to be seen with you anymore." Jarena put her arms around her, sobbing into her shoulder. "I'm so desperately unhappy about it."

"I'm sorry. That makes me very sad. But we could still be friends in secret, right?" Annaveta pulled back and looked into Jarena's eyes. They shimmered with tears.

"Yes. I'd like that." She nodded, took out handkerchief, and dabbed at her eyes. "There's something else I wanted to tell you. Remember the day we were out riding, you were curious about the area on our land that my papa said was dangerous?"

Annaveta's ears perked up, curious as to what she found out.

"Well, I decided to look around one day when my parents were gone. I threw some heavy rocks all around the area, making sure there weren't any land mines or anything. I found a secret entrance to a tunnel, behind two large trees."

"That's so interesting, Jarena." Annaveta didn't know what to make of it all. "Did you find anything down there?"

"Sadly, I only got about half way down the stairs before I heard the sound of a carriage. I rushed up and saw that my parents had arrived home early. So I put the board back in place and covered it up with dirt and leaves like I found it."

"That must have been a surprise to find a secret passageway in the middle of your land." Annaveta's curiosity wouldn't be held back. "Wouldn't it be great to see what is all down there?"

"That's exactly what I was thinking. Of course, we need to do this without my papa knowing." Jarena looked up at ceiling. "I have an idea that might work. I know that papa leaves again tomorrow and won't be back until the next day. How about if you came just after the sun has set. That way no one will see you."

"That would work. I'll sneak into your yard and wait for you." Annaveta was excited about being able to look around in this

tunnel. She had a feeling for Jarena it was more about assert-
ing her independence from her father and being able to do
her own thing. But for Annaveta, it was a search for hidden
secrets. They might even find something that would help
stop Mr. Barinov from buying Uncle Roman's land where the
shelter was.

"I better go. I think I hear my father's voice." Jarena picked
up some linen as if carrying it somewhere. "See you tomorrow night."

Annaveta stayed where she was until she was certain the
coast was clear. All kinds of thoughts filled her mind of what
she would discover inside that tunnel.

"I'll stay here with the horses, miss." Pavel whispered to Annaveta as she dismounted and began to walk toward the trees
lining the edges of the Barinov estate. Annaveta looked back
and waved to Pavel, grateful he was brave enough to help
her out. She hadn't told Aunt Esther or Uncle Roman about
where she was going, and she had asked Pavel to keep quiet
about what they were doing. She knew he risked his job to
help her, so she told him to not feel pressured. She could
figure out another way. But Pavel seemed determined to help
her. He told her he would do his best to keep the horses
quiet until she returned.

Annaveta walked a full mile before she neared the small
copse of trees where she waited for Jarena. It wasn't long
before her friend approached.

Jarena had a big grin on her face. An unlit lantern was in her right hand. Annaveta realized that for her friend, this was more of a lark. Jarena didn't realize how serious Annaveta was about finding hidden secrets here. For her, it was life and death. There was something that Mr. Barinov, Misha, and Monsieur Arnaud wanted bad enough that they were willing to kidnap a young girl and threaten Uncle Roman to get. She concluded that the prize must be very valuable.

"Here, I'll go down first. Hand me the lantern when I'm closer to the bottom will you?" Together they moved the board that covered the entrance to the crudely dug hole in the ground. Jarena started down, and when she neared the bottom, Annaveta handed her the lantern.

Annaveta covered up the hole as best she could with the board and started down. The light from the lantern cast its glow over the dirt walls. Both of them gasped in surprise at what they saw. All different types of guns sat on wooden shelves lining the hard-packed dirt walls of the tunnel.

"So this is what Papa is buying and selling." Jarena's eyes were wide as she took in all the hand guns and infantry guns, including the new Winchester models. There were also ten large Russian machine guns filling one entire wall. Grenades and other small devices were also in the line up. "Now I know why he makes so many business trips and had the money to buy new things for the house, us, or himself. I wonder just how much of a profit he is making selling these weapons."

Annaveta wondered the same thing. They moved down the corridor of the long, hollowed-out cave. Jarena stopped and held up the lantern. Annaveta's eyes followed the light's soft glow which showed a coarsely-hewn wooden door at the far end of the tunnel. Looking down the dirt passageway, it seemed like the rows of guns went on for a long time until they reached the end. There was a little room off to the side. Annaveta noticed that it was different than the rest of the corridor because there were a couple of chairs and two long tables against two of the walls. Under each of the tables and stacked really high on the top of each were wooden boxes of what looked like paper.

Annaveta followed Jarena into the room, where she put down the lantern and started looking through the boxes on a tabletop.

"We'll just look and see what we can find here. What other secrets has my papa kept from me?"

Annaveta looked at the boxes stacked under the table. In most of the boxes were papers that gave descriptions of the guns they purchased and those they sold. Names and places and pricing were marked clearly on each one.

"I would be interested if you find anything that tells us the details of land purchases." Annaveta searched tirelessly through the papers under the table.

"Sure, I'll let you know. Wow, I can't believe all the money Papa and his friends have made from this. The details of all the transactions are listed here," Jarena whispered.

Annaveta went through all the papers at that one table and moved onto the next one. Behind one of the boxes she saw two more that were made of metal. She tried pulling them forward, but they wouldn't move. So she pulled herself under the table and peered into each box. She was so surprised by what she saw that she jumped back, bumping her head on the table.

"Jarena, come here. You won't believe what I found." She

motioned for her friend to come closer with one hand and rubbed the swelling bump on her head with the other. "Take a look." She pointed at the two heavier boxes.

"Bars of gold," her friend whispered. "How do you think they got their hands on two big boxes of gold?" She picked up one gold bar. "It's heavy. Feel how heavy it is."

Annaveta held one in her hand, one part of her curious where the gold bars would have come from and the other part of her scared to find out.

A scuffling noise came from the other side of the wall.

"Did you hear that?" Annaveta handed Jarena the gold bar. "Here put this back. We should get out of here. Someone might be coming."

They got out from under the table and Jarena double checked that the papers were put back in the boxes. They stared at each other as the sound of voices got louder through the wall.

"Let's get out of here. Now." Jarena picked up the lantern and the went to the stairs. Jarena went up first and moved the wooden board out of the way. Annaveta handed her the lantern and followed the rest of the way to the top. They quickly snuffed out the lantern and moved the wooden board back in place, making sure they put leaves and dirt on top of it.

They walked toward the tree line and crouched behind two of the thickest bushes there.

"That was close. We don't want to be caught in there," Jarena whispered. "But I'm so glad we found out more of what my papa has been trying to hide from me."

"I wish we could come back and go through the rest of those papers on the other table," Annaveta whispered back, hoping her friend would agree.

Without warning, the board that covered the hole to the entrance of the tunnel moved. Annaveta saw Misha's face pop up above the ground. He looked around as if trying to search for someone. Terrifying memories tossed around in her mind of Misha and all he had done to hurt both her and Alex. She couldn't believe he was out of prison.

How could anyone so evil be allowed to escape?

Annaveta held her breath. She didn't expect to see Misha's face. Would he discover them?

Soon he went below and moved the board back in place.

"That was a little scary. He's Papa's business partner. I don't like him. He's more than a little mean." Jarena breathed a sigh of relief. "I want to come back, but we'll have to wait a little while now. Looks like they know someone went through their stuff, so we'll have to back off for a little while until we can try again." Jarena grabbed her hands. "But we will come back again, I promise."

"Thanks, Jarena. Send me a note when you have a chance and let me know how you're doing and what's going on, okay?" Annaveta hugged her friend, her hands and legs still shaking from fear.

"I will. And don't worry, we'll come back here and get the answers you need." Jarena pulled away and started walking in the opposite direction toward her house. Annaveta waved one last time when she looked around and followed the tree line back to Pavel and the horses.

Her mind raced with a thousand unanswered questions.

Who did they sell all those guns and ammunition to? Was it the military? Where did they get the gold bars? Did they trade cash for gold? If Misha was working with Jarena's father, who else was involved in this Black Market scheme?

Annaveta needed more answers, but she knew from experience, they would be hard won.

Chapter Twenty

Alex had been back on board the *Imperatritsa Mariya* ship for six weeks and they had not seen any action. They pulled back into port at Sevastopol for new fittings for the ship and to work on some general repairs. Admiral Kolchak had told the sailors that the ship was bow-heavy, and they needed to reduce the amount of ammunition for the forward twelve inch guns and for the five inch guns. The Admiral said he hoped that would slow down the large amount of water that the ship pulled through her forward casemates.

Alex walked off the ship to go get more of the tools they needed to fix some minor repairs his men were working on. Suddenly he heard some of the sailors on the boat yell out.

"Fire!"

"Grab some water! Quickly!" He heard Midshipman Ignat-yev's voice call out to his sailors. The sound of buckets of water being poured in the ship's forward and the dissonant sound of many voices was cut short suddenly by a loud explosion. Alex ran across the deck to the railing to get a better look at the front of the ship. A few minutes later another explosion erupted near the torpedo compartment. Alex saw the front end of the ship go down.

Alex ran to find his lieutenant. They needed to help save the ship. Soon many of the men followed Alex back to the railing. They were shocked when they saw the *Imperatritsa Mariya* list to starboard and capsize a few minutes later. Alex couldn't believe his eyes as the last of the ship went under the sea.

The sailors beside him sprung into action. Alex went with them to take the small boats out to the where the ship was.

"If any men are still alive, we'll bring them back to shore," First Lieutenant Vasilyev called out from the lead life boat.

"What happened?" Alex looked at a sailor who had run off the ship just before Alex heard the explosions.

"As far as I could tell from what I overheard, Engineer-Mechanic Ignatyev and his men saw a fire and managed to flood the forward shell magazine with water before it exploded." The sailor's voice choked up as he spoke. "If they wouldn't have flooded the shell magazine, it would have meant a massive detonation. They put their lives on the line to save many others."

The men in the boat rowed toward the last place they had seen the ship.

"The Admiral said to just wait to see if someone resurfaces. Only the divers are to go below." Soon the divers went into the water. Alex watched the bubbles surface on the water and wondered if there would be any life found down there. He still couldn't believe how fast it all happened. They waited with the other two life boats ready to help any survivors who came to the top.

After what seemed like hours, all five divers came up, one

after the other. The lead diver, took his mouthpiece off and spoke.

"There were no survivors, sir." He spoke to the lieutenant in charge. "We searched through the compartments that we could get to, but all were flooded, and all the sailors we saw there were already dead."

The survivors stood still for many minutes in silence, lost in the memories of the sailors who had given their lives.

"Rest in peace, comrades." First Lieutenant Vasilyev's words seemed to echo through time to all those who had given their lives. After another moment, he picked up his oar. "We'll need to let the admiral know. He'll let us know what to do next."

Alex rowed with the rest of the sailors back to shore. The rest of the day was spent in a whirlwind. By the next day, they had the Navy beginning their investigation of what went wrong. For the next couple of weeks, they stayed at Sevastopol and waited for the new ship to arrive. One week before the expected arrival of the new ship, Lieutenant Levinson arrived back at port. Jude sent for him.

"Glad you're back sir." Alex saluted the lieutenant when he found him in the officers' building.

"At ease, sailor." Jude gave him a big smile and Alex relaxed. "I'm happy to be back and doing something productive. I'm finally doing well enough to do something other than lay around and sleep."

"Good to hear, sir." Alex looked at his head. The swelling was gone, along with the bandages. "Your head looks much better."

"Yes, Mama is a force to be reckoned with. When she wants something done—even something as simple as healing my body—it usually happens." Lieutenant Levinson winked at him. "But you know that already."

"I appreciate Mrs. Levinson, sir. She is a wise woman, and she's given me work at a good and honest wage." Alex's thoughts switched to Annaveta, but he didn't know if he should ask about her.

"Spit it out, Wagner. I can tell you want to ask me something. It wouldn't have anything to do with a certain red-haired cousin of mine, would it?"

Alex's neck and cheeks suddenly felt hot.

Jude laughed. "When I left, she seemed to be doing well. She's still busy helping at the shelter and keeps Papa's bodyguards working hard. But she has been extra careful ever since one of the bodyguards was found dead the day before I left."

"What? What happened?" Alex paced, worried more than ever about Annaveta.

"The police were still investigating when I left, so I don't know all the details." Jude stared at him. "Stop pacing already. You don't need to worry. My father will see to it that Annaveta is protected."

"Sorry, sir, but I can't help it. I worry about her." Alex stood still, hands behind his back, and met Jude's gaze.

"I'm sure she'll be fine. Now, how are your men taking the loss of their comrades?"

He was back to being Lieutenant Levinson once again.

"My men are taking it hard, sir. Especially the new sailors. It's not easy to lose friends."

"True." Jude nodded. "Looks like we'll be getting a new ship in a week. It will be good to sail with you again, Wagner."

"You too, sir." Alex saluted.

"Oh, I almost forgot. Annaveta asked me to give you this letter. She wrote it before she heard the news about her bodyguard, I think." Jude handed him the letter.

Alex's fingers closed around it, excited to read her words.

"Thank you, sir." Alex saluted one last time and walked out of the room. He could hear the echo of Lieutenant Levinson's laughter at his eagerness to read the letter as he walked down the hallway of the officer's building. He opened it as soon as he left the building.

Dear Alex,

I miss you. I got spoiled having you here for two weeks, and now that you're gone again, I miss our talks and playing detective together. Although, I must tell you, I am still somewhat of a spy. Jarena invited me to look at an underground tunnel she found on their estate. We found all kinds of black market stuff. Guns and ammunition, along with paperwork that proves they are making a tidy profit from each sale. However, it's what we found in the back corner of this tunnel-like cave that you might find interesting. Bars of gold. And lots of it. Where would this come from? And what does the BH plan to do with it?

I have many questions, and I plan on getting answers. But they are taking longer than I thought, mostly because my aunt and uncle are hovering and I can't go anywhere. It's weird that their hovering is endearing and annoying all at the same time. I know you'll be pleased to hear that.

David Saratov has been very helpful in all this. The families at the shelter are staying warm and well fed. Also, the big news is that Dassa is back with us again. The police found her freezing near the edge of the city limits of Odessa. All she'll say is that she got lost. We'll sort this mystery out yet.

Hope you are well. Stay safe and come back to us soon.

Yours, Annaveta.

Alex read through the letter again, relieved to know she was doing well. He just hoped and prayed she wasn't so brave that she would do something foolish to put her life at risk.

The *Shevstafi* dreadnought battleship was close to the same size as the *Imperatritsa Mariya*. He'd overheard one of the engineers say that this ship was a slightly enlarged version of the *Potemkin* and had an increase in armour as well as more guns. When the war began, this ship—along with other *Evstafi*-class ships—were the most modern ships and formed the core of the fleet for the first year, but then the newer dreadnoughts entered service. It took Alex about one week to figure out where everything was located and to help the men under his leadership learn the differences of this new ship from the last one. New sailors joined them, but for the rest of the crew it was a grim reminder of the two hundred twenty-eight sailors who had lost their lives.

Admiral Kolchak took the Black Sea fleet to search along the boarders of the Ottoman Empire. They chased away a few Turkish ships, but they were losing ground in the war. That seemed to be the talk that Alex heard among the crew as the year switched over to 1917. They read in the newspapers that the Russian army was beginning to crumble in the face of massive casualties and defeat on the battlefield. Talk of revolution spread through the ranks, and plans for a new offensive against the Ottoman Empire had to be forgotten.

It was late February when Admiral Kolchak delivered the news that the Russian revolution had overthrown the Tsar and replaced the Romanovs with a provisional government. He said for the time being, the provisional government wanted to stay in the war. Most of the sailors grew discouraged from the changes happening within Russia, and from the defeat of their fellow soldiers in the army.

For the next few months they continued their blockade of the Turks and continued to stop any progress the Turkish army made on land. By April, they began laying more mines, even using an expanded fleet of seaplane carriers to carry out some bombing attacks.

Alex agreed with Admiral Kolchak that the new way of warfare with seaplanes was really the way of the future. However, the raids and all the mine laying didn't seem to be making that much of a difference. The morale and the discipline of the Russian Black Sea Fleet started to cave in on itself.

Alex talked with his comrades in mess hall and overheard many of them talk about the Germans and Austro-Hungarians occupying Russia.

"We're worried we're going to lose this war," Moeshe said. "Just look at all the battles we're losing on land. And now the

Germans are beginning to occupy some of our ports."

"True, but don't forget that we've got the Allied Power on our side," Alex reminded Moeshe. The other sailors didn't seem encouraged by that.

"How come we never see them, if they are supposed to be on our side?" One sailor stared at his plate of the common Navy rations—beans with a side of bread. He looked up at Alex.

"I don't see them, either, but I've read the news and have overheard the officers talking." Alex lowered his voice. "In the newspapers, they are saying Russia's economy is crumbling. In St. Petersburg – or Petrograd – many are going without food. Not only that, but things are pretty tense now that the Tsar was no longer in power. With how unstable and poor our country is right now, it doesn't seem like we'll survive this war. And yet, some of the reporters have heard that our Allies are starting to gain more ground."

"All I know is I'm getting pretty tired of this war." This comment from another Sailor had most of the other men nodding their heads in agreement.

"Maybe this revolution that's begun in Petrograd is a good thing," Moeshe said. "It can't get much worse than how we have it now, can it?"

"I don't know, Moeshe. It might just get worse before it gets better." As Alex spoke, a sense of foreboding came over him. He wondered, not for the first time, what the future would bring for those fighting as well as those at home.

Chapter Twenty-One

Annaveta reread the same page through for the third time. She was distracted today.

Early that morning she began going through the large pile of files Aunt Esther had given her. Since Uncle Roman had developed a fever late last week, he hadn't been able to work. At first, Aunt Esther had talked with their clients, but then Uncle Roman took a turn for the worse. Since then, Aunt Esther had stayed by his bedside.

Annaveta had somehow managed to talk to a new client earlier that morning who had invented a new type of plow for the fields and wanted to see if there was interest in some of the other countries. She went through the list of things to ask, just like Uncle Roman and Aunt Esther had taught her. She was surprised her interview with the farmer had gone smoothly, and she had been able to negotiate a fair price for the shipping of the first two products and any future products. Business had slowed down considerably since the start of the war, but since she had begun talking with other Russians who wanted their products exported, she had suddenly gained a few more clients for her aunt and uncle.

It felt good to have some success in helping them in their

business. This past year had been quite hard on Uncle Roman as he lost a ship during the war, which had meant they had been operating at a loss. Annaveta was happy she could help them out for all they had done to help her since she arrived in Odessa.

Doing the paper work helped keep her mind busy so she didn't constantly worry about Alex. It had been too long since she last heard from him. He had written a letter right after cousin Jude had delivered her letter. It had been written just before they set sail again in the new Navy ship. Annaveta wished she could hear from him again, just to know that he was okay.

She also worried about the people at the shelter. This past week she hadn't seen any of them because she had been so busy helping her family. She hoped everything was all right. She had asked her aunt's driver to bring supplies to them last week and asked if he could check in on them to see how they were doing. He had come back saying each of them were helping the others in some kind of way, so Annaveta wasn't too worried about it.

However, her biggest fear was that someone else would be hurt at the shelter. Uncle Roman had spoken to the police about the bodyguard that was killed, but they said they hadn't been able to find any leads on who did it. Her uncle told the police who they suspected, but without proof, nothing could be done about it.

She finished up the last file just as there was a knock on the office door.

"Luncheon is served in the breakfast room, miss." Larson nodded to her.

"Thanks, Larson. Would you let Aunt Esther know I'll be right there?" Annaveta nodded to the butler and put away the completed files. She hurried to the small breakfast room, which sometimes doubled as a lunch room when there were only a few people.

"There you are, my dear." Aunt Esther waved for her to sit across from her at the small table. Annaveta walked up to her aunt and kissed her cheek before she sat down. She noticed the dark circles under her Aunt's eyes.

"How are you doing today?" She worried about her aunt and all the hours she spent nursing her sick husband. Annaveta had been helping to take care of uncle Roman in the afternoons while her aunt had rested.

"Tired and weary of this illness. I'm happy the nurse comes today to help with your uncle." Aunt Esther sighed in relief.

"I'm glad about that. You need a break already." Annaveta tasted Cook's borscht soup, savouring every mouthful. "So if the nurse is coming today to help with uncle's care, you won't mind if I go and see David will you? He said he had some new information about Zaydeh's property."

"I wonder what that is? It's always been a bit of a mystery to me. I remember papa saying the land they bought held some secrets." Aunt Esther eyes misted. "Then Papa and Mama were killed in the Pogrom of 1905, and I never knew what they were."

"David says he has learned more about that." Annaveta looked up to see her aunt frowning.

"What is it?"

"Be careful of David. He might be after more than just helping you."

"Aunt, you know Alex and I have an understanding. David and I are just friends. Nothing more." Annaveta's cheeks turned red at the insinuation. "Anyway, I really want to find out the reason why these papers are missing."

"You will, I'm confident of that. I didn't realize my sister raised such a strong, determined daughter. That makes me happy." Aunt Esther squeezed her hand.

"I don't feel strong or determined." Tears welled up in Annaveta's eyes and slipped down her cheeks. She wiped them away. "I feel weak. Many times I think I should quit trying anything because I usually get into big trouble somehow, but more importantly, those close to me always get hurt. I feel like I have this curse hanging over me." Annaveta wiped away more tears and thought of all the horrible events that had happened to her and those close to her in the past.

"Listen to me. Let me help you regain some sound judgment." Aunt Esther reached over and wiped the tears from Annaveta's cheeks. "The Torah says when you were made in your mother's womb, you were not cursed, but made beautiful."

Aunt Esther's voice was passionate, and Annaveta listened closely. She really wanted to believe all that her aunt was saying.

"I suppose I have been thinking too much of what went wrong in my past instead of focusing on the truth." Annaveta thought of her words and squeezed her aunt's hand. "Thank you."

Aunt Esther nodded, and they finished their luncheon together.

"I'll ask Larson to have the carriage brought around." Aunt Esther left to talk to Larson while Annaveta went to get her wrap.

A blast of cold air hit her when she walked outside toward the carriage. Annaveta wrung her fingers as she wondered what David had discovered.

As soon as the maid answered the door, she was ushered into the library. David was waiting for her when the maid showed her in.

"Ah, Annaveta. It's always good to see you." David took her right hand and kissed it. "Come, sit down. Would you like some tea?"

"Tea would be wonderful, thank you." Annaveta sat on the couch nearest the fireplace to get warm. David pulled the cord that summoned the maid into the library. After he ordered tea and biscuits, he joined her.

"I'm sure you're curious about what I've found." David rested his elbows on his knees and leaned over.

"I am." Annaveta tensed and waited.

"I found the name of the man who had the land before your Zaydeh owned it. Vassily Krupin. He had a wife and one son. The wife died a few years ago, but his son, Maxim Krupin, is in the Navy. We found paperwork at the land office, which said that he sold the land directly to Mr. Barinov."

"That can't be true. To claim that would be the same as saying my Zaydeh and Bubbeh never lived in that house on that land at all. Something's not right." Annaveta stood up and paced. They were missing something, but what could it be? The maid came in and put the tea tray on the small table.

"I know. It doesn't make sense at all." David frowned. "Come, sit. I'll pour some tea for both of us."

Annaveta stopped pacing and sat. She was tense with unanswered questions. What had gone wrong with the paperwork when her Grandpa had bought the land?

"Here's what I'll do." David's calm voice soothed her. "I'm going to ask my father's friend, who has worked with the judge before, to look at this document. Something is not right, but I can't put my finger on it. There's got to be some way to find answers to our questions."

"That would be a big help. The documents with my Zaydeh's name on them are still missing. I'm going to keep doing all I can to find them." Annaveta put down her tea cup and found her reticule. "I should be going. I wanted to go to the shelter. I have a lady coming to help teach the older girls and ladies to sew. That way they can take in sewing and earn their own money."

"You are like their guardian angel. And much like you're helping them, I'm going to help you today." He walked with her to the door and put on his coat as she did the same.

"I'm driving you to the shelter, and then I'll take you home." David opened the door for her. Somehow as she felt cool air hit her face, it didn't feel so cold anymore. The day was brighter because she had someone else on her side.

It didn't take long for them to get to the poorer section of

Odessa. Annaveta's heart melted when she saw little children without shoes and proper clothing and older women so thin, their ragged clothes hung on them like potato sacks.

"I'll come back for them after I drop you off at the house."

"Let's see what is happening here today." Annaveta frowned when she got out of David's motorcar. She opened the door to the shelter and headed inside, followed quickly by David. She was pleased to see the table already in use for drawing and cutting patterns to make new clothing. The seamstress was teaching one lady at a time how to sew. She had asked Aunt Esther if she could bring their sewing machine to the shelter for the women to use. She smiled watching Dassa's mama at the machine. It looked like she had taken a shine to sewing already.

David left the house for a few minutes and returned quickly with the women and children they had seen on the street. Soon they were content with some hot food. And Dave was pulled to the floor to play a game of marbles with two boys.

Annaveta watched some girls busy cleaning in the kitchen and other women doing laundry. They had even put up a few lines of strong string across the one corner of the room to hang their clothes to dry. One room on the main floor had been made into a sitting room. Right now, all it had was one rocking chair and an old worn out couch, but the nursing mom on the rocking chair and the children playing at her feet looked happy and content.

She made her way back to the kitchen and eating area. Annaveta studied the practical dresses that had already been sewn when she heard an anxious voice behind her.

"It's happy I am that you're here, Miss Travotsky." Mrs.

Chernoff struggled to get her words out clearly. Her hand shook as she held a note in her white-knuckled grip. She hurried up to Annaveta, her youngest son hanging onto her skirts. "One of the bodyguards just found this note stuck to the door of the house. I can't read, so I don't know what it says. But I'm worried just the same."

"Thank you, Mrs. Chernoff." Annaveta took her hand to try to calm her. "Please don't be worried. I know all of you have had to deal with some hard days already, but I want you to know we're doing everything we can to see that justice is done. We want you to be safe here." Annaveta squeezed her hand and smiled.

"I know. And I thank you for me and my children, Miss Travotsky." Mrs. Chernoff's own tears soon had her youngest son crying. When the mama went away to take care of her children, Annaveta walked over to the corner of the room to read the note.

This is your last warning. If you don't have a bill of sale ready for this house and land within three days, you'll be sorry. Failing will mean not just one person dies, but all who live in this house. Remember what happened to the bodyguard? We can make that happen again, and on a much larger scale.

Annaveta shook at the threat they made. She knew they meant it. They would stop at nothing to get this land. If she didn't get Uncle Roman to sign his name to a bill of sale, the Black Hand would kill all the innocent person living there. She didn't want their blood on her hands.

David came up behind her, and she handed him the note. "We don't have much time." Annaveta put her coat on.

"No, we don't. Let's get going." David followed to the motorcar. "We need a plan."

Annaveta nodded.

There had to be some way to save these people who had become her friends.

Chapter Twenty-Two

Alex hurried up the stairs to the upper deck.

Captain Levinson, who had just been promoted, told Alex to meet on the upper deck of the ship with Admiral Kolchak and a few others sailors. He wondered what the reason was for this special meeting. Maybe the Admiral had a plan to bring more order and peace between the sailors. All the sailors in the Black Sea Fleet had been fighting each other and feeling confused since they heard about the February Revolution in Petrograd. Alex had read in the newspaper that there had been industrial strikes and bread riots and mass demonstrations in which people fought with the police and the last loyal forces of the monarchy. He wasn't too surprised when the Provisional Government forced Tsar Nicholas II to abdicate the throne. A Provisional Government was formed made up of liberals and socialists who wanted to change how the country was run. Russia was going through changes, and he wondered what kind of trouble waited for them all.

He knocked on the door, and it was opened immediately by another sailor. He looked around the crowded landing. Admiral Kolchak and a few other officers sat around a round table while the other sailors stood to the side and against the walls to listen. Alex went to stand near Captain Levinson. Maybe he would help him understand what this was all about.

"Men, I have news." Admiral Kolchak stood, his voice ringing out firm and stoic. "I've been relieved of command of the Black Sea Fleet." Loud gasps were heard around the room at this unexpected announcement. "I've been asked by the Navel Minister Alexander Kerensky to give a report on conditions in the Navy to the Provisional Government. So I leave for Petrograd as soon as your new Admiral arrives in about three days time."

The Admiral gave the sailors time to digest that news before he continued. "The reason you were called to this meeting is because there are a few other fleets that need the special skills you have. I said there were a few sailors I could recommend who were skilled in the areas of engineering, reconnaissance, translation, and more. Some of you will be transferred to the *Aurora*, and some to other ships in the Baltic Fleet. When you leave here today, I will give each of you new orders. That is all." He looked around at the group of men and saluted. "You are dismissed."

The sailors filed out the door, each receiving new orders from the two sailors stationed at the door.

"Why are we being transferred?" Alex asked Captain Levinson who walked behind him.

"There is a bigger need where we're going than we have here in the Black Sea Fleet." Captain Levinson received his paper and kept walking.

"Sub Lieutenant Wagner." Alex announced his name and the sailor in front of him handed him his orders. "Admiral Kolchak has promoted you to Lieutenant Wagner." Alex saluted and left to walk down the hallway.

"Where are you headed?" Captain Levinson had been waiting for him and walked beside him down the stairs to the main deck.

"The *Aurora*. She's in Petrograd. It seems they need someone who can translate German for them." Alex sighed and looked at Jude. "Where are you going?"

"Same ship. They need help with reconnaissance during patrols, so I'll be in charge of that."

"A promotion, then. I'm not surprised, sir. Congratulations." Alex turned to head back to his station. "I'll see you on the train tomorrow morning." He saluted and walked to the gunnery to check on his men. His mind was filled with thoughts of what it would be like to be back in St. Petersburg—Petrograd. Now he would be even farther away from Annaveta. He knew he needed to write her a letter. He worried for her. He worried about his transfer to the *Aurora*, too.

He couldn't quite put his finger on what was wrong. All he knew was that he had a feeling something wasn't quite right.

Alex stepped off the train and went to pick up his bag. About half of the sailors had been transferred to either the *Aurora* or another ship located off the shores of Petrograd. He followed the other men as they boarded the tram to take them the rest of the way to the shipyard.

"Does it look different than when you were here last?" Captain Levinson sat beside him.

Alex looked out the window as the tram rumbled down the street toward the Naval base.

"The buildings are the same, a little older maybe, but seeing the lineups of mamas with children hungry desperate for food is not only different, it's appalling." Alex stared out the window of the slow moving motorcar, shaking his head at the many people dressed in rags wondering the streets. He remembered the pictures in the newspaper of the *February Revolution* which showed workers walking the streets holding picket signs that read, *Peace, bread and land!* and *End the war!* and *All power to the Soviet and All land to those who work it!* In another picture, armed workers escorted captured policemen to holding cells.

The people were tired of how Tsar Nicholas II ran the country and all they had to show for it was poor wages, very little food, and little to no freedom for the common workers. It was this pressure that caused the Provisional Government to force Tsar Nicholas II to abdicate the throne just a couple of months ago. The new government had taken over the leadership of the country. It was an alliance between liberals and socialists that most likely wouldn't last.

"The revolution has begun." Captain Levinson shook his head as he looked out the window and saw the chaos in the streets.

"I'm glad of it. Now maybe we'll have some fair wages." A sailor sitting behind them voiced his frustration. Other men agreed and began to talk about how Russia was in desperate need of change.

"This war needs to come to an end. I read that since Kerensky became Minister of War at the start of May, he's been at the front, speaking to each division, urging the soldiers to do their duty."

One sailor laughed. "I don't think his convincing speeches are going to have any lasting effect. Why just last week, I talked with the wife of a soldier friend who is serving at the front. He had written her that many men are just up and leaving their posts and going home. Many soldiers believe it's a hopeless war for Russia. They hoped the Provisional Government would put an end to Russia's part in the war, but when that didn't happen they decided to desert."

Alex listened to his comrades talk until they reached the port. They were each shown to their new quarters on the Aurora. He was glad his friends Moeshe Abramovitz and Boris Olenev had also been transferred to this ship. Moeshe's skill with numbers got him transferred there to help keep track of supplies, and Boris had become Quartermaster Olenev because of his skills with the larger guns.

Early the next morning, Alex sailed away on the *Aurora* on a routine mission to look for any enemy ships.

"Lieutenant Wagner." Senior Lieutenant Gapon, a short dark-haired older man with broad shoulders, stood in front of him as he entered the gunnery where he'd been assigned.

"Yes, sir." Alex saluted the senior officer and waited for his new orders.

"I see you were transferred to the *Aurora* for your skill at speaking and translating German." He eyed Alex under dark bushy eyebrows.

"Yes, sir." Alex wondered why he was asking him stuff that

was already written in his transfer papers.

"Well, most likely you won't be needing to translate German any time soon, sailor, unless we suddenly have a bunch of German prisoners. I see you were transferred here by Admiral Kolchak." At Alex's nod, the Senior Lieutenant continued. "I hear right at this moment, that traitor is making his right wing Bourgeoisie ideas known to the Provisional Government." He stepped closer to Alex and looked straight into his eyes. "A little friendly advice. If your political views match those of the former admiral, I'm afraid you will find service on board the *Aurora* quite unpleasant. Most of us here follow Lenin. We are Bolsheviks."

"Yes, sir." Alex spoke the expected words, but a surge of anger filled him at the strong arm tactic.

"Good, then. I'm glad we understand each other." Senior Lieutenant Gapon stepped back. "I've assigned fifteen new cadets to your command. Let's see what you can do with them."

"Yes, sir. Thank you, sir." Alex saluted and walked toward the gunnery where his new cadets were waiting. He shook away the nagging thoughts about the differences from his last post.

"Attention." One of the sailors called out as Alex entered the gunnery area in the aft of the ship.

"At ease, sailors. I'm looking forward to working with you all. I'm Lieutenant Wagner." Alex introduced himself to the new cadets who stood at attention in front of him. Most of them looked eager to learn their new duties, which made his job much easier. He spent the rest of the day teaching them.

This remained Alex's routine for the next few weeks while

the *Aurora* was at sea. The ship had been undergoing some major repairs. The cruiser *Aurora* had been part of the battle of Tsushima in 1905, and many times had suffered mechanical difficulties. At the start of the war, the *Aurora* operated in the Baltic Sea performing patrols, and then was sent to Petrograd for repairs. So this was the first time she'd been put out to sea since the repairs were completed. They didn't encounter any German ships while they were out patrolling the waterways near Petrograd.

Each day, as he ate in the mess hall with his fellow officers, Alex overheard talk about the revolution. Some sailors wanted the Provisional Government, believing it past time to bring law and order to the chaos of Russia.

"I think if Kerensky becomes Prime Minister, he will be able to bring order from this mess. To bring democracy and fair wages to our country." An older officer shared his views with the sailors his table.

Alex sat at the end of the table and listened to the ongoing arguments.

"You think Kerensky can actually help pull Russia out of this mess?" One sailor turned red and nearly choked on his food. "I think Lenin's Bolsheviks have it right. Lenin's *April Theses* outlines better changes for our country. The workers should control the banks. The land itself should be under the control of the the country. Production and distribution of land should be taken over by the workers. I think he has it right that the war can only be ended properly if capitalism itself is erased."

"What? That's the backbone of this country. The farms and businesses are what bring money and jobs to the workers here," another sailor pointed out.

"What jobs? Look around you. There are people everywhere in Petrograd and in other cities who wait in line for hours for one small loaf of bread to feed their large families. Most people don't make enough money in their jobs. They work hours that are way too long and live in freezing cold one-room apartments with many other people. I know because my mama and sisters live together in a small apartment. They work in the factory everyday while Grandma stays with their five children. And they are barely surviving. Something has to change."

"I agree. Something must be done to help people get back up on their feet. But I think there is a way to do that which will be positive for everyone." Alex needed to try to get his comrades to listen to reason. "I grew up near the Volga River and we worked hard to farm, but we were fairly poor until Pyotr Stolypin began his agricultural reforms in 1906. When he began to get rid of the commune system and made it easier for common peasants to own their own private land, it began to change people. They became more grounded and more profit-minded. There was less unrest. I read statistics just last year that thanks to Stolypin's farmers, Russia's grain exports were more than thirty percent of countries like Argentina, United States, and Canada combined." Alex took a deep breath. "That was what was done for farmers. He also worked on improving the lives of urban workers and increasing the power of local governments. Stolypin's ideas to 'wager on the strong and sober' seemed to have worked. What if something similar was done now to help workers and businessmen? I think society would begin to grow stable again."

"With the chaos that's going on right now, you think that would work? I think you're crazy." Seaman Lipatov spat his angry reply. "You are nothing more than a bourgeoisie capitalist, like Kerensky and his followers. What's needed right now is something radical, like what Lenin and his Bolsheviks are offering."

Alex didn't say anything in return. Unless he missed his guess, Lipatov was close allies with those sailors who were gaining more control over others on this ship. They were all big supporters of Lenin.

Two days later, Captain Eriksson returned the *Aurora* to port. Alex was treated with anger and rudeness because his opinions didn't match that of the Bolshevik sailors. As soon as each sailor left the ship for their barracks, Alex heard hurried footsteps behind him. He turned to see Captain Levinson.

"Sir." Alex stopped and saluted.

"At ease, sailor." Captain Levinson started walking and Alex continued beside him. "You know, all your talk in the mess hall might just get you in trouble yet."

"I was just speaking my mind, just like all the other sailors." Alex glanced at Jude and noted the troubled expression on his face.

"I know, and I agree with what you said." Jude stopped him before they reached the barracks and looked around as if concerned one of the men would overhear his words. "I've just heard talk from some of the officers. What you said made sense to some of the sailors. Now the officers who are Bolsheviks are talking about how they can get you to be silent."

"You mean they want to send me to some other Navy duty that's far away from the crew of the *Aurora?*" Alex shook his head frowning.

"Maybe. Maybe a lot worse. Some of the sailors they mean to

silence anyone who doesn't agree with their Bolshevik views. I'm just telling you to try to keep you safe. I'd get in trouble with my cousin if I didn't." Jude slapped him on the shoulder.

Alex settled into his barracks. His sleep that night and for the next few nights was restless as changes seemed come at him from all sides. The Provisional Government was in crisis. The Kadets had walked out of the meeting with the Menshiviks, and the Socialist revolutionaries and had threatened to breakup the government coalition. Most of the sailors, soldiers, guards and citizens wanted the war to be over, especially since two hundred thousand Russian soldiers had recently died in the Galician offensive. Alex heard the discontent from workers in the city and from the sailors around him.

"Some sailors and soldiers are going tonight to a secret anti-government conference." Moeshe entered his room and paced after another busy day. "Boris is going. He's tired of the unfair working conditions he grew up with and wants this war to be done. I want the war over, too, but I don't want to be part of whatever they're planning."

"I agree." Alex got up and looked out the window at the street below. "I don't have a good feeling about where this unrest and discontent is headed. All I know is that I don't want be in the middle of it. But it might be that we're already too late."

Alex and Moeshe both had the following day off, so they decided to go see more of Petrograd. After breakfast, they took one of the back streets to get to Petrograd's popular street, Nevsky Prospekt. As they got closer, Alex heard rapid footsteps and many voices shouting. He motioned for Moeshe to follow him up the side stairs of an old hotel so they could get a better idea of what was going on.

Alex looked down on the street at women and men—sailors, workers, and soldiers—demonstrating against the government and yelling for Russia to get out of the war. Their picket signs read, *All Power to the Soviets! End the War! Fair wages for workers!*

At least a hundred thousand revolutionaries swarmed the streets, all calling out for big changes in their country.

Troops came down the side streets to try to stop the demonstration. To his horror, Alex heard gun shots and saw hundreds of people either killed or wounded. The soldiers disarmed workers, disbanded the revolutionary military units, and began to arrest the insurgents. Alex's eyes grew wide and bile rose in his throat as he saw the blood of innocent people covering the streets.

"Let's get out of here." Alex turned to leave, and Moeshe followed him down the stairs and toward the back alley. They hurried back to the barracks where shouts of anger and disagreements between sailors were heard through the walls. Alex tried to not get involved in the heated arguments that followed.

The next two days were full of news. The printing plant of the political newspaper *Pravda* and the Bolshevik Central Committee headquarters had been destroyed. Minister of War Kerensky ordered the arrest of Lenin and other leading Bolsheviks. He accused them of starting the revolt with German financial backing. The news reported Lenin had successfully gone into hiding, but other leaders like Trotsky, Kamenev, and Lunacharsky were arrested. Days after that, Prime Minister Lvov resigned and Alexander Kerensky took his place. No longer did the Soviets have dual power with the Provisional Government. Peaceful resolution of the revolution now seemed impossible.

The next couple of months were spent helping with repairs to the *Aurora*, and in the middle of October, they took her out on the water. By then, the Russian Navy mirrored the unrest and revolutionary ideas happening in the city. The ship's master, Captain Eriksson, had to have the permission of the ship's committee to take the ship anywhere.

Alex wanted to be off this ship and out of Petrograd. It was high time for the war to be over. Germany began to advance and take over some cities in Russia, but with the unrest and food shortage, Alex expected a full scale revolution to soon commence.

In the mess hall later that day, things got out of hand.

"Alex, do you still insist that if the Bolsheviks take over the leadership of this country, it's a bad idea?" Boris Olenev sat across from him, slurping his meagre soup with the rye bread.

"I can't see how any long term good can come from a government who wants to take away each individual's freedoms. A government that insists that the farmer or the business owner doesn't have the right to own their own business—to contribute to creating more jobs and making a better life for their families—is taking away the only real incentive people have to work hard to build a better world for themselves and the people around them."

Boris frowned. "I don't agree. All I've seen is the backs of the poor people, like my mama, being broken by hard labour while the rich have gotten richer and the poor even poorer. That's not right." Boris had a lot of sailors at the table nodding in agreement at his words.

"That's not how it should be, you're right. When I think of

how hard some people have had it here, I start to understand why there have been lootings and crimes. It's pent up rage of over three hundred years finally coming to the surface. But there's a better way. My uncle Leo lives in Canada, and he's been able to take pride in owning his own land, and year after year it gets better for him. I think we could make similar changes here, instead of making all the land and factories and everything owned by the government." Alex spoke passionately because he believed it to be true.

"If you've got the guts and a little know how, you can take what you feel is owed you without waiting for it to be legal. My own papa didn't wait for a revolution to get paid twice on the same land." Maxim Krupin, a tall, broad shouldered sailor, sat beside Boris.

"What did he do?" A couple of sailors asked the same question.

"He had originally sold the land he owned in Odessa to a Jewish man back in 1898, and the papers were filed at the land office. Then he got involved in a secret society, and one of the members there wanted the land that he owned. So after the Pogrom in 1905, which killed the family in that house, much confusion ensued, during which he took the papers from the land office and switched the signatures to say the land was still in his name. Then a friend of his bought the land from my father again at double the price. My papa made a lot of money from that land." Maxim laughed at his own joke. "Isn't that brilliant?"

"Maybe it was a good deal for your papa, but it wasn't so great for the people who should have received payment for their land." Moeshe spoke up. He had a Jewish background and family in Odessa. Alex could tell by the set of his jaw that he wasn't impressed.

"Oh, get over it Sub Lieutenant Abramovitz." Maxim mocked the other sailor. "At least my papa was civil about it. No one got shot. No one looted stores. Names changed and he made some money. Sounds like a good idea to me."

"You would think that's a good idea." Another sailor clapped Maxim on the back and laughed.

One of the sailors on the ship's committee, Engineer Petty Officer Zlatogorsky, spoke up. "Alex, I like Maxim's idea better than yours. You are nothing more than an enemy to the people who work hard in this country. I hope your fair words keep you company when the Bolsheviks arrest you and lock you up in a lonely prison somewhere. Because if you keep talking like that, that's where you're headed."

Alex resumed eating his soup. As soon as he was done, he headed to his quarters. He wasn't on duty until the early morning, so he thought he would get a little sleep.

When he heard loud angry voices coming from the upper deck, he went to see what was happening. Captain Eriksson and the four sailors who formed the group that controlled what went on in the ship were arguing.

"We're ordered by Milvrekom to sail the *Aurora* up the Neva River to a mooring by the Nicholas Bridge." Acting Commodore Pavlovitch's angry tones could be heard loud and clear.

"Well, I'm unsure of the soundings in that part of the river. I fear if we go there, we'll ground the ship." Captain Ericsson's shaky voice matched his shaky hands. Alex could see their faces and body movements by the glow of the full moon. He wouldn't want to be in the captain's shoes.

"We've been ordered to go there, *Captain*. We'll lower some boats and get some sailors to row up the Neva river to take the soundings so we know the cruiser can make it to the bridge."

They didn't wait for the Captain to say anything, but instead called out for some sailors and lowered the boats.

It was only a few hours before they returned.

"According to the soundings we took, the *Aurora* is able to sail to Nicholas Bridge. So let's get going." Victorovich Belishev looked at Captain Ericsson.

"I don't think it's such a good idea to head there. So close to the Winter Palace and palace square. It might not be safe." The captain tugged on his naval cap.

"Listen, either you sail this ship to that bridge, or we will. It's up to you." Commissar Belishev leaned closer, his angry tones vibrating to where Alex stood in the shadows.

Alex wondered what they were up to. What was the real reason that they wanted the *Aurora* to be so close to the Winter Palace?

The Captain, visibly shaken, ordered the Cruiser to sail up the Neva. Alex knew he should probably go back to his barracks, but he was desperate to discover what these sailors were up to.

"How do we know when to fire?" Someone whispered, just loud enough for Alex to hear above the sound of water lapping against the side of the ship.

"We got the command earlier to surround the Winter Palace

along with the Red Guards and other Soviets. We're in this together, and this time we will win!" Alex heard the fervor in Belishev's voice as he spoke to the men gathered around him. "Men, it's time for all Bolsheviks across Russia to take back what's ours." The men whispered furiously among themselves.

Alex realized they were about to put their plan into motion. He needed to get out of here before they discovered him. Turning around, he saw the huge form of Maxim Krupin standing there, his arms folded across his chest.

Too late.

"Not so fast, Lieutenant Wagner. Not only are you a Jew lover, you're also a spy. It's time your commanding officers knew. Turn back around and start walking." Alex felt the hard, cold edge of steel push against his neck. He stumbled forward, fear causing beads of sweat to trickle down his forehead.

Alex looked around him as he was pushed forward. The four sailors who were part of the committee that ran the ship stood in front of him. He was surprised to see Lieutenant Levinson beside Captain Ericsson a little farther away. He must have been ordered to help the Captain navigate through these narrow waters.

"Look who I found, lurking on the stairs, spying on our conversation." Krupin stood behind him, the gun still pressed hard against his skin.

"Is that what you were doing, Wagner? Spying on us?" Petty Officer Zlatogorsky walked up to him, his hard gaze staring into his own. "I must say, I'm not surprised. All your fancy words of how we might change things in this country without the Soviets winning this revolution has lead me to believe you are nothing more than a bourgeoisie. An enemy of the people. What do you say, Commodore Pavlovitch, should we get rid of him?"

Sweat dripped into Alex's eyes. He saddened at the thought of never seeing or holding Annaveta again. He looked at his superiors, accepting his fate.

"We've arrived at a mooring by Nicholas Bridge, Commodore Pavlovitch." Lieutenant Levinson's firm and sure tones rang out like safety beacon in the dark night air.

"Thank you, Lieutenant Levinson." Commodore Pavlovitch looked the other men. "Looks like we're ready for action. Let's make our presence known at the Winter Palace." He smiled. "Take Sub Lieutenant Wagner down to the hold. We'll let him repent of his sins, and then when we're done here, we'll get rid of him."

Krupin held the gun to Alex's head and urged him down both sets of steep stairs until they got to the brig. He shoved Alex inside and locked the door behind him.

"Time for you to start repenting of your many sins, Wagner. You don't have much time left." Krupin strolled away whistling, flicking the keys in his right hand.

Alex sat in the cold dark room, surrounded by metal bars on every side.

I'm sitting here, waiting to die. I can't believe it's come down to this sad end. And all I did was stand up for what I believe, just like all the other soldiers were doing. But according to them, I'm on the wrong side. They see me as their enemy. So now I must die.

Alex's last prayer was that Annaveta would be taken care of.

Chapter Twenty-Three

Annaveta finished her supper at a frenzied pace.

"You seem to be in a hurry tonight." Uncle Roman sat at the table, finally feeling better after two weeks of illness. He eyed her as he took a sip of his wine.

She set her fork down and toyed with her glass.

Slow down. You have to try to look relaxed and unhurried. If you don't, they'll just ask more questions. And that's something you don't want.

"I'm just extra hungry tonight. Cook has outdone herself again." Annaveta took a sip of her water and smiled at her uncle. "I'm happy you're well enough to eat with us, Uncle Roman. You gave us all a scare."

"Well, I'm too ornery to be kept sick in bed for long." His cheeks still looked a little sunken. and his skin was a little too pale from the effects of pneumonia. She smiled at him, loving his spunk despite how sick he'd been. She glanced at Aunt Esther, whose dark circles under her eyes revealed all the stress and worry she had suffered.

The maids began clearing the plates. It seemed to take them forever.

I can't tell them that I'm going to Jarena's house, so I'll have to think of some other excuse to leave.

"Let's go to the parlour and enjoy the fireside before we settle in for night." Aunt Esther got up and moved to help Uncle Roman.

Annaveta walked on the other side of her uncle to help out. She knew her aunt expected her to stay with them when they had family time in the parlour. She hoped it wouldn't take too long. They sat and talked about what was going on with the war and the negative effects it had on their business. Uncle Roman was encouraged that Annaveta had managed to get a couple more clients. It wasn't long before they talked of their friends, and Annaveta yawned.

"If you're tired, dear, you don't need to entertain us. Go on to bed." At Aunt Esther words, Annaveta stood up, kissed them goodnight, and walked to her room. She hurried to change into her riding habit. At the last minute she put on a sweater to keep her warm against the cold wind. Since her room was on the ground floor and far away from her uncle and aunt's room, it was easy to slide out the window without being heard.

Jumping into the brush below, she hoped it didn't make too much sound. She hurried toward the far road, where David said he would wait for her. Together, she and David came up with a plan to search through older documents that had Annaveta's grandfather's name—Mordecai Goldstein—on them. David said this was necessary so they could prove the land Mr. Barinov claimed was his really belonged to the Goldstein family and their descendants. She finally saw David's Model-T and rushed over to him.

"Sorry. Dinner and parlour time took longer than usual." She slid into the seat while he waited.

After she had settled in, he turned to her. "I still don't think this is such a good idea, Annaveta. What if something happens to you? Alex and your aunt and uncle would never forgive me. I can't be responsible for that." David didn't move the car.

"Listen to me, David." She had to try to get him to see reason. "We only have three days to get the proof we need, so that Jarena's papa and anyone working with him won't be able to do anything with that land. I was already down in the tunnel once before, and I saw all the important documents they have there. I have a feeling they have what we're looking for. A couple nights ago I dreamt I had found the treasure I was looking for. So that feels like a confirmation that I'm on the right path."

He looked like he was relenting his first stance.

"And besides, you're coming with me, so what could possibly go wrong?"

"What, indeed?" He grimaced at her, cranked the car, and drove to the other side of Odessa where Jarena's papa had his estate. They left the car on the side of the road and walked up the hill a little ways toward the backside of the house. Annaveta knocked on the small door that led into the little sitting room Jarena had attached to her room.

"What took you so long?" Jarena had her hands on her hips and looked exasperated. "What's he doing here?"

"Jarena, I'd like you to meet David Saratov. A trusted friend."
Annaveta hoped she would understand. "David offered to
help us look for those papers."

"You can come along. My step-brother might not like it,
though. He's very possessive of that tunnel, as I recently
discovered." Jarena looked from David back to Annaveta and
sighed. "Yes, Anton said since I couldn't get in from outside,
he knew of another way to get down there and he'd show us.
He said we needed to do it when Papa and my step-mama
were away."

"We're ready. Lead the way." David smiled at Jarena, who
frowned. She didn't seem too sure about him. They followed
her to the library.

Annaveta's eyes adjusted to the dim lights and saw Anton
standing next to the fire, crutch under one arm, wine glass in
his free hand. He frowned when he saw David, but he quickly covered it with a smile.

"Ah, Annaveta, you are here at last. I thought maybe you
would have been too scared to venture down into the dark
again. And how nice that you brought a friend along."

Annaveta heard the impatience in Anton's tone, but too late
realized she should have said something about bringing David before she'd gone there. "I'd like you to meet David. He's
trusted friend, and he wanted to help." They would just have
to make the best of it.

"David." Anton shook his hand and looked David over briefly. Just as quickly, he changed the subject. "I think we should
have a little bit of tea to calm our nerves before we go down."
He pulled on the rope that brought the maid. It was late, but
she was still up. It didn't take long before she brought back a

tray of tea that Anton took from her.

Annaveta didn't really want to waste any more time, but tea wouldn't take long. She sat on the couch beside David and looked up at Jarena, who was on the couch opposite her. She seemed to be eyeing her stepbrother. Annaveta hoped they wouldn't fight before they went into the tunnel.

Anton handed each of them their tea. They talked about how dark and scary it was last time they were down there. Jarena said she had put together a bundle of what they needed to take with them.

"That was quite nice." Annaveta put her empty cup on the tray. "I think now I'm ready to see what we can discover."

She stood up and walked over to the door, where there was a big pile of lanterns, picks, and blankets. She picked up what she could carry. Soon everyone did the same, and Anton walked over to the wall of books that went from floor to ceiling and pulled out one of the books. One part of the wall slid open revealing a secret passage. Anton took a lit lantern into the passage. Jarena stepped through next. Then David, with Annaveta following close behind. They walked into a separate, secret room that had one small table, two chairs, and a large wooden cabinet with many drawers. Anton waved for them to follow him. He lifted a latch on the wall, revealing a much smaller door that led into a dark tunnel. They each had to crouch to make their way through.

"Suddenly I feel lightheaded and very tired," David spoke as he bent over to go into the tunnel. "I think I'll just stay here until I feel better, Annaveta."

"I'll stay with you until you're feeling better." Annaveta helped him back through the small opening toward the secret room.

"No. Just go. You need to find those papers. I'll be fine here." David sat on the chair and put his head on his arms on the table top.

"All right, if you're sure." Annaveta saw him yawn and close his eyes.

I wonder why David's suddenly not feeling well? I really didn't want to go down into the cave without him. But it can't be helped. I have to uncover more information.

With a backward glance at David, she saw he was sound asleep. She went back through the small door that opened to the tunnel and closed the door behind her. She hurried to catch up with Anton and Jarena. The tunnel was long, with just enough room to walk with her head down. The hard earth beneath her feet was lumpy in places. Stumbling, she put her hands on either side of her on the cold, packed earth. She worried about David.

Annaveta was terrified to walk in the darkness. She hoped it wouldn't take long to find those missing papers with the deed. She didn't want to be stuck down here in this dark dungeon for too long.

Her skin prickled.

Memories of Misha holding her captive in the dungeon of Baron Yakov's castle still haunted her. Her feelings of hurt and anger over what he had done to her and to Alex became fresher in this dark place. Three days of agony. The taunting, the sickness, the fear. Most of all, the fear. Misha made sure she got regular doses of fear and reminders of how worthless she was. It was on the third day in that dungeon, she had come to the end of herself. She wanted to die. That's when she'd seen the angel who reminded her that she was valuable and loved. He helped her escape so she could help Alex get away, too.

Her feet stumbled over a big lump of dirt, and she almost fell. Her fears were distracting her. There was no reason to be afraid. She was here with her good friend Jarena and her step-brother. It was just her own memories and vivid imagination that made her scared.

Control your fear, Annaveta. You'll be fine. You'll just find the papers and then you'll be out of this dark hole. Nothing to be afraid of.

"Annaveta, are you there?" Jarena's voice snapped her out of her gloomy memories. She hurried forward until she saw the light of the lantern. Not for the first time, she wished Alex wasn't on that ship. Now he was even farther away than ever. She would have to be brave. Alex would want that.

She finally reached the small hole that had been made into a larger room. Anton had the lantern on the table and was going through the large stacks of paper he saw there. Annaveta moved to where Jarena searched through documents at the table on the other side of the small room. She started going through the documents under the second table. Rubbing the back of her neck with one hand, she tried to soothe the tension in her muscles. It took a few minutes before she realized why she was so stressed. She overheard Anton muttering to himself.

"I can't believe they kept so much information from me. Next time Papa asks for my help, I'll demand to be in on all the details." Annaveta stiffened as Anton kept going on and on, muttering under his breath about what he didn't get. "I deserve to be given all the inheritance that's due me as his only son."

Annaveta saw the tendons standing out on his neck and shuddered. She worried about how closely aligned Anton was to his father's corrupt ways and what details he was getting from him. She was tired of all the violence she had seen.

Anton stopped his mutterings for a while, and Annaveta sighed in relief. She continued to look through the documents, carefully inspecting each one. It seemed like hours of searching without any positive clue to lead her to the papers she was looking for. So far the pages she read through had been about the Black Hand and the contacts they had in different countries, as well as how much money they made on each of the guns and ammunition they sold on the black market. She had found plenty of documentation to incriminate Jarena's father and his associates, but she still hadn't found the paperwork she needed about the land transactions, and her hope and energies were waning.

She reached for the last document-filled box and pulled out the first few pages. She began to read through land titles and deeds, but so far none of them were about property she was interested in. Annaveta looked at each page closely until she neared the end of the box. There she found what she was looking for—three pages of documentation on the land that was sold to one Mordecai Goldstein in 1899. It said that this land was sold for one thousand rubles to Mordecai Goldstein by Vassily Krupin. The next few pages under this one was a duplicate title deed of what was at the land office saying that Boris Barinov bought the land for ten thousand rubles. A note was attached to this title deed. *This is the official document at the Land Office in Odessa.*

"I found it." Annaveta gasped in surprise. She stood up and

showed Jarena the title deed. "See, it says here that it was my grandfather who bought this land way back in 1899." Annaveta pulled out more documents. She had Jarena looking at the documents over one shoulder and Anton over her other. "This other paper, the official document from the land office, doesn't have my grandfather's name on it at all."

"Here's something else." Annaveta read through a letter that had been behind the other land deed. "It's a letter signed in Vassily Krupin's signature. It says, *Now that you've paid for that Jew's land, at triple the normal price, it's yours. Here's the paperwork, in your name like you wanted. You'll need to figure out a way to replace the official document with Goldstein's name on the land title, with this new document that has your name at the Land office. In the end, it looks like we both got what we wanted. I got a lot of money to help me retire in luxury and you get the land and revenge on a people group whom you despise. It's been good doing business with you.*" Annaveta put the letter against her chest, and stared wide-eyed and unblinking at Jarena. "I just can't believe that they got away with this."

"How do you know that what is written on these papers is the true story?" Anton limped away from them and ran his hand through his hair. He nearly knocked the lantern off the table with his jerky movements.

"I don't know for sure. But David Saratov is a lawyer and with his help, along with a few other people, we will be able to either confirm or deny if these papers are authentic."

Anton stared at her and then looked off into space. Annaveta looked over at Jarena, whose smile had all but disappeared. She saw herself in the haunted, long-suffering look in her eyes. She knew first hand the betrayal of a father.

"I'm pleased for you, but sad and angry at my father. I'm

sorry he did this to your family." Jarena ran a shaky hand through her hair. "You are helping others, while he's taking from them. You deserve it." She straightened her shoulders. "I'm glad you've found these documents. Now the next step is to get someone to look at these land titles."

"Thank you Jarena. You're a good friend." Annaveta moved closer and squeezed her hand. "After all this time, I am so happy to have finally found some proof that my Grandfather owned this land." Annaveta nearly danced into the next room, the papers fluttering in her hand. The people at the home would be saved now. Because if it was true that Mr. Barinov bought her Zaydeh's land knowing that the legal land title was still in her grandfather's name, then more than likely he had done that with other properties as well. And with all the illegal activities stacked up against him, he would no longer pressure Uncle Roman to sell the house to them. Those people who lived at the shelter now would be free to stay without any worries of being evicted and having to leave. She twirled again in the small space and bumped into Anton. He hovered over her, a scowl on his face.

"I'll take those." He yanked the documents out of her hand and put them behind his back. "I just realized I can't let you keep them."

"What?" Annaveta backed away from him, shocked. "That's what I came here tonight to find. You said you would help me." She shook her head in confusion over Anton's change in attitude.

"I know I said that. But do you think I really meant it? No. I did it to lure you down here, so that you would find the papers. I know what your plan is. You want to get your grandfather's land back, and by doing so, you will ruin my father. And I can't let you do it." Anton's eyes hardened.

"Anton, what are you doing? Those are Annaveta's documents. Give them back." Jarena tried take them from her step-brother, but he pushed her so hard, she fell down to the cold, hardened earth.

"I don't understand." Annaveta stepped forward to help Jarena up from the ground. She heard some shuffling and turned around in time to see Anton reach for one of the guns on the shelf.

"I know you don't understand, so I'll explain. You see, with this injury, I'm no more than half a man. Which means I will need my inheritance to live the way I want, and for my future family. At first I thought that could be you, my dear Annaveta, but that's just not possible when you are the one person standing in the way of getting what I want. So I need to get rid of you. Since you surprised us by bringing your friend, I had to give him some drugged tea so he wouldn't come with us. I'll need to finish him off when I get back to the house." He searched for ammunition needed for the gun in his hand and looked over at Jarena, who had tears trickling down her cheeks. "Sorry, sister. I never meant for this situation to go so far, but Annaveta has given me no choice. I commend your loyalty to your friend, but in the end, your devotion to her will be the thing that takes away your life." He started to load the ammunition.

Annaveta looked around the dark, cold cell to see if there was any way they could get out of this. She saw a metal canister labeled Tear Gas. She snatched it and threw it so it landed right beside him, then she covered her face with her sleeve. Anton stumbled in the muted light of the underground tunnel, blinded by the gas.

"You shouldn't have done that, you little savage. You'll regret it." Anton started shooting at the wall, his aim missing both her and Jarena.

Annaveta grabbed Jarena's arm to pull her away from the falling shelves, but one of them fell on top of her friend.

Anton kept shooting at them. One of the bullets hit Annaveta in the arm. She managed to hide behind a bunch of large metal sheets that had been behind the shelf. The rocks and ground from the wall seemed to hold most of the sheets up, but a couple of them fell on her legs, bruising them. Just as quick as the shooting started, it stopped. She heard the click of the empty gun and realized Anton had run out of bullets.

She heard him shuffling around, hindered by his limp leg.

I know he's coming to see if I'm dead. I want to get out of here, but I can't move without yelling out in pain.

She closed her eyes and waited for the inevitable.

Without warning, a loud thump and what sounded like a gunshot sounded at the place where the tunnel connected to the house.

"Looks like there's more intruders I need to take care of. If you both are still alive, just know I wish you a long, slow death." Anton shuffled away, taking the big lantern with him. The sounds of his departure echoed for several minutes, bouncing off the earthen walls and returning to her time and again. Each time she thought it was safe to move, she heard another noise and held herself still.

Finally, the tunnel was silent. Annaveta opened her eyes after his footsteps had faded into the distance. They were still alive. She let go of the breath she'd been holding.

Sharp pain cut between her eyes and in the arm that had been shot. Screwing her eyes shut, she braced herself against the jumble of emotions that plagued her—fear, anger, and physical pain. She will herself to move, choosing to focus instead on how to survive. With her good arm, she managed to pull her legs out from under the metal. Once her legs were free, she wrapped her arm as best she could to help stop the bleeding. The silence that followed was eerie.

"Jarena, can you hear me?" Annaveta whispered, but it sounded loud as her voice echoed off the walls. She dragged herself using her one good arm over the cold dirt and tried to find her way in the dark. Another small lantern had been hidden against the wall behind the shelf. She groped her way to it. A matchbook had sat not far from the lantern, so she searched until she found it. She took a match and pulled it against the zipper she had on her riding habit. It took about ten tries with her good arm to get it to light. She managed to get the lantern lit and then sat for a minute, catching her breath.

A soft moan emerged from where Jarena lay. Annaveta got up and cleared the debris with her one healthy limb. As soon as Jarena was freed, Annaveta checked her pulse. It was soft but steady, and Annaveta sighed in relief. Jarena was all right. She leaned against the dirt wall. What if no one found out they were here? They would more than likely die there.

Two friends had been hurt today. Because of her. No matter how she tried to do what was right and help others, she still managed to be the reason people got hurt. She remembered the conversation she had a few days ago with Aunt Esther.

You are not a curse to others, but a blessing. You were made beautiful. Once you accept the truth, you'll find your greatest treasure.

It was hard to believe those words while she sat gazing at the gray earth around her. She looked at the chaos that covered the floor. Guns and ammunition that once sat on shelves littered the hard packed ground.

It feels like I'm sitting in a ready-made tomb.

She looked at the wall Anton had shot, and she was surprised to see a different colour. She picked up the lantern and brought it close to the wall. Yellow glittered in the light. She put her finger on it and knew what it was.

It's gold. That's where all the gold bars must have come from.

Annaveta remember sitting on Zaydeh's lap as a little girl as he told her stories. Once he told her that beneath their house was a secret treasure. "Someday you might discover it, if you dig deep enough. In the same way, we search for hidden treasure inside of ourselves, and if we don't give up, we find the gold that was in us all along. Nothing is worth as much as the treasure inside of you, little one."

Annaveta slid to the dirt floor and wept. She was currently trapped inside this dirt grave, but something inside of her had shifted.

Chapter Twenty-Four

Alex cringed at the deafening boom of the canon exploding from the *Aurora's* forecastle guns.

Captain Levinson walked into the hold right after the heart-stopping noise. Alex looked behind the captain to see if someone had followed him.

"You sure got yourself into a bad spot this time, Wagner. They are serious about getting rid of you. They see you as a traitor to their cause." Captain Levinson stood in front of his cell, hands balled on his hips.

"I know. I was trying to get them to see things from another angle, but that failed." Alex shook his head and stood up. He walked to where Jude stood and put his hands on the bars, his eyes misty. "Would you write letters to my family? And tell Annaveta I love her. Tell her to have a good life for both of us." Alex closed his eyes and took a big breath. "Will you?"

"You'll be able to tell my fair cousin yourself. It turns out that I don't agree with their plans for you. Besides that, I owe you one." Jude put a key into the lock and jiggled it.

The prison door swung open. Alex gaped.

Jude grimaced. "Hurry, we don't have much time. We have to get out of here now, while everyone else is busy making bad decisions."

They hurried to the top level of the ship, trying to keep themselves from being seen or heard. They made their way to the back of the ship without anyone noticing. Many of the sailors were at the front of the ship, cheering loudly about the success of their attack against the Provisional Government in the Winter Palace.

Jude tied a rope to a hook in the floorboard of the ship. "Go down the side and start swimming for shore. I'll follow."

Alex hurried down the side, and Captain Levinson followed close behind. They slipped into the cold Neva River and started swimming to the shore.

As soon as they reached the shoreline, Alex overheard someone yell out that the prisoner had escaped.

Jude looked at him, and they both ran in the direction of Petrograd. It seemed hours before they got there. Alex and Jude ran to the train station. They hid in the shadows of two buildings, waiting for an opportunity to jump on one of the empty cargo bays of the train. Soon they saw that all the men had left. The train blew the whistle and chugged slowly forward. As soon as it had a little more speed, they came out of their hiding place and ran toward the train. They were slowed down a little by their wet clothes, but they were able to catch up to it.

"Halt! You can't go on there." One of the men in charge yelled after them, but he was too late. Alex clambered aboard first, and then he helped Jude.

"Well, at least we're out of there." Alex tried to slow his breathing and looked at Jude, who was smiling. "What's so funny?"

"We lost those guys from the Navy and the two old guys running after us from the shipyard. Their red faces were a sight to behold." Jude laughed and slid down the side wall to sit on the floor. Alex smiled at the picture they had made. He thought of the couple of men from the *Aurora* who had chased them into Petrograd. They had zigzagged down a few different streets to lose them before they went to the train. It must have worked, because it seemed like they lost them.

"Do you think the Navy will try to track us beyond Petrograd?" Alex asked.

"Of course." Jude took off his jacket, bunched it up, and lay down. "That's why we'll have to catch a bunch of different trains before we sneak into Odessa. We'll try to lose them. Get some sleep, you're going to need it."

"Good idea." Alex lay down on the hard plank floor, the rumble of the train lulling him into a restless sleep.

"We'll need to jump off before the train reaches the station." Alex shook Jude so he woke up fully. "It's slowing down toward Odessa now."

After five days of hopping trains and trying to catch what sleep he could, Alex was glad to finally be there. He walked over to the sliding door, happy to see the familiar lush farmland. Jude walked up and leaned against the corner of the door.

"It's time." Jude jumped and Alex went right after him, rolling into the wet grass in the ditch. They got up and started walking in the direction of Jude's parents' place.

"I can't wait to eat some of Cook's fresh bread with jam again." Jude hurried his pace and Alex had to practically run to keep up. The morning sun was just peeking over the horizon, and workers took advantage of the sliver of light to gather the last of the crops before winter set it.

Soon Alex and Jude trudged up the hill toward the Levinson estate.

"We should sneak in through the stables." They walked through the trees until they were close to the stables. The smell of hay and the snorting and whinnying of horses had never felt so good.

Jude watched the groom finish giving the horses their morning feed. "Hey, Pavel."

The groom jumped and dropped his pail.

"Ah, Captain Levinson." Pavel picked up the pail and put it over by the feed. "You scared me. I didn't know you were coming home."

"We didn't, either. It was a sudden decision." Jude pulled his hand through his hair. "Could you go to the house and see if my papa and mama are awake yet. If they are, can you ask them to come to the stables to talk to us? And I'd consider it a favor if you didn't tell anyone else we're here just yet."

"Oh, they are awake, sir. Their niece didn't come to breakfast and they don't know where she is." Pavel spoke and started walking toward the open barn door.

"What? What happened to Annaveta?" Alex grabbed the groom's shoulders as fear coursed through his body.

"They don't know, sir. She just wasn't there this morning." Pavel started to move toward the door.

"I've changed my mind, Pavel. Jude, I'm heading to the house. I've got to find out what's happened."

Jude handed Alex an oversized barn coat. "At least put this over you and put hood on. And go in through the back kitchen door in case Mama has called the police already." Jude looked exasperated with him, but Alex didn't care. He had to find out what was going on.

He hurried to the back door and let himself in. He didn't think anyone had seen him. The smell of fresh bread caused his stomach to growl.

"Mr. Wagner, you're here." Cook looked at him, eyebrows raised. Her hands were full of flour as she kneaded another batch of dough. "Here. Take some bread." She gestured to a fresh loaf.

"Thanks, Cook." He was so worried, he didn't think he could take a bite. He went through the kitchen doors to the breakfast room. No one was there. He heard voices in the parlour, so he waited and listened.

"I'm going to go talk to the police. I don't know what else to do." Roman's deep voice sounded rough with worry.

"Yes, that would be best. Check also with the women at the

shelter to see if they've seen her." Esther's voice cracked.

Alex knew she was doing her best to hold back tears. He didn't hear anyone else in the room with them, so he walked toward the sound of their voices. Alex was about to speak, when he heard the sound of hurried footsteps.

Jude came from behind him and entered the room first.

"Papa. Mama." Jude walked up to them and hugged them both. "We'll find her."

"Jude. What are you doing home?" Esther Levinson hugged her son and then paused as she saw Alex. "And Alex. What has happened that you are both home?"

Jude explained about their escape from the Navy and how it was important they didn't let the police or anyone else know of their whereabouts until they decided on a plan.

"Of course." Esther sucked in a rough-edged gasp, her wide-eyed gaze flittering back and forth between them. "We can't find Annaveta. When she didn't come to breakfast, I checked her room. It was empty. Her bed looked like it hadn't even been slept in."

"I'll help you find her." Alex offered.

"But you shouldn't be seen." Esther remarked. "We can get the police to check."

"I'll wear a disguise so no one will even recognize me." Alex assured them both. "Besides I know of a couple of places she might be that the police won't even think to check."

More tears trickled down Esther Levinson's cheeks. Roman

put his arm around her shoulders.

"I'll do everything I can to bring her home. I promise." Alex assured her. He walked to the closet to put on a different jacket and a fedora hat.

Roman asked Larson to order the carriage for them. "I'm going to go talk to the police. But I can ask the driver to take you wherever you need to go."

"Thank you, sir." Alex pulled his fedora low on his forehead and felt like his disguise was complete.

"I'm coming with you." Jude pulled on one of Roman's coats and a hat. Soon they were off. "So where are we going first?"

"If you could get the driver to bring us by David Saratov's home, that would be helpful." Roman nodded and soon they had pulled up to his house. Jude and Alex climbed the stairs to the Saratov home. Exhaustion weighed down Alex's every step. He hoped David knew where Annaveta was. He had asked him to help take care of her while he was gone. Did he slack off in his duty?

A uniformed maid answered the door at his knock.

"I'd like to speak with David Saratov, please."

"Wait here, please." The maid disappeared and was back a few minutes later.

"Judge Saratov would like to see you in the library." Alex wondered why he was being asked to talk to David's father. The maid led them to the library.

"Got away from the Navy, did you? Well, it couldn't be better timing." He waved his hand in the direction of the two armchairs that sat across from him. "My son is missing. And I need your help to find him." The old man peered across a layer of cigar smoke to stare at the two of them.

"David is missing, too?" Alex stood up and started pacing. So David had done as he asked.

"What do you mean 'missing, too?' Who else has disappeared?" The judged barked out the words and took another smoke. "And sit down young man. You're making me nervous with all your pacing."

"Sorry, sir." Alex grimaced at Jude and sat down again across from David's father.

"My cousin, Annaveta, is also missing, Judge. My parents are very worried."

"And so they should be." The old man grunted. "So what are you going to do?"

"We'll keep looking until we find them, sir." Alex squirmed a little under Judge Saratov's fierce scrutiny.

"So you will." The older man stood. "It looks like you've got work to do." He pulled the cord that called the maid. "If someone gives you any trouble, just send them to me."

"Thank you, sir." Alex shook the Judge's hand. They followed the maid to the door and walked out into the brisk early morning.

"Let's go to the shelter," Alex said. "If they aren't there, then I have another idea of where to look."

Jude raised his arm to hire a hackney driver and coach. They got in and soon they were at the shelter.

"This old building is what my father bought a long time ago." Jude's eyes glanced over the dilapidated house as they got out of the carriage. "Annaveta uses this run down house as a shelter. But for whom?"

"She's been helping mostly women and children who have fallen on dire straights because of the war. Last I heard, eight families live here." Alex knocked on the door and the body-guard opened it. Recognizing Alex and Jude, he went back to his post.

Alex went to each one of the adults and asked if they had seen Annaveta. Most of them said it had been at least three days since they'd last seen her. He gave them each a description of David and asked if he had been here.

"Oh, yes, he was with her last time they came," Mrs. Golov said. "Very nice he was, playing with little Tommy here. But I couldn't tell you what has happened. We will pray for them that they will be all right."

"Thank you, Mrs. Golov." Alex tipped his hat and he and Jude left. "There's one other place we need to go. But we'll walk there."

"We're going tromping in the woods, are we?" Jude pulled his jacket closer and his hat down. Alex grinned at his friend's obvious discomfort.

"Maybe a little. Don't worry. We'll get where we're going soon enough." They had crossed the street, and were walking past many of the poorest houses in this part of Odessa. Suddenly, Alex had a prickling sensation that made his hair stand up on the back of his neck. "Don't look behind you, but I think we're being followed. Let's turn right here and walk between these two houses."

Jude led the way into the dark shadows of the two houses and they kept walking until they could turn again.

"I took one of Papa's handguns, just in case we ran into trouble." Jude said as they stopped and moved against the house. He peeked his head quickly around the corner. "The motorcar is still parked there, but it's now empty."

"They're on foot. See those trees over there? Let's get to them as quick as we can." Alex whispered, then he ran, with Jude at his heels, the ten yards to the trees. They stopped and hid themselves behind some thick brush. Soon two men appeared.

Monsieur Arnaud and Misha!

Of course. It all began to make sense. They were in business together with Boris Barinov, the other Black Hand member in these parts. He knew Misha wouldn't give up. He was desperate to get back at both him and Annaveta.

"Where did they go?" Monsieur Arnaud's gruff voice brought back to mind the pudgy overseer attacking Annaveta at the Shremetev Estate. He had meant to violate her innocence. She had been so scared. Alex had been so glad to pull Arnaud off Annaveta and save her. That was the day he fell in love with her.

He had to find her. What if she was sick or something worse had happened to her?

"If you would have moved faster out of the motorcar, we

could have caught up to them. Now I don't know where they went." Misha yelled at his cousin. "Let's go up the street a bit farther and see if they came back through the other houses there."

As soon as the two men were out of sight, Alex waved his arm at Jude.

"Let's go, before they decide to circle back." Alex and Jude hurried through the thicket, jumping over fallen trees and moving aside dead branches that blocked their way. Alex remembered Annaveta telling him about the secret tunnel that Jarena had shown her on her yard. She told him there were incredible secrets down there. She didn't want to write what she'd found in a letter that might be read by someone else, but she had written she wished he could come back to her soon so she could tell him everything.

Alex saw the cluster of trees that stood apart from the rest of the trees along the edge of the property, and he knew it was the place that Annaveta had described.

"That's it. That's where we need to go. I don't hear anything, but they might be down there." Alex looked around to see if they were being followed. He didn't see or hear anyone. "Let's go quickly." Alex hurried toward the bush. He looked down and saw dirt. It confused him. He thought that was where the entrance was. He bent down and felt around in the dirt. His hands brushed against something hard. It was a large, flat piece of wood. He pushed on it and moved it until it completely uncovered a large hole. A ladder descended into the blackness. He didn't want to call down, for fear of being overheard.

"I'm going down. I need to see for myself." Alex told Jude, who had crouched down. He held the gun and watched for any movement in the trees.

Jude followed him. "I don't see anyone around here. Maybe we lost them. I'll close the trap-door."

Alex entered the deep cave. He heard Jude behind him and soon the room turned dark. After his eyes adjusted, he noticed a flicker of light coming from across the room on the floor. Alex tripped over big mounds of dirt, pieces of wood, and guns until he saw Annaveta lying on the ground. Her eyes were closed, and her face was still and pale under the glow of the lantern.

"Annaveta." Alex breathed out her name like a prayer and hurried over to her. His fingers shook as he touched the side of her neck, feeling for a pulse. Feeling the soft, steady rhythm of blood pulsing through her veins, he breathed a sigh of relief.

"Annaveta. It's me, Alex. Can you hear me?" Alex whispered a little louder as his fingers stroked through her hair. Her eyelids fluttered open.

"Alex?" She tried to sit up, but faltered when her arm collapsed beneath her weight. Alex helped her sit up and saw her wince when he touched her arm. Then he turned toward moaning coming from the other side of the room.

"I heard it, too," Jude said and moved toward the sound. Knowing Jude would find out where the moaning was coming from, Alex moved closer to Annaveta.

"What happened to you?" Alex saw a fresh flow of blood come through a bandage already stained with dried blood. "Who did this?"

"Jarena's step brother, Anton." Annaveta's eyes opened wide. "Jarena. We need to help her. Is she all right?"

"I don't know. Jude is helping her right now." Alex kept one arm around Annaveta, and with the other hand he moved the lantern closer to Jude so he could see.

"Annaveta?" Alex heard a weak voice calling from across the room.

"I'm here, Jarena. Alex and my cousin have come to save us."

Alex stood and picked her up.

"Yes, we have, and we need to hurry out of here." Alex carried her toward the ladder. "Jude, you have Jarena?"

"Yes. I'm right behind you." Jude's heavy footsteps followed him.

"No, wait. We must find David." Annaveta's urgent whisper stopped him before he climbed up the ladder.

"Where is he?" Alex waited for Annaveta to catch her breath.

"He's back through the tunnel in the secret room behind the Library. Anton drugged his tea."

Alex realized what she was saying and realized they needed to go back.

"Is this who you're looking for?" A low, menacing voice spoke from behind him. Alex turned around slowly and saw Misha holding a gun to David's head.

Beside him Annaveta sucked in a deep breath.

"Annaveta, you look pale. What, you didn't think you'd see me again?" Misha taunted from his place of control. A glint of steel glittered in his hand.

Every muscle in Alex's body shook. His brain twisted from numb to panic. He could smell his own fear. He felt like a dog being stalked by a coyote, knowing death was on his heels.

Chapter Twenty-Five

"Why, Misha? What do you want from me? From all of us?" Annaveta moved out of Alex's arms and stood on shaky legs.

"Annaveta, you more than anyone should know what I want." Misha looked at her long and hard. His eyes looked glassy, even in the dim lamplight. "But since it looks like I can't have what I really want, I'll settle for making you all suffer just like I have. I want to see to it that you don't get this land. Instead, I'll see to it that you're buried here along with all your friends. A fitting end, don't you think?"

"Misha, just take me and let everyone else go. I'm the one you really want." Annaveta waved her hands at everyone standing around her. "They've done nothing to you. Just let them go."

His eyes seemed to waver at the offer. "No. I won't let you change my mind, as tempting as the offer is." He shook his head and gripped the gun even tighter. "There have already been too many mistakes made this time around, with Anton deciding to take everything into his own hands and my dear cousin unable to follow orders." His sarcastic words were directed at Monsieur Arnaud who stood a little behind David. Monsieur Arnaud's pudgy cheeks puffed out, and he sputtered.

"So now I have a new plan." Misha looked at them all individually with contempt, his calm tones a bold contrast to the sneer marring his features. "Everyone move over to this side of the room." When no one moved, he jabbed the cold steel of the gun into the back of David's head. Annaveta saw David wince, and she started toward the other side of the wall to where Misha pointed.

"That's better." Misha shoved David toward Alex. David stumbled forward, and Alex caught him before he fell. Misha grabbed Jude's gun from his waistband. Jude still held Jarena's wounded body and couldn't resist. "There. Now that everyone is where I want them, here's what's going to happen. My cousin and I are going to go up the ladder, and you are all going to stay here. If you move before we get to the top, I will shoot you. If you stay where you are, you will have time to say your last prayers." Misha pulled a rounded, pineapple-shaped cone out of his pocket. "I'm quite proud that I was able to get one of these new Mills bomb grenades from one of my contacts in England. Today will be the first time I test it and see if I got my money's worth." His loud laugh echoed off the walls as he backed up toward the ladder, keeping the gun fixed on them. "Of course, we won't be staying to die with you. You understand."

Annaveta watched as Monsieur Arnaud climbed the ladder first, pushing back the flat stone that covered the hole. Misha started up the ladder, still training the gun on the five of them.

Chills ran up her spine at the certainty of their death. She grabbed Alex's hand. She didn't know what they could do. All the guns kept in this cave were at least ten feet away from them. If one of the them ran to get one, it would mean certain death. She saw Alex looking around to find some way of escape.

Annaveta saw the shine of moisture on David's forehead, saw Jude's face was pale and tense. No one knew how to get out of this. They were all about to die.

"Say your prayers." Misha pulled the pin out of the grenade and threw it down the hole. Annaveta was pushed back along with Jarena. To Annaveta it seemed like everything happened in slow motion after that. The grenade launched through the air. Alex took off his jacket to try to cover the grenade as he had seen a sailor do with his helmet on their last mission. The jacket missed it's intended target. Jude and David each tried to pick up a gun. Through all the chaos around her, Annaveta watched an angel fly over them, snatch the grenade mid-air, and blow on it. As suddenly as the angel came, it was gone, and the grenade landed on the ground. They stood there, each of them quivering, waiting for the bomb to explode. But nothing happened. After waiting for a few more minutes, Alex asked Jude for his jacket, and he threw it over top of the grenade. Still nothing happened.

"It looks like it might have been a faulty grenade. For which we're deeply grateful." Alex looked around at everyone. They were all starting to breath normally again.

"We're saved." Annaveta let out the breath she'd been holding. She knew the grenade hadn't been faulty. She'd seen the angel save them all.

"Hurry, let's move over to this side of the cave in case Misha and his cousin decide to come back." David waved his arm for them to follow him. "We don't know if they're still up there listening. If they're going to come back and check on us. If that grenade will still explode."

Jude walked over to peer up through the hole that led to the surface. "I don't see or hear anyone." He whispered. "We probably just need to wait a few more minutes before we go up."

"What if this explodes? We need to get out of here." Jarena finally spoke. She sat shivering on a mound of dirt, both hands rubbing her head.

"Didn't you see it?" Annaveta looked at Jarena and noticed everyone listening intently.

"See what?" Alex frowned.

"The angel." She saw the disbelief in their faces. She sighed and explained. "I saw the angel suddenly appear in the room. He was going as fast as the grenade. He put the grenade into his hands, blew on it, and let it fall to the ground. Then he disappeared. You didn't see that?"

"No. You might have been seeing things because of all the stress, cousin." Jude walked toward the opening to see if Misha and his cousin were actually gone.

Annaveta saw the others shrug and nod as if agreeing with Jude.

"I believe you, Annaveta. And I'm grateful we're all okay." Alex hugged her gently. "I'm happy that's over."

Annaveta decided she would just need to come to grips with the fact that they didn't believe her and let it go. After all that had happened, she was just grateful to be alive.

"It's time we all got ourselves out of here and above ground." David wiped his forehead with his arm. "I am definitely ready to get out of here."

"Jarena, let me help you." Annaveta walked over to Jarena who was shivering.

"I'm just a little dizzy from the blow to my head, I think." She stood up and stumbled as she walked forward.

"We'll go up the ladder together." Annaveta held onto her friend from behind.

"I'm going above ground to hunt down Misha and his cousin, to bring them to justice. Are you men with me?" Alex picked up one of the many guns that lay scattered on the ground, and David and Jude followed suit.

Alex peered through the opening. "All clear."

They each climbed to the top of the ground, grateful for the fresh air and sun once again. Then shouting came from the Barinov Estate.

"David, do you mind taking Annaveta and Jarena to the hospital and summoning the police?" Alex hurriedly kissed Annaveta on the forehead. "Jude and I are going to see what we can do to catch these guys."

Annaveta limped toward the trees with David and Jarena, watching Alex and Jude as they zigzagged along the tree line toward the Barinov Estate.

Gunshots echoed across the estate. Annaveta stopped in her tracks.

"I don't see them. David?" Fear clogged the flow of air in her throat until she felt like she could hardly breathe.

"Stay here. I'll go check on Alex and Jude." David hurried away while Annaveta took Jarena to a fallen tree low enough to sit on. She waited impatiently to hear news, worrying endlessly over what might have happened to Alex and Jude.

"They are smart and strong. They'll be okay." Jarena whispered. "Annaveta, I'm so sorry about what happened in that cave last night and this morning. I still can't believe it. I was so sure Anton wanted to help us. But then he turned on us. I mean, I've always known he was greedy, but I never realized he was so desperate that he would stoop to murder, too. You don't know how sorry I am about that."

"Jarena. It's not your fault. You couldn't have known. So stop feeling guilty." Annaveta hugged her friend. "I, too, feel betrayed that Anton stole the documents to the land title. But I'm reminded of what my mama used to tell me. 'Stop dwelling on all that's gone wrong, and start being thankful for what's gone right.' So let's agree to focus on what we have to be thankful for. One big detail for which to be grateful is that we got out of there alive."

Loud voices came closer to them. Annaveta stood up. She saw Alex with a shirt tied tight around his leg being supported by both Jude and David.

"What happened to you?" Annaveta rushed to his side and helped him to sit on the log.

"Misha, Monsieur Arnaud, and Anton had a fight. At least, that's what it looked like when we got there." Jude spoke. Alex was catching his breath and winced in pain, holding his leg. "We saw Anton shoot Monsieur Arnaud, who shot back but missed. Then Anton shot Misha, and Misha killed Anton. We got there and Misha was already down but managed to fire one last shot at Alex."

"So they're all dead?" Annaveta felt guilty as weights seemed to lift off her body. She shouldn't be happy for anyone's death, and yet those men had caused such havoc in her life.

"It looked that way. We're going to get the police out here to check on them." Sweat broke out on Alex's forehead.

"It's time that we went to the hospital." Annaveta stood. Jude helped Alex and David assisted Jarena.

When they finally got to the hospital, the nurses took Alex, Jarena, and Annaveta all to separate places to look at their wounds. A few hours later, Aunt Esther came to see them and talked the doctors into releasing all three of them into her care at home. She hired a nurse on the spot.

As they were leaving the hospital, David stopped to talk to Annaveta. "I found these under Anton's coat. I believe these belong to you and your aunt." Tears filled Annaveta's eyes when he handed her the original documents for the land deed. She thought she'd never see them again.

"Thank you so much, David. This means so much to me and Aunt Esther." She pressed the papers against her heart. It felt like she had recovered a portion of who she was along with the papers. "I need to send a note to those men to tell them I have proof they have been swindling property from previous owners, and that they need to stop all attempts to try to get the land that the shelter is on."

Annaveta looked at David, who shook his head in disagreement.

"How about if I do that for you? I can put it in legal terms that will put the fear of God in them." David grinned.

"You're right, of course. That's something that should come from a lawyer who can say it in a way that will alarm them. Thank you, David." Annaveta rubbed her chin and thought about the shelter. "What if they try to strike back? Maybe I'll ask Uncle Roman to put more bodyguards at the shelter for the next few days."

"You do that. And I'll get started on that letter." David nodded at her and left. Soon Alex, Jude, and Jarena followed Aunt Esther out of the hospital. Annaveta got in the carriage with them and headed for home.

It wasn't until luncheon the next day that they saw each other again.

"Tell us again how you managed to get away from the Navy and from what the newspapers are calling the biggest revolution to hit Petrograd and the whole country of Russia?" Uncle Roman wiped his mouth with a napkin after finishing his soup. His head was tilted so he could hear his son's response.

"Well, it wasn't planned. I realized when the Committee Sailors on the *Aurora* decided they were going to kill Alex that it was my chance to repay him for saving mine. So we escaped and came home by train."

Uncle Roman shook his head, a slight smile on his lips.

"I should let you know the Naval authorities might try to follow us here," Jude warned his papa. Annaveta noticed the resigned look in her uncle's face.

"Well, first we need to get you all well before we worry about any other plans." Aunt Esther spoke in firm tones, as if she had any control over the situation.

"Yes. Quite right." Uncle Roman yielded to his wife's wisdom.

"I don't know what my papa will say when he and my step-mama get home." Jarena frowned. Annaveta noticed she had hardly eaten a bite of her borscht soup.

"I went this morning and left a note explaining where you were, so they wouldn't worry." Jude explained.

"I don't know if that will do any good. It might even make things worse." Jarena rubbed her head, something she had done a lot of for the past two days.

"Well, we won't think about that right now. We need to get you better." Aunt Esther waved one of the maids over to her. "Help Miss Jarena to her room, would you please?"

The maid put her arm around Jarena's shoulder and they walked together out of the dining room.

Aunt Esther, Uncle Roman, Jude, Alex and Annaveta sat and drank tea together, enjoying the quiet midday air. A loud knock broke the tranquility.

"Larson, wait just a moment before you answer that." Aunt Esther waived the maids over to clean up the house. "Alex and Jude, go to your rooms and lie down in your beds quickly." She got up, motioning for them to go.

"What? Mama, what is the meaning of this?" Jude's voice could be heard complaining as he walked down the hallway.

"Never mind. Just do as I say." Aunt Esther's tense reply made Annaveta nervous.

She tensed when she heard the loud male voices talking with Larson at the door. Uncle Roman stood up to go see what was going on, when Larson appeared at the dining room door with two policemen.

"I'm so sorry, Mr. Levinson. I tried to stop them, but they pushed their way inside."

"That's fine, Larson." Uncle Roman nodded at the anxious butler and crossed his arms, frowning at the men who stood before him. "I hope you have a good explanation for coming uninvited into our home."

"I'm sorry, Mr. Levinson. But I have a good reason. I've just been informed by Navy personnel that there are two deserters from this house. I've been ordered to keep them in custody until they can stand trial. I have their names here. Captain Levinson and Lieutenant Wagner."

"What?" Roman Levinson eyed the papers in his hand. "Let me see those." He read them over just as Aunt Esther walked back into the room.

"What do these officers want?" Aunt Esther looked at her husband, who handed the documents over to her. "Seems like our two young men are wanted by the Navy to stand trial for desertion."

Aunt Esther's face paled and her lips quivered.

Fear snaked it's way down to her Annaveta's belly. She knew what it meant to stand trial for desertion, she read of what happened just a few weeks ago to two sailors who had been convicted of it. They had been immediately taken to stand before a firing squad and shot to death. Annaveta's hand shook as she took a sip of water.

"Well, you'll have to wait then, if you want them so badly. They are lying in bed sick with the Spanish flu." Aunt Esther spoke in firm tones to the officer. "If you want, I'll take you to them and you can see for yourself. However, I must warn you that Spanish flu is very contagious and most people who get it never recover."

"Ah, I see. No, we'll just leave them here until they are well, Mrs. Levinson. However, we'll have to post guards at the exits around the house to ensure their, ah, safety." Officer Kuschev put the tip of his fingers to his hat and nodded at Aunt Esther and Uncle Roman. "Good day to you."

"Good day, Officer." Uncle Roman sighed in relief after Larson let them out.

"Oh, Aunt Esther, you gave them more time. But now what are we going to do? They are placing guards around the house." Annaveta walked over to her aunt. She hoped there would be a way out of this mess.

"I do have a plan, but we need to wait just a few days until Alex is feeling better from the gunshot wound." Aunt Esther began to explain what was going to happen.

Three days later, a little after midnight, Jude, Alex, and Annaveta carried their packed suitcases down the stairs. Many tears were shed as they hugged Roman and Esther goodbye.

Jarena had left yesterday. David had taken her to visit her papa in jail. Judge Saratov said there was enough evidence against Barinov to hold him for a long time. David told her Monsieur Arnaud had died from his gunshot wounds as had Anton. The rumour going around about Misha was that his Papa had picked his body up to bury him at his home.

Annaveta couldn't stop the tears as she hugged Aunt Esther for the last time.

"I'm going to miss you so much. You've been so good to me. Like my own mama." Annaveta kissed her cheek one last time and then did the same with Uncle Roman. "Do something wonderful with your papa's land. There's real treasure there, I saw it for myself."

"We will do something in memory of Zaydeh and Bubbeh. He would've been so pleased that you took to heart all those lessons he taught you when you were a little girl." Aunt Esther kissed her cheeks and then waved her off. "Now, go. And Adonai be with you."

"Write to us and let us know how your journey has gone." Roman Levinson kissed both her cheeks, hugged his son, and shook Alex's hand.

"Remember all the signatures and money you need is in here. You can start setting things up as soon as you get there." Roman handed his son a small leather suitcase and then gave Jude, Annaveta, and Alex a hug.

"We will do our best, sir." Alex replied. "Thank you for helping me through my own parents' deaths, and for taking such good care of Annaveta."

"Ah, son. We're *mishpachah*. We take care of each other."

Aunt Esther kissed Alex on both cheeks. "Now, go, you three. And write to us so we know where to send letters." Aunt Esther called after them as they walked through the tunnel door and out into the night air.

All three were silent, careful to walk lightly on their feet. They took the back way around the Levinson estate by the trees and then down the hill to the port. They found a small boat that Uncle Roman said would be waiting for them. Soon they rowed their way to Uncle Roman's merchant ship. As soon as they reached the ship, someone let down a ladder along the side.

"Annaveta, climb up. I'm right behind you." Alex followed her up the ladder with both of their bags.

As soon as they were on board, they went to the two-room cabin they had been assigned. They each decided they would hide their bags under the lifeboats on the side of the ship until they were fully underway.

Dawn was just beginning when they placed their bags under the lifeboats.

A horn blasted. "Halt, by order of the Soviet Navy. We're coming on board." Jude pointed to each of the three lifeboats and they each hid under one. Annaveta lay there shivering, praying they wouldn't be found out.

"We've been informed that two men under house arrest have escaped, Captain. We're here to do a search." At the sound of heels clicking and sharp commands, the search was underway.

Orders were given and soon there was loud cursing everywhere.

"You've searched everywhere?" The lead man asked.

"Yes, sir. And we found nothing. No hint that they were even on board."

"Well, that's what we'll tell the Commander then. He won't be happy about it, but that's the best I can do. Captain, carry on." The officer and his men went back down the ladder and soon the sound of the small engine to their boat could be heard going off in the distance.

Annaveta heard knocking on her lifeboat. "You can come out now."

She squirmed out of her hiding place along with Alex and Jude.

They were sailing past the last port in Odessa, when Annaveta spotted someone familiar standing on the edge of the pier.

Misha.

He wasn't dead after all. He stood there looking at her as if planning his next move. She closed her eyes and turned away. She hoped he wouldn't try to find her. Now that they all had to leave their mother country, she hoped they would finally be safe.

Twisting the bracelet from Alex, she blew out the bad thoughts and breathed in the good.

Alex came to stand beside her and held her hand as they looked forward toward their new destination. "Canada will be good to us, my love. And we to her. It's a fresh start."

"I'm excited and scared all at the same time, Alex." Annaveta put her head on his shoulder and thought about all she had left behind. Family, friends, and some powerful enemies.

Loneliness and fear wrapped around her like an invisible shroud.

A new course was already in motion for both her and Alex, whether they wanted it or not. She knew from experience that new beginnings didn't come without sacrifice.

Was she ready for what lay ahead?

Enjoyed Anchoring Annaveta?

Thanks for joining Annaveta and Alex on another adventure.

Did you enjoy *Anchoring Annaveta?* **Here's what you can do next.**

If you loved this book and you have a moment to spare, I would really appreciate a short review. Your help in spreading the word is gratefully appreciated. Reviews make a huge difference in helping new readers find the series.

Anchoring Annaveta **on Amazon.com**

Anchoring Annaveta **on Amazon.ca**

More Romance books by Lorna Faith coming soon...

You can sign up to be notified of the next book as well as pre-release specials here:

http://www.lornafaith.com/get-my-free-book

Author's Note

I love to blend history and romance together and season it with action, adventure with a dash of the supernatural.

Research is also one of the most fun parts of being an author. I find learning about the past inspiring and enlightening as it guides us to make better choices for today. Interesting aspects that were woven into this book: the Pogrom(killing) of hundreds of Jews in Odessa in 1905; Russian Navy and their skirmishes with the German Navy and Ottoman Empire in the Black Sea; innovations of Volga German farmers in Russia; diving deeper into the political unrest and the forced abdication of Tsar Nicholas II in 1917; and details on the life of the wealthy who lived in Odessa in the early 1900s.

Books I found helpful as I studied this time period in history include: *Peasant Russia,* by Christine D. Worobec; *A Brief History of 1917 Russia's Year of Revolution,* by Roy Bainton; and *Life on the Russian Country Estate* by Priscilla Roosevelt.

I also drew inspiration from stories my dad told about his parents and grandparents way of life in Russia in the early 1900s.

I love writing romance stories that include suspense and mystery. My stories reflect main character's who learn to overcome tragedy and obstacles to develop into people of strength, wisdom and confidence. I love stories where good wins over evil and happy endings. If you do too, welcome to this cozy corner of the world.

Grab a cup of coffee, get comfortable by the fireplace and let me tell you a story :-)

Acknowledgements

I'm grateful to so many people who gave their support and encouragement to me through the process of writing this novel - and those who support me every day through love and friendship.

Robin for helping me with tons of ideas for the original outline.

Brenda… for your great tips on how to make this a better story. Thanks for being a Beta Reader.

Tribe Writers Fiction Writers group… for your encouragement to keep writing.

Staci… for editing this book. Appreciate your patience with me and your helpful advice on how to make this a better book.

Domi for designing this amazing book cover.

For my readers… for your inspiration and encouragement. Love you all.

Qualan, Atlee, Saejal and Coral… for being the best kids a mom could ask for.

And, last but never least, Murray… for speaking confidence and belief into me daily and most of all just for being you. I love you.

About Lorna Faith

Lorna Faith has a Bachelor's Degree in Music from the University of Lethbridge with a major in Voice and a minor in Piano.

She taught voice and piano lessons at the University Conservatory and then for many years from her home studio. In the past four years, she has rekindled a dream she had as a young girl to write stories.

Lorna also loves hiking in the mountains with her family, drinking green smoothies and soaking up culture and history wherever she is.

She and her husband along with their four children live in Southern Alberta, Canada near the Rocky Mountains.

You can sign up for updates from Lorna and be the first to know of new releases and giveaways for Romance books - Historical, Western or Contemporary - by clicking here: http://www.lornafaith.com/get-my-free-book

<u>Connect with Lorna online:</u>

(Email)<u>lorna@lornafaith.com</u>

(Twitter) <u>https://twitter.com/lornafaith</u>

(Facebook) <u>https://www.facebook.com/LornaFaithBiz</u>

(Pinterest) <u>https://www.pinterest.com/lornafaith/</u>

(Google Plus) <u>https://plus.google.com/u/0/+LornaFaith/posts</u>

(YouTube) <u>https://www.youtube.com/user/lornafaith</u>

For Writers:

Lorna's business <u>http://www.lornafaith.com</u> helps people uncover their writing voice, storytelling ideas, tips and strategies and learn how to self-publish and market their books. She has blog posts, podcasts, videos and a new online course for writers which you can find on her website.

www.ingramcontent.com/pod-product-compliance
Lightning Source LLC
Chambersburg PA
CBHW051331250626
47155CB00007B/2544